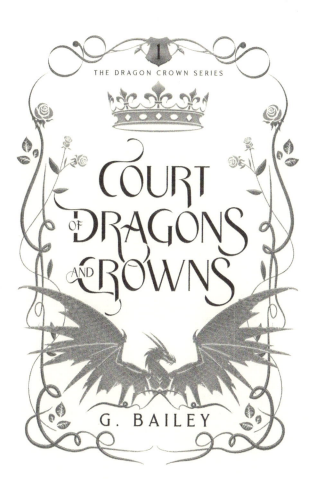

1

THE DRAGON CROWN SERIES

COURT OF DRAGONS AND CROWNS

G. BAILEY

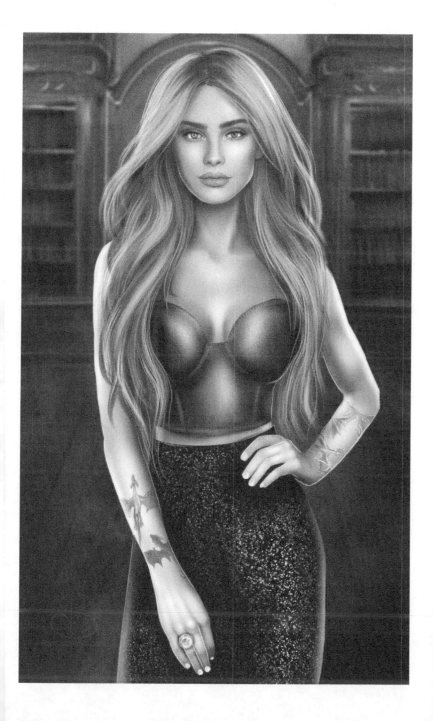

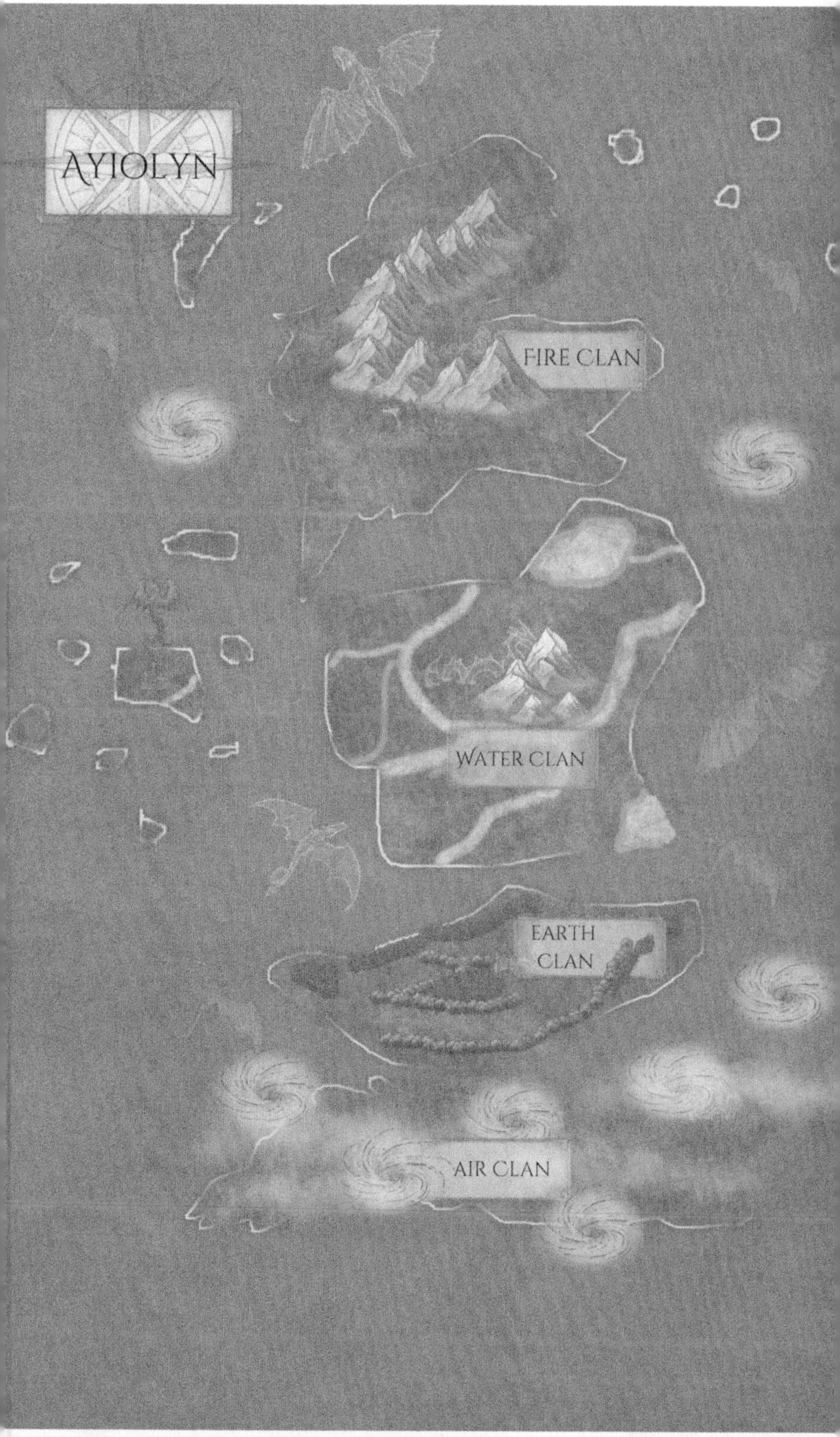
AYIOLYN
FIRE CLAN
WATER CLAN
EARTH CLAN
AIR CLAN

COURT OF DRAGONS AND CROWNS

THE DRAGON CROWN SERIES
BOOK ONE

G. BAILEY

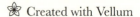

CONTENTS

DESCRIPTION

**The dragon kings need a queen, and they
have chosen me to compete in their race.**

Four gorgeous dragon shifter kings break into my
home and kill my ex-boyfriend before taking me
to their world to compete to be their queen. Once
every thousand years, the dragon kings come
together to find human brides from Earth, and if
they don't have their brides in one hundred days,
their courts will lose their magic. I didn't know the
world of magic and dragons existed, not until I'm
thrown headfirst into it and expected to compete
in a deadly competition to be one of their four
brides.

Arden, Emrys, Grayson and Lysander are cruel, entitled, and I don't want anything to do with them.

In this world of glittering dresses, sharp teeth, and claws, I need to become stronger than the dragons themselves.

They want a bride—but I'll be nothing but a nightmare when I win.

This is a full-length enemies to lovers fantasy romance with dragon shifters, a badass heroine and possessive alpha males.
Perfect for fans of spicy fantasy whychoose? romance.

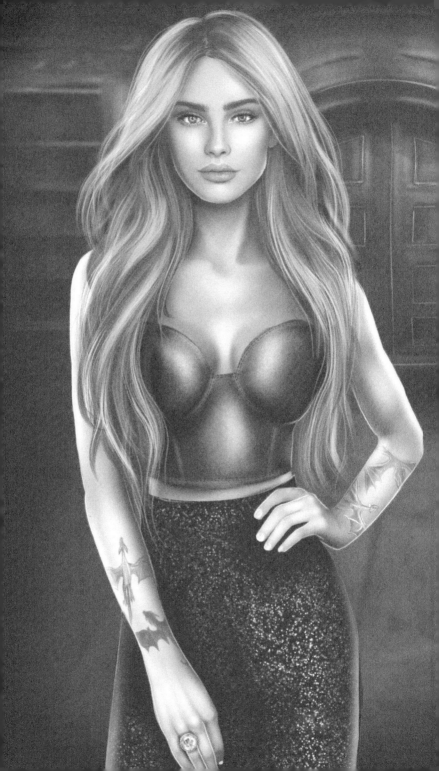

CHAPTER 1

"*T*here's a dragon in the sea. Can't you see him?"

The waves brush against the stone steps, smothering the bottom two until they can't be seen anymore as the local crazy man walks past, muttering to himself about sea dragons and magic. The cold, beautiful coastline of Silloth stretches out for miles, wrapping around a small corner of England, but it feels like it's a million worlds apart from the rest of the busy world. It certainly is in the middle of nowhere, for me at least. The sky fills with bright, vibrant oranges and yellows that reflect across the calm blue sea as the sun sets. This is my favourite part of the day, but it fails to make me smile, to make me feel less lost and alone today. I wrap my tanned arms around my short legs, breathing in the familiar sea air, and try to forget today. It doesn't work.

"Ellelin!"

Fuck. I knew hiding here wasn't a good idea, as he knows it's my secret spot, away from the visiting tourists. This is the end of the promenade, where it meets the old lighthouse. I climb to my feet, just as my boyfriend—no, ex-boyfriend as of half an hour ago—stumbles to a stop in front of me, sand spraying onto my worn boots. He's handsome, so my grandmother says, six foot tall with blond hair and honey brown eyes. She also told me the pretty ones always, always fuck up in the end.

She was right.

"I can explain. If you'll just listen—"

I chuckle, wiping a stray violet lock of my hair out of my eyes. Dying my black hair violet was one of the only things I've done for myself in a long time, and I love the colour. Finley said he preferred it black. "Explain what, exactly, Finley? You want to explain how you slept with a friend of mine? I don't think that needs to be explained. We're over."

I turn around and leave. I'm done with him, and this damn town I've been trapped in since I was six and my grandmother took me in. The sad truth is this is the only place I have ever known, and I don't have any friends except for my ex-boyfriend and my friend who he slept with. I don't have anyone but my grandmother, and something about that fact makes me sad. I can't remember my life before I was six, and my grandmother won't tell me anything about where I lived before that. I only know that my parents died tragically after travelling for years but that my mum was born here, in Silloth. I've been stuck here with my grandmother, my only remaining family, and I've never left.

School finishes soon, only three days away from graduating, and then I can leave. I can get out of this small town, see what the world has to offer me. My grades are high, and I've been accepted to several universities from Edinburgh to London. I just need to make my choice exactly how far I want to go from my grandmother. She still needs my help, but I'm not sure I can be here to help her without giving up the chance of leaving this town. The stubborn old lady refuses to let us have any carers in.

Finley scrambles up to my side, grabbing hold of my arm to pull me to a stop. "Let me go," I demand, loud enough to turn the heads of several people nearby. Finley looks around, noticing how many people are looking, and roughly lets me go. I shake my head and turn away, walking back to my house.

"Ellelin, please, just listen to me!"

I pause, turning back to look at him standing on the edge of the road. "Look, we were going to break up. I'm going off to university, and I'm sure not staying around here for you. Just go and live your life. We both know your life is here with your family. Just leave me the hell alone."

"But I love you," he weakly protests.

I chuckle as I walk away. I've always told him not to say that to me, because I don't believe you can fall in love at eighteen, or at least, I never felt that way about him. Love is destruction, according to my grandmother and every romance book I've ever read. So no thank you. I want security, a decent apartment, and money to travel the world. Not a life trapped in a small town, popping out babies with a man I don't really care that much for as he cheats on me. That would be my life here with Finley, and I'd rather have no life than that.

I look at Finley once last time, remembering that he was charming and made me laugh once, but every one of those good memories is now tainted. "You certainly didn't love me when you were screwing my only friend. It's over. Leave me alone."

Finley looks like I've broken his heart as I tuck my hands into my pocket to warm them up and cross the road, hoping he doesn't follow me this time. The bitterly cold sea breeze blows against my black hoodie and leggings, reminding me I shouldn't have left without my thicker coat this morning.

I head down the streets until I come to our small, terraced home, the street quiet and empty. All the terraces around here are a multitude of colours like a rainbow, and ours is yellow. The yellow paint now is chipped, faded, and cracked in so many places, and the windows look close to falling off, but I love this house. It's quirky, like my grandmother, and I've never not felt at home here. Our house stands out in the row as every other house is freshly painted, but we don't have the money for that, and our neighbours make sure to mention the paint every time I bump into them. One day, I'm going to have a good job and be able to repaint the house for my grandmother. One day.

Unlocking the latch, I open the door and head inside, where the warmth of the lit fire makes me sigh. "Nan, it's me."

I take my coat off and rub my eyes. I'm exhausted after cleaning caravans for two hours after school to give us a bit of extra money for food, as my grandmother tries her best, but everything is expensive. Between work and school and caring for my grandmother, some days I feel like I never rest. No wonder my boyfriend cheated on me. Never have enough time to be with him—with anybody, in truth—which makes it sadder that I decided to surprise him by walking to his and sneaking in through his bedroom window today.

My grandmother doesn't reply to me, and I frown as our cat, Jinks, jumps up onto the back of the sofa. Jinks is pure white with strange red glowing eyes, but the vet swears it's normal. I swear he looks like the devil, especially in the middle of the night. I stroke the back of his head as he purrs at me for food. "Alright, Jinks."

I feed him in the small kitchen at the back of our house before going to search for my grandmother in the garden, where she usually is. The thick grey clouds above suggest it's going to rain soon, and the sun has nearly set completely. The solar fairy lights around our garden flicker to life along the path as I walk down the long stretch. The garden stretches all the way back, and my grandmother has filled it with beautiful flowers, trees, and bushes. I find my grandmother at the back of the garden, on a metal bench, wrapped in a pink knitted blanket, watching the sky above. Her sea-coloured blue eyes, the same as mine, fall on me, and her wrinkled face lights up with a loving smile. Her grey hair is messily pulled up into a bun, exotic, multicoloured flower slides clipped in, and she is barefoot even when it is a cold late summer day.

"Elle, darling. How was your day?"

I sigh, sitting next to her and crossing my boots. "Finley cheated on me with Daisy. You were right about him."

Her hand picks up mine and she pats it twice. "I don't like being right, dear. He was never good enough for you."

I lean my head on the rotting shed behind the bench. "How did you meet this one true love of your life you tell me about? How did you know you loved him?"

She sadly smiles at me, looking away after a moment. "You simply know when you meet the one who will turn your life upside down. I knew because I couldn't stand your grandad. He was arrogant, annoying, and always two steps behind me. He drove me around the bend most of the time. But one day I realised it wasn't that I hated him, that I loved him, and I didn't want him to ever stop annoying me. We built a life together, had your mother, and we were happy until his stupid heart packed out on me. Typical. Men always leave first."

I smile at her, enjoying her story. "I don't think I ever cared about Finley all that much."

"I know, dear. That's why you are allowed to feel sorry for yourself tonight, and tomorrow you're going to face the world with a smile. He isn't worth crying over. When you meet the man that is, you won't ever be able to move on. You will just exist."

For a moment, I see her sorrow, and in a blink, she hides it. I'm all my grandmother has left now everyone else is dead, and sometimes I think I'm lucky I don't remember my parents or grandfather. I don't have to mourn them like she does. I change the subject, as I don't want to upset her. "Are you going out tonight?"

She stands up. "Of course. Dorris needs her ass kicked at bingo. If I don't go, who else would put her in her place?"

I chuckle, standing up and linking my arm through hers as we walk back to the house. "I'm going to curl up on the sofa, watch some disgustingly cheesy movie about love, and eat chocolate ice cream, because that will make me feel better."

My grandmother kisses the side of my head. "Leave some ice cream for me, dear. When I'm back, we can share and talk shit about Finley."

I laugh, breathing in how she smells like mint and garden herbs, which makes me relax. This is home and I'll miss it, but I'm ready to get out and see the world.

A few hours later, I curl up on the sofa after my grandmother has gone out and turn on the TV to search for a good movie. I just pop open the lid of my chocolate ice cream when there is a frantic banging on the front door. I groan, putting down the tub as the banging continues. I know exactly who it is. Finley knows when my grandmother goes out to bingo, as it's usually our time alone. I unlock the door, intending to tell him to piss off, but he barges in without asking. I slam the door shut behind him.

"You're interrupting my ice cream and crappy movie. What do you want?"

Finley runs his hand through his hair, and I smell the alcohol on him. Great, he is drunk. "To talk to you. You have to give me another chance. You just have to let me fix us. I love you so much."

I roll my eyes, going back to the door to open it, but he grabs my arm to stop me. He's always been a bit grabby when he's had a drink, and considering he's twice the size of me, I can't do much as he pulls me away from the door and back into the living room. For the first time, I realise that I should not have opened the door to him. "Let me go, Finley, and go home. We can talk when you're sober."

"No," he angrily snaps, tugging me against his body. "Look, you just need to listen to me. She kissed me and then one thing led to another. I was just horny and stupid, but I love you. You have to forgive me, Elle."

I try to pull myself away from him, but his grip is iron-tight, borderline painful. "No, I don't. We can talk tomorrow, Finley. Let me go."

Instead of letting me go, his thick hand wraps around my throat as he tries to kiss me, and I panic, trying to push him away. My voice comes out frantic, and I scream, "Let me go!"

Finley doesn't listen, pushing me backwards towards the sofa, kissing my cheek and mumbling about loving me. Dread pools in my stomach as I struggle in his arms, trying to get away and fearing what will happen if I can't. Dating Finley was a big mistake, but I was never scared of him until now. I manage to lift my leg and I knee him hard, making him groan in pain and let me go.

He trips on the sofa, falling to his knees and cupping his balls. "What the hell is wrong with you? Get out of my house and don't come back!"

He glances up, and the look he gives me sends chills down my spine. He's going to hurt me for that. "No, I'm going to make you listen to me. You're mine, Ellelin, and we are not breaking up!"

I back away towards the kitchen, knowing I'm going to have to leave and run. He is drunk, so I have a good chance of escaping through the garden if I run fast. At least if I scream outside, my neighbours will come and see what is happening.

I hear the back door unlock, and my shoulders sag in relief. My grandmother's back from bingo early, and maybe the shock of seeing her will make Finley leave. Finley rises to his feet as I stumble away, and he pauses, looking over my shoulder to the kitchen. All the colour leaves his face. A shocked scream rips out of my throat as a silver dagger swiftly flies past my cheek and slams into his chest, blood spraying across the carpet between us. His scream is bloodcurdling and terrible, as I freeze in shock. Red hot fire spreads out from the dagger, burning him so quickly that, within seconds, he's nothing but ash falling softly on the blood-stained carpet. The dagger falls with a thud, and my scream dies away as I turn around slowly.

My heart pounds in my chest as I face the four massive men standing in my tiny kitchen. The man in the middle lowers his hand, smiling at me through waves of shiny thick black hair as his red, fiery eyes meet mine.

"You can thank me later."

CHAPTER 2

"*Y*-you killed him?" I sputter, taking a step back in shock. I'm shaking from head to toe as the men all look between each other.

"Humans don't like murder, dumbass," the red-haired man says, patting the shoulder of the man who threw the dagger. He is wearing a black shirt tucked into black trousers that scream money. "Arden, you broke this one. You can deal with her. The last one bit me."

Arden groans. "I'm not dealing with this one, Lysander. I'm already bored."

Arden leans against the wall, picking up another dagger from his long trench coat and playing with it, throwing it up and down in the air. Lysander looks at the other two. One of them watches from the darkness of the back of the kitchen, and I can only see his outline. The other steps forward, a playful smile on his lips as locks of white hair fall into his moss green eyes, and he pushes it aside. He goes to say something when a deep voice speaks from the back of the kitchen. "She's going to run, and then she's my problem."

"She's not going to run, Grayson. Arden just saved her from whoever that fucker was," he murmurs. "I'm Emrys. You're Ellelin, right?"

"Boyfriend. That was my ex-boyfriend, and you just murdered him," I croak, snapping out of my shock. "How did you do that? How did you burn him?"

Arden's laugh is deep and taunting, just like his eyes as they meet mine. "We are dragon shifter kings, babe. Fire is my skill."

"Arden, you're being a dick and scaring her," Emrys mutters, stepping closer to me with his hands in the air. He is wearing a dark blue jumper and dark jeans. For some reason, I get the feeling they don't wear clothes like this often. "He forgets humans don't know about magic and dragons. We aren't here to hurt you."

Lysander sits down on my grandmother's chair, crossing his legs at the ankle. "Just let Matron explain it all. We burnt her boyfriend to a crisp; she isn't going to believe anything else we say."

Emrys ignores him. "We're dragon kings from four courts. We're not from this world. Your world is connected to several worlds, including ours, and we can travel between."

My hands feel sweaty as I cross my arms. "What does this have to do with me?"

Lysander grins. "You've been chosen. All you need to do for now is come with us through a portal."

I lower my arms. "I'm not going anywhere with you." I step back and accidentally stand in what is left of Finley. I step aside, cringing as I rub my shoe on the carpet.

Arden laughs, the sound echoing. "She just stood on her piece of shit boyfriend. It's almost funny."

I narrow my eyes at him. "Fuck you."

He meets my gaze, running his eyes up and down over me. "Anytime, princess."

My cheeks burn as I take another step back, looking between them all, focusing on the shadow outline of the man in my kitchen. For whatever reason, he feels like he's the most dangerous of them all, and I can't even see what he looks like from here. They all look pretty dangerous, and I'm not sure how I'm going to get out of this. They're all muscular, ridiculously tall, and handsome. All I can think about now is how they just burnt my ex-boyfriend to a crisp in the middle of my living room. How is that even possible? And now they're talking about kidnapping me.

I steel my back. They aren't taking me anywhere without a fight. "I'm not going with you. Get out of my house."

Emrys tilts his head to the side, his forest green eyes softening. "I know this is creepy and you don't trust us, but we don't want to harm you. You have been chosen to come to our world and compete in an event. This is an honour. There are several bloodlines in this world that came from ours, including yours. Your bloodline was sworn to the same magic we are bound to, allowing us to find you and bring you back to our world. Four of the chosen will become our brides. Become dragon queens. More will be explained later."

I feel delirious as I chuckle and then laugh. "I'm pretty sure I'm going mad. I must be dreaming. Going completely mad. You're kidnapping me to become your dragon queen, and I have to compete for the honour? I'm not fucking doing that. Find a girl the normal way."

"I like this one," Emrys laughs.

Arden throws a dagger at him, and swiftly he catches it midair. "I don't."

Emrys pockets the dagger before he runs his hands over his face, looking frustrated. "We are wasting time here. Let's just knock her out and go home."

"Agreed," Arden replies, leaning off the wall. I don't think, only act, as I turn and run. The front door lock melts as I run for it, so instead, I fly around the banister of the stairs, lugging my ass up the steps as fast as I can, my heart pounding.

"Arden, go after her. You freaked her out by killing someone!" Emrys demands.

"He was going to attack her! She should thank me for killing his worthless ass!" Arden all but growls.

"I will go and fix this mess," Lysander sighs, my grandmother's chair creaking, "while you two fight like children."

"Good luck!" Arden shouts while laughing.

I get to the top of the stairs, stumbling around the corner and pulling the bathroom door open, slamming it shut behind me and locking it. I don't know what use the locks are going to be against—what did they say they were? Dragon shifters? Are they actual dragons, wings, and scales and all that? No, this can't be real. No, none of this can be real. I'm going mad.

I hear Lysander's heavy feet thudding up the stairs after me. He is real, and I have to find a way to escape. I look around the room for anything. Anything at all to defend myself with. My eyes flicker to the small, frosted window. I've never climbed through it. It's thin and I'm not sure I will fit through it. Fuck it. I have to try. I start cranking it open when I hear the bathroom door handle being twisted, the door shaking. My mouth parts in surprise as clear water runs up the door from the bottom, smothering every inch of it. I don't move as the water suddenly turns to ice, the door shattering in shards of wood and ice. Lysander stands on the other side, leaning against the frame, his thick arms crossed. "Running is completely useless, Elle."

"Don't call me that. You killed the last person who called me that!" I snap. I might have hated Finley for cheating and attacking me, but he didn't deserve to burn to death.

He raises an eyebrow. "I don't control fire, Elle. I'm the water dragon king, so you can't blame me for that one. If it matters, I agree with Arden. He deserved to die for laying a hand on a woman. I would have done far worse with him if we had more time."

For a moment, he lets me see past the charming smile to the true darkness hidden in his soul, and it scares me. I'm not going with them. No fucking way. "Don't make us chase you. It's boring and pointless. You can't escape."

"Fuck you!" I snap, picking up the nearest thing and throwing it at him. My nan's multi-coloured squeaky duck flies pathetically through the air, and he catches it. Lysander's lips twitch in amusement before he squeaks it once and throws it over his shoulder. "Fine. We'll do this the hard way if we must."

He steps into the bathroom and reaches for me. In a split second, I look around quickly for anything and grab the top of the toilet lid, lifting it and smashing it straight across his head. He looks so surprised for a second, right before he collapses onto the ground, blood pouring from a deep cut on his forehead. "Holy shit."

I drop the toilet lid on the floor, wasting no time as the others might notice. I go to the window again, propping myself up on the ledge and pushing my legs through first. I manage to squeeze right through the window as I hear them running up my stairs. My heart pounds as I softly shut the window and lie down on the tiles of the back porch, listening to them for a second.

"Whoa, the little human princess knocked him out. How the fuck did she do that?" Arden questions.

Emrys laughs. "Make sure Grayson doesn't do anything stupid, while I heal him. She's impressive, that one. Make sure she doesn't hurt herself trying to escape."

"It was the toilet seat," Arden laughs, and I hear him picking it up. "Or was it the rubber duck in the hallway? Either way, it's hilarious."

"I'll get her," Grayson's dark voice states.

The others go silent. Emrys clears his throat. "Don't hurt her."

His voice is like death. "The brat hurt us."

"Gray!" Emrys shouts, but Grayson doesn't reply. Dammit, he is coming for me, and I've wasted too much time. I slide down the roof panels, some of them clicking under my weight. Rain begins to pour out of the sky, making the roof slippery. A cry escapes my throat as I slip, sliding off the roof and slamming hard onto the grass. Ignoring the pain in my ribs, I climb to my feet and start sprinting straight up the garden. All at once, thick green vines shoot out of the surrounding ground, coming out of everywhere, and one trips me. I fall over, only to be caught in the vines. I fight them as they are wrapping around my legs, arms, and chest. I manage to snap a few of them, but more just keep appearing until they're wrapped so tightly around me, squeezing me until I almost can't breathe.

Grayson's face comes into the moonlight. He is gorgeous with thick brown hair, dark golden skin, but there is a harshness to his silver eyes that matches the cruel smirk he gives me. He looks at me like I'm pathetic. "You're going to die first in the Dragon Crown Race. You're clearly stupid."

"Let me go, you fucking monster!" I scream, struggling and wriggling the best I can. He smells like the earth itself and a mixture of sandalwood that reminds me of forest walks. "Let me go! Let me go! HELP! I'm being kidnapped by crazy magic men who think they are dragons! HELP!"

"Shush, brat. You're just embarrassing yourself and giving me a headache," he mutters, picking me up with the vines like I weigh nothing. He throws me over his shoulder. "It's time to go."

My eyes widen as he twists around to look at the others, who are walking up the garden path to us. There's something in the middle of our garden. It looks like a shimmery wall, almost like it's water, but it's gold, illuminating and bright on the other side. Creatures fly through the air around the mountains and castle in the distance. They are too big to be birds. They are dragons. Actual dragons. Through it, I can see tall mountains and a silver castle nestled right in the middle of them. Orange fields surround the mountains, luminated by the night sky full of glowing yellow stars. I scream, panicking as Grayson turns and begins to walk towards it.

"Will you knock her out, Emrys? She is pissing me off," Grayson growls. *I'm pissing him off?* They are literally kidnapping me and making it sound like a chore. I hate them so much. What is my grand-mother going to think when she comes home, finding a pile of ash and that I'm missing? She is going to be so worried. She has lost everyone else.

Emrys walks up to me, his eyes surprisingly soft as I keep screaming, hoping someone will come and help me. No one is going to save me from them. Oh my god. "I'm vaguely impressed with you, Elle. I hope you win."

He touches my cheek, and suddenly I can't breathe. I gasp for air right before everything falls away into darkness, where I can hear wings.

CHAPTER 3

*E*very inch of me feels groggy as I wake up, my mouth dry. There is a stale taste of something almost earthy in my mouth, and it's cold wherever I am. I breathe in the scent of fresh linen as I open my eyes, blinking up into the dim darkness. I jolt, memories of the men who kidnapped me coming back to me in a flash as my eyes adjust to the light. Those bastards kidnapped me.

My head smacks into something metal, and I look up to realise I'm on the bottom of a bunk bed. The sheets I'm lying on are dark red, soft, and expensive. Where the hell am I? There's another matching, empty bunk bed a few feet away, and the room is small, with two dark wooden doors.

The walls are silver stone, and there is a breeze coming through, explaining why I'm cold. I throw my legs off the bed, thankful that I'm still dressed in the clothes I came in when those dragon shifters kidnapped me.

Dragon shifters? Oh, my god. It was real. It was all real. "Don't freak out. You're okay."

I look over to see that I'm not alone and three pairs of eyes are watching me. There are three other girls in the room, all similar ages to me. One with long curly blonde hair and a friendly smile comes over. She is slim, much taller than me, and very pale, making the freckles on her cheeks stand out. Her eyes remind me of honey. She sits down on the bed. "I'm Arty. Well, my full name is Artemis Wood, but that's a mouthful. I prefer Arty. Yes, my parents loved Greek gods, before you ask. I don't like the goddess of the hunt personally. She historically killed a lot of people, and animals, and I don't like violence. What's your name?"

I'm thankful she stops rambling. I gasp, placing my hand over my mouth as I remember Finley. I'm not going to cry over him, as he was going to attack me, but I've known him since I was six years old, and his mother is the sweetest woman. Her son is dead, and she won't know that. He is just going to be classed as missing, along with me. Even if I manage to get back home from this place, she won't believe the truth. I barely believe it happened, and I was right there. Arty's hand hovers in the air near my shoulder for a second before she puts her hand on my shoulder and awkwardly pats me. "I'm sorry about whatever made you sad right now. I hope it wasn't me. I'm not sure if this is helping, but I—"

"Please stop talking," I snap, moving away so she stops patting me. "Did they kidnap you too?"

She pauses, hurt flashing in her eyes, and she nods. "Yes, but I was expecting it, so does it really count as kidnapping if I went willingly after saying goodbye to my family?"

"No," I deadpan. "You willingly went with those assholes?"

One of the other girls laughs, and Arty ignores her. So do I. "Of course. My mother said it was most likely going to be me, as she waited and they didn't come for her."

"Some of the idiots here wanted this," the girl that laughed dryly comments. She has short, pixie cut, black hair, several piercings in each of her ears, and her lip is pierced too. She is wearing black shorts and a white crop top with an over-sized dark blue hoodie. "I didn't want to go with them either."

"Livia, I'm not an idiot. You two just don't understand," Arty sighs. "We were chosen for this great honour. You were both meant to be told of this and prepared. It was a message sent through the bloodlines. One day, the dragon kings of Ayiolyn will awaken the old magic and come to the mortal world to claim their brides. Then the curse on the land will be lifted until the new heirs are born and it begins all over again."

I roll my eyes at her. "That sounds like a fucked-up fairy tale."

"Yes, it does, but it's real and you're here. The dragon kings are very handsome, and being a queen doesn't sound all too bad," she wistfully replies. She is crazy. I'm stuck with crazy person number one.

"Those dragon assholes killed my ex-boyfriend in front of me and then kidnapped me," I dryly respond. "They aren't nice, and I don't want to be a bride for any of them. How can you want that?"

She smiles sadly at me. "My life wasn't all that great back home, but I was taught to make the best of every day of your life. You aren't promised the next."

I go to reply when the girl who hasn't spoken a word stands up. Her long sleek black hair falls down her chest in two braids, but everything else about her clothes suggests either she has been here longer than us or they kidnapped her from Harry Potter World. She has black leggings, a short black top tucked into them, and a cloak clipped around her shoulders, with symbols lining the edges and a pulled-up hood. I catch a flash of dark blue eyes. All of them have English accents like me, but I don't know hers. "Matron will be in here soon, so stop whining. She only gets pissed off when you do, and trust me, we want her on our side, or we are already dead."

"Who the hell is Matron?" I demand. The door clicks before sweeping open, banging on the wall, and an old lady hobbles in. She's got a silver walking stick that clicks on the stone ground, her wrinkled hand tightly clutched around it. Her back is slightly arched, so she is almost constantly looking down, and she has no hair on her head at all. Wrapped around her shoulders is a black hooded cloak that matches the other girl's, and it's too long, brushing the ground as she shuffles in. On the edges of the cloak are four symbols, crests maybe, and they are each an element: fire, earth, water, and air. She lifts her eyes to look at each of us, and I blanch when she meets my gaze. Her eyes are pure black, like a winter's night.

"Come. You are the final ones to awaken." She turns around, her walking stick loudly clicking on the ground as she leaves.

"That was Matron."

I ignore Livia's dry comment as I look at the open door. They haven't locked us in, and if I can find—

"Don't bother," the cloaked girl coos at me, her tone patronising. "You're not on Earth anymore. You can't escape your fate here."

"This is Hope," Arty introduces us. "Hope has a bad attitude and told me to shut the fuck up when we met. I'm sure the two of you will get along like a house of straw on fire."

"That was a strange metaphor," Livia adds from where she is leaning on the wall, her ankles crossed. "Where are you from exactly, doll?"

Hope glares at us and snaps at Livia as she heads to the door. "Move."

Livia holds her hands up in mock surrender, arching an eyebrow at me as Hope storms out of the room. Livia follows after her.

"Are you coming?" Arty questions, looking back at me. "It's going to be okay. My parents told me it would be. Let's just go and listen to Matron explain everything. One step at a time?"

I look down at myself. I'm still covered in bits of vines that have ripped several pieces of my clothing off, and I look pretty awful. "Fine."

I climb to my feet, following her out and into a long, slim corridor with matching stone walls and a carpeted red runner leading to an open archway. There are eight other doors in the corridor, all of them open, leading to rooms like I woke up in, but no exit other than the archway, where I can hear the chatter of the others. There are no windows for me to climb out of either. Arty touches my shoulder. "I'm sorry about your ex-boyfriend. From what I understand, humans are considered less than dragon shifters, and I imagine the dragon kings wouldn't think twice about killing us."

"And you want to be one of their brides?" I ask. She can't be that stupid. "You're human, right?"

"Yes, I do, because being a queen means we could make changes and protect the humans here. It is a great honour for our family, and I would be remembered forever. It's a great honour for you, too," she replies, bumping my shoulder with hers.

I frown at her. "Please don't touch me."

"Okay," she says with a sigh. "Well, I'm your friend. We're sharing a room and will do till the end of this."

"I don't have friends," I coldly reply. Not friends as crazy as she clearly is. There is no point getting close to anyone. I'm leaving this place as soon as I possibly can.

Arty keeps babbling on about the dragon kings as I tune her out. The corridor is plain, but the ceilings are high with swept arches that lead all the way down. The arched doorway leads to a large communal space. It's a circular room filled with dark red sofas, thick rugs of matching colour, and a few curved dark wooden bookcases crammed with old books, littered around walls. There's an enormous fireplace with two stone dragons making up the mantel, with their spiked backs, their tails curling around the base. Above the fireplace is a stone crown cut out of the wall itself.

The room is full of girls all the same age as me, and there is only one sofa space left—nearest to the fire and in front of the waiting Matron. I pause at the door, my eyes wide as Matron looks right at me and clicks her staff on the floor. I hear the clicking of rock and turn back to see the archway is suddenly filled up with stone bricks, looking like the surrounding walls. Magic is real. Dragons are real. If I keep saying it, maybe it won't be so goddamn scary. I tell myself to think of what my grandmother would do in this moment. She wouldn't cower and run. She would face this head-on and pretend everything is okay.

Never cry in front of your enemies, she told me once.

Arty nods her head at the empty sofa, and I follow her over, sitting as far away from her as I can get. Of course, she moves closer and looks at Matron like an eager puppy waiting for a treat. Someone save me from her. We are definitely not going to be friends. She is way too happy about all of this, and happy about this means she must obviously be insane.

"Everyone sit down," Matron commands, and her tone says she is not to be argued with as dozens of empty stools appear around the room. Magic. Magic is real. I don't think I'm ever going to get used to that. As a little girl, I used to wish magic was real so I could bring back my parents and leave Silloth. Matron's eyes turn to me for a second too long before moving around the room. Even though she looks old and fragile, something about her tone makes me a little frightened of her. I cross one of my legs over the other as everyone takes the empty seats.

"Welcome to Ayiolyn. Some of you were prepared by your families for this day," Matron begins, her voice croaky and a little difficult to understand. "Some of you were not, and I understand this must be a shock. So, we'll start at the very beginning. There are mirror worlds, hovering over each other like a pile of plates. Earth is one of those worlds, mostly ruled by humans, and magic is gone. Lapetus is another, ruled by gods in wolf shifter forms, much like our own dragons. There are six in total, and you now belong to this world. Over three thousand years ago, this world was cursed by a sorcerer from another world. Our dragon kings refused to bow to him, and he made sure there would be a price paid for that before he was sent back to his own world at the cost of the dragon kings' lives. The price was paid by the heirs."

The room is silent as she continues. "No one has magic in this kingdom, no one is anything but mortal, unless the dragon kings hold a competition called the Dragon Crown Race and each chooses one from the four mortals left to be their mate. The winners will become dragon queens, filled with magic, and have their own powers based on their genetic line. There are four courts—"

"There used to be five," Arty whispers to me. I frown at her. I couldn't care less. Matron briefly pauses. Whether she heard Arty or not, she doesn't show it. "The Water Court of the south, the Fire Court of the north, the Earth Court of the east and the Air Court of the west. Each of them has their own dragon king, and I'm sure you have all met them briefly. For future reference, you must bow when you are in their company."

I snort, and several heads whip my way. I'm not bowing to them. Fuck that. Matron narrows her eyes on me. "The test will take a hundred days. In this time, they will get to know you and you will compete against each other in a series of magical tests they decide on, as well as attend a class to learn the ways of this world. Be warned, the tests are designed to find the strongest among you, and they are deadly. This also gives you a chance to make friendships that will be needed to beat the odds against you. Friendships with the other three you share a room with are a good way to start."

"How deadly are the tests, exactly?" a girl asks, but Matron ignores her.

"In between the tests, your classes, and day-to-day life, there will be royals and high-class dragons around the castle looking to meet you. When you are crowned, you will need to know many of these people. So be friendly," she warns. "The former queens will be around as well, the two who are still living. It is a great honour if they speak to you. There have only been two tests in our history, and all eyes are on the twenty-four of you."

A random blonde girl puts a hand up, her Welsh accent thick. "How can there have only been two tests? Surely if it's been three thousand years since the curse, there'd be like thirty queens, as we only live to a hundred if we are lucky."

"Dragons have much longer lifespans than most," she coolly replies, "and once some of you become dragon queens and bond with your mates, your lifespan will be longer."

Another girl puts her hand up high in the air. "What about the tattoos on our backs? What are those, and how do we get rid of them?"

Tattoos? They best not have done that to me. Matron frowns. "Why would you wish to be rid of them? Markings are blessings from dragon gods and are special. When you came here, we took a tiny bit of your blood from your finger and swore you into the test. The markings are proof of that and a great honour. When you complete each test, you will get another mark on your wrist in the form of a dragon."

"How many tests are there?" Arty questions. *So, she doesn't know everything.*

"There are four tests for marks to be earned. When you complete all four, theoretically, there will be four of you left. If not, you will kill each other until only four stand."

My skin goes cold, and any whispers around the room go silent. What kind of crazy Hunger Games shit is this? "Most of the time, there are only four left by the end of the tests, so this hasn't been an issue in the past. Our blessed dragon kings can choose their brides from the winners. The dragon kings will be living here, and it is best you get to know them. Make yourself aware of who they are and the future they offer in their courts for you. They can be very informative."

I raise my eyebrows. This is completely insane. I stand up. Every pair of eyes turns to me, including Matron's. She tilts her head to the side. "Yes, Ellelin Ilroth?"

"What if you don't want to enter? What if I want to just go home to Earth and say screw this race?" I demand, placing my hands on my hips.

Matron almost seems to smile at me, so quick that I could have missed it if I wasn't staring at her. "That option is not available for you. For anyone here. Your bloodline was chosen by the sorcerer and sent to Earth, along with thousands of others. Your ancestors came from here and, a long time ago, made the choice for you to compete in this test. You are from here. Your blood is from here. You have dragon magic in your soul, wound into your very essence and blood. Everyone here does. Maybe you want to leave, but a part of you longs for this world. Search for that part of you and embrace it."

I try not to laugh. "I'm not called to this place. I want to leave. I didn't sign up for this!"

Matron closes both hands over her walking stick in front of her. "As I've said, that is not an option."

"So, what happens to the people who lose?" I question. "You said there can only be four dragon queens. So, if we lose, we go home, right?"

I can just give up and—"No, you die or win. There is no going home."

There are gasps around the room, and some people start crying. My eyes just widen as I still stand, even as my legs feel weak. My heart pounds in my ears, drumming out the sounds around me as the word *die* repeats over and over until it's all I can hear. I don't know why I expect her to say anything different.

"We might die?" Arty nervously questions. I look down at her, and she is pale, no longer as happy as she was. Now she gets it. This isn't a blessing.

Matron nods. "Yes. These tests are deadly and not easy to conquer. You will need to be smart, quick, and brave, all traits a dragon queen will need to excel in. You've been grouped into fours; work together as a team and survive to win the greatest prize of all—to become a dragon queen who will be remembered forever."

Matron disappears. Nothing but smoke that looks like mist left in the middle of the room. Suddenly, a lump of black clothes and two black knee-high boots land on my lap with a thud. I look at Arty, who is silently crying, clutching her own bundle of clothes that match mine. I don't think she knew about the dying thing, either. Her parents didn't tell her everything, or they didn't know. I can't imagine they happily sent their daughter into a death competition just to be a dragon king's— what did Matron call it—mate. I assume that's like a wife. I'm not interested in belonging to anyone—especially not them. Somehow, it makes me feel a tiny bit better that not everyone knew about this. "Back to your rooms." Matron's ancient voice echoes around the room. "Change and get ready."

No one moves for a minute as I clutch my clothes and boots, and stand. I all but run, feeling sickness rising in my throat, back to my room. I count the doors down until I get to the one that I woke up in and head inside, slamming the door shut behind me. I know my new roommates are following, but I can't breathe, can't think straight, and everything is blurring in front of me. I can't breathe. I can't breathe. There's another door at the opposite end of the room, and I run to it, throwing the door open to find a small bathroom. I go inside, shut it behind me, dropping the pile on the floor.

I pull my top over my head, turning my back to the mirror. A massive black-ink tattoo covers my back, and right in the middle is a crown with swirls going around my ribs, up my shoulders and to the swell of my back. No, fuck no. I flick the waterfall shower on, letting the cold water spray over me before I scream and scream until my voice breaks. The water gets hot as I kick the wall, slam my fists against it as I let out all my anger, fear, and panic. If I die here, my grandmother will never know what happened to me, and if I survive, I'll belong to someone without any choice in the matter. I don't want to be a dragon queen for those arrogant bastards.

"Arrogant bastards, you say?" Lysander's voice makes me jump. I pause, slowly turning to look at him through the steamy bathroom as he leans on the wall, his arms crossed. It crosses my mind I'm just wearing a bra and I don't know what is more concerning. My lack of clothing or him being in here. His red hair is tied at the nape of his neck, and he has stubble on his jaw I didn't notice before. A black cape falls off his thick, massive shoulders, and he is wearing a crisp white shirt tucked into tight black trousers that look more from my world than this place. My hair and clothes are soaked, and Lysander's green eyes linger far too long on my body before rising to meet my eyes. "Not many are brave enough to call us that. Not to our faces, at least."

I steel my back, hearing nothing but the pounding water falling down my back. How did he get in here? Was he always in here and I didn't notice? I'm not scared of him. Well, he can't see that I am.

"Trust me, everyone you've met has said that and worse about you behind closed doors," I snarl, my hands shaking. "Now get out!"

Lysander laughs, watching me with interest. "You're like a caged, trapped animal. Do you find us all that unattractive?"

I frown. "How did you get in here?"

"Magic," he sarcastically taunts with an arrogant smirk I want to smack off his face. He straightens and walks over to me, leaning around to switch off the shower, his arm brushing mine. For a moment, my backstabbing, stupid heart pounds for another reason. I can't help the fact that he's absolutely gorgeous, inhumanly gorgeous, and I can't see a single flaw on his perfect face. I've never read about dragon shifters, but I know there are books about them. Paranormal romance was never really my thing though. Neither was fantasy, and yet here I am, in a shower with a freaking dragon shifter.

Taking the small distraction, I run to the door, and just as I reach for the handle, Lysander's hand snaps around mine, pinning my arm above my head as he presses his body into mine while I push at him with my other hand. "You can't leave yet. We need to talk. I want you to do something for me, Elle."

He knows that's the nickname Finley used. "Fuck you."

He growls at me, the sound unnatural, and I freeze in fear. "I'm the dragon king of the Water Court, and no one speaks to me that way without being drowned. I'm being nice, Elle, but don't push your luck."

I shiver from the threat and how I can see he means it. He would kill me without blinking. A lethal smirk tilts his lips up, and he leans closer to me. Too close. "I can hear your heart pounding fast. I can sense the change in you that went from being utterly fearful of me to being a bit aroused in that shower. It's a damn shame you ran. We could have explored that."

I glare at him as he picks up a strand of my purple hair. This reminds me of Finley, of how he grabbed me, of how he was going to take what he wanted without my permission. I can't breathe. I can't breathe. "We won't be exploring anything, Lysander. Let me go."

I'm surprised when he does just that, letting me go and standing back. I suck in a deep breath. He crosses his thick arms. "I need a spy within these stupid little games, and you, Elle, are going to be that for me. I want you to get close to Arden—ridiculously close—and make sure he trusts you. When you're sure he trusts you completely, you're going to kill him. I want it to hurt. I want him to imagine a future with you, trust you, right before you kill him."

"No," I gasp, my mouth dry.

"Yes, you are, and in exchange, I'll help you stay alive in the tests," he continues. "That way, we both win. I'll even mate with you in the end and let you go home."

"You'll let me leave?" I quietly question. I stand a little straighter. "And if I don't do this? What if I just find Arden and tell him you want him dead? He might offer me a better deal."

He narrows his eyes, and I feel the water on my clothes go cold, almost tighten against my skin. "Your sweet little grandma lives all alone. So mortal, so helpless. Wonder what would happen if she accidentally fell into the sea on her morning walk while my dragon was swimming by?"

"No. No, don't, please," I beg, my heart pounding.

He offers me his hand. "We have a deal, then?"

I nod, but I don't take his hand. He eventually lowers it, stepping back. "Do as I ask. Get close to him. Make him trust you. Make him fall for you. It will hurt so much better when you stab him in the heart."

He disappears into mist, and I slide down the door, dropping my head onto my knees before I let myself burst into tears.

CHAPTER 4

Staring up at the bottom of the top bunk, I try to fall asleep again without seeing Finley burning. Without seeing those dragon kings kidnapping me, without imagining my grandmother frantically looking for me. She will be wondering if I'll ever come back home, and I can't get out of my mind the haunting, lonely look that will be on her face.

I can't sleep. Nothing works.

I listen to two of the girls' light snores and Arty's much louder ones from above me where she sleeps. She snores like a banshee caught in a net. Holy fuck, banshees might be real. Fairies might be too. The sound of them snoring is a little comforting, even if they are strangers...they are strangers in the same boat I'm in. When I close my eyes this time, I see green eyes staring back at me. Lysander. His threat is burning into my mind, and how I wish I could find a way to refuse him. But I can't risk my grandmother's life. She is all I have left, and I owe her so much. She didn't have to take me in, not at her age, not when she hardly had enough money to look after herself. But she did, and I cannot be the reason she is killed.

Now I'm going to have to get close to Arden. He killed my ex-boyfriend without even hesitating. That's how little humans mean to him. I don't want to flirt with him. I've never been any good at that, and I've been told I constantly wear my feelings on my face. Considering I hate the bastard, I'm not sure I'm going to be able to fake interest in him. He seems like an arrogant prick, so he might be used to girls throwing themselves at him. No, I need to think of a different way to get close to him. For my grandmother and the possibility of getting back to her at the end of all this.

Lysander said he'd send me home, but I don't think he has the power to do that. The only way I'm going to get back is by winning this goddamn test and making sure I marry one of them that won't force me to stay here. I should get to know the others. I don't want to be a queen—a dragon queen. I don't want magic. I don't want any of this shit. But perhaps if I do win, I might have enough magic to get myself back to my own world. I could disappear with my grandmother on Earth or maybe one of the other mirror worlds Matron talked about.

The door swings open, slamming against the wall, and a cold breeze blows through the already freezing room. I sit up, rubbing my sore eyes. I barely slept a wink all night, and I feel like shit. I guess that's our wake-up call, along with how the room suddenly fills with light, and I can't tell where it's coming from. It's almost like the stone bricks are glowing.

Hope looks over at me as she sits up on her bed, picking up her cloak and heading into the bathroom, slamming the door behind her. "Good morning to you, too."

Livia rolls her eyes at me as she easily jumps off the top of the bed, heading over to the mirror at the end of their bunk bed and beginning to braid her hair into a crown. I frown at her back, wondering how she learnt to braid like that as a happy, chirpy voice fills the room.

"Good morning, everyone! I wonder what we're going to be doing today! I'm so excited!" Arty all but squeals as she climbs off the bed and stretches her arms above her head.

"Lessons," Livia declares.

"How do you know everything?" I ask her, suspicious. She looks over her shoulder at me as she finishes her hair.

She raises an eyebrow. "Wouldn't you like to know? I'm not bothering to tell you, because you will be dead by the end of the day."

"That's not very nice!" Arty defends me. "I'm sure there won't be a test on our first day. I expect a slow day."

The bathroom door opens, and Hope comes out with her hair perfectly straight and a frown on her face. "I hope they have coffee to make up for waking us up this early. Really, really good coffee."

Arty grins at her. "See, I can't even drink one cup of coffee without climbing the walls like Spiderman on crack."

I listen to Arty explain how coffee sends her batshit crazy as I pick up my cloak and run my fingers through my knotted hair while I head to the bathroom. Coffee sounds wonderful and I hope they have some. Arty is still ranting about coffee as I walk past her. "I've never been good with caffeine of any sorts. My mum says it's inherited, because she's never been good with caffeine, and once——"

I shut the bathroom door behind me and quickly freshen up, taking off my black shorts and vest and dressing in the leggings and long-sleeved black top left out. The boots are snug, but I admire the soft leather for a moment. I pull the cloak over my shoulders and tie the knots around my neck. I run my fingers over the fire crest, which is a simple flame inside a circle of flames. Though, as I look closer, I see the outline of a small dragon in the middle of the flame.

When I come out of the bedroom, Livia links her arm through mine as Arty slips into the bathroom. "We should be friends. Artemis talks too much."

I unlink my arm from hers. "I don't talk or make friends until I've had breakfast and coffee. Two cups on bad days like this. Hell, I might even need a whole jug."

She laughs, inclining her head. "My kind of person. Still, we should be friends."

Livia walks out of the room, her cloak sweeping around her, and it looks much better on her than me. Arty comes out of the bathroom, her hair in two braids, and she has the same clothes that I have on. It's got to be a uniform, as if they need to be sure these are the humans they stole and forced to compete to be their dragon queens. "Ah, so you're not a morning person? I am one, I've been told. Go ahead, I just need to make my bed and I'll catch up. My mum always said to start the day by making your bed to clear your head. I always remember it because it rhymes!"

I head to the door, shaking my head but smiling. Arty is quirky, a little annoying, but she has a good heart. I walk out into the corridor where several more girls are coming out of separate doors. I notice a girl with long blonde hair that is as straight as mine, but hers falls right down to her ass and is still silky smooth despite a long night. Mine is not that smooth this morning, but I couldn't care less. I don't have my straightener here, so it's all downhill from here. The girl joins me as I walk down the corridor. She doesn't have a cloak on, and she must be freezing. She's just wearing the thin black top and has black leggings with boots like we all have. I realise that everybody is wearing the exact same clothing.

"Hi. What's your name?" she says in a familiar accent.

"Ellelin," I reply. "Are you from Cumbria? I recognise the accent."

"Yes!" she says, smiling widely. She reminds me of my grandmother; they almost look similar.

"Whereabouts are you from then?" I ask her.

"Penrith," she says. "I grew up there and was about to leave for Glasgow University. Guess I won't be going there now." She clears her throat. "What about you?"

We move aside as four girls come out of one of the rooms, arguing with each other. "Silloth. I've been there since I was six."

She fondly smiles. "I used to love going there. The arcades are the best."

I smile tightly at her as I used to love going there with Finley, and now all I can see when I think of Finley is him cheating on me and then being burnt to death. "Oh, what's your name, anyway?"

"Katherine. It's good to have someone from home here."

We walk through the archway back into the domed room. Instead of there being sofas laid about, now there are four rows of tables littered with food and drink machines. I feel like I'm on autopilot as I use the coffee machine to make myself a cup of lukewarm coffee that tastes like shit. The one perk of working at the caravan site cleaning was the free Costa coffees I could sweet-talk out of the cafe.

I sit down, already drinking it, and Katherine sits next to me, sipping on her cup of tea. I help myself to some bacon, sausage, eggs, and beans to make a full English. It's been a long time since I had food this good. I'm not starved, but we never had money for expensive food like this. I only wish there was tomato sauce. The moment I think it, a bottle smacks right in front of me. I raise my eyebrows, looking around before carefully picking it up like it's not real. But I smack the bottle of tomato sauce on the end, and it comes out on my plate, so I dig in. Katherine chooses a giant load of fruit to put on her plate right before Arty comes and sits on my other side, grinning.

"The food looks amazing! Doesn't it look amazing, Ellie?"

"It's Ellelin," I respond, but she ignores me or doesn't hear me.

"I could make myself sick eating everything here. It's so nice," Arty continues and looks over my plate. "And who's this?"

"Arty, meet Katherine, and vice versa," I introduce them and look at Katherine, who is nibbling on an apple slice, her eyes a million miles away. Most of the girls in here look like that—or they're crying. I want to cry again, so I get that. "So, did you know about all this crazy stuff before it happened?"

Katherine snaps out of it. "Yeah, in a way. I always assumed my parents were telling me some sort of fairy tale and it wasn't real. I honestly thought it was a joke they made up to mess with me."

"I would have thought it was a joke if I was told it too," I agree. Maybe if my grandmother knew, that's why she never told me. I guess it could be from my father's side, and after he died, there would have been no one left to warn me of this.

We finish eating in silence, other than the sobs echoing around the room. I make myself a large glass of water before two more archways appear in the room on either side of the tables, replacing the brick walls. I can see dark red wallpapered hallways lit up with hanging lanterns that are shaped stars made of metal.

"I think that's our cue to leave," I grumble, pushing away from the table and standing up. Arty stays close to my side, and Katherine follows behind us as we go down the right corridor. There are several framed paintings on the walls of the long corridor, all of them of various coloured dragons flying around water or mountains. I pause when one of the paintings catches my eye. It's a dark green dragon, curled around a large willow tree, its mouth full of leaves as it gazes at the ground.

Arty stops with me, looking at the painting too. "Earth dragon, I bet. Beautiful."

"Or terrifying," I say. Arty is right. There is an elegance to the smooth, thin, but massive dragon that makes me want to stare for longer. I shake my head and carry on walking with Arty, noticing how she smells like roses and the strawberry milkshake she drank for breakfast. The hallway leads to an entrance hall with several wooden staircases going in different directions, but the one in the middle is the biggest, and the steps go high up.

At the bottom of the middle staircase stands a tall woman, who is so still she could almost be a statue. She is wearing a stunning, almost glittering white cloak, covered in the same crests that are on my own cloak. That same crest, as I'm learning, must be for the elemental courts, probably each of them marking where the dragon kings come from. At the collar of her cloak are two dragons made out of silver metal, holding the cloak together underneath her neck, and she has on a slim white dress that falls to her feet. Her silver hair is held up in a tight bun, and even though she is dressed as an angel, I get bad vibes from her. Pulling her thin lips back, she narrows her eyes at us all as she clamps her long-fingered hands together. "Welcome, queens in training. It is an honour to meet you all. Your sacrifice is honourable."

Her voice is almost robotic. She lifts both her hands high in the air, arching her neck back. Words I don't understand come out of her mouth. "*Sit draco deos suos victorem eligere.*"

Katherine leans closer. "That's Latin. My mum spoke it, but I only understood *dragon*."

The woman looks back down at us, her eyes now glowing a soft red. Not a scary red like Arden's. "I am your tutor, and you may call me Desmerda. I am here to teach you, guide you, so you are ready for when the tests are over. I will teach you about this world, the politics and past, so you are prepared to leave this castle. My first lesson is the castle itself."

She pauses as we all look around. "It was said to be made by the sorcerer for this test, and it knows you. Not everyone believes that story, as it was aid this castle once belonged to another court. This castle appears only when the test is in play, and it will only allow those it wishes within the walls. The castle was designed to help you. It under-stands what you need. Ask and it will decide if it wishes to give it to you, but do not abuse the power or you might find yourself lost forever in these walls."

That's not creepy or anything. Arty steps closer to me, her shoulder brushing mine.

"The castle scares me. For real," Arty whispers to me. For once, I actually agree with her.

"Please follow me to your classroom, and we will begin. Every other day, I expect you here after breakfast for our lessons, and if you are late, there will be punishments."

She turns around and all but silently glides up the steps, her heels not even clicking on the stone. We all hurry to follow after her, because she might look as scary as a mouse, but there is a vibe to her I can't shake, and I swear there was a hint of excitement in her tone when she said *punishment*. She leads us up the stairs, which twist around in a circle, looping backwards on itself before coming out to a balcony where there is only one door. She opens the creaky old wooden door, slipping into the dark room.

I'm stuck in the crowd as we head inside, where it isn't as dark as I thought it was. Inside is a large room filled with dark wooden desks and tall-backed leather chairs, and I think there are enough for all of us. The walls are as old as the rest of the castle, made of the same stone, but one wall is a massive stained glass window. The glass is broken up into sharp triangles of every colour, and light blasts through, casting rainbows across my boots.

I walk over to the window, needing to have a look outside to check I'm still not on Earth. We're high, maybe in a tower, and there's nothing but rocks surrounding a field of grass below. The mountain eclipses everything else around, hiding the world from this angle.

Arty follows me over and I barely notice she's staying at my side until she steps back from the window, shivering. "I hate heights."

"I bet this height is nothing to dragons, though. I'm yet to actually see a dragon close up since we turned up here. Have you seen one?"

"No," she replies, shaking her head and turning from the window. She still looks pale. "But they're definitely real."

We head over to the desks where people are sitting down, and I go to sit at one when Hope slides into the chair, propping her legs up onto the desk and crossing her arms. "Find another one."

I tilt my head to the side, wondering if punching her is a good idea, but Arty grabs my arm and all but pulls me away as I mutter, "She's a bitch."

Arty sighs. "I don't know her very well, and my mother taught me to never judge people's actions as anything but a reflection of their own feelings, but I'm inclined to agree with you."

"You can call her a bitch, Arty." I grin at her. "If the boot fits and all."

Her cheeks redden, and she shakes her head. "I don't swear. I was taught not to, and throwing insults is mean."

I shake my head at her as we both find a desk, and Arty sits right behind me. Katherine moves to sit a few desks away and waves at me. Desmerda walks around into the middle of the room before holding her hand in the air. Mist pours out of her hand, shaping itself into a dragon that flies around her in a circle, hovering in the air at her side. Wow. I'm speechless as I watch her effortlessly use magic, and I don't think there will be a day I don't find the fact magic is real as spectacular.

"As you're aware, dragons are real, and as long as dragons rule in Ayiolyn, their blood-sworn subjects can share their magic. The easiest way to imagine the connection is like a tree. The dragon kings are the trunk and branches, and the people of their court are the leaves. The leaves come and go, as the dragon king allows, and the dragon king can choose how much power a leaf has. If you have been listening, you should be aware there are four courts in this world. There is the Fire Court with the last heir, King Arden, who has had the throne since he was young. King Lysander rules the water kingdom, but there are many heirs to follow his line. King Emrys rules the Air Court and fought hard for his position at a great cost. Finally, King Grayson rules the Earth Court, who are the smallest and most secretive court in our world. Not much is known of them, therefore preparing you will be difficult."

She stops and clicks her fingers. The dragon shapes itself into a map. It almost looks like the UK, but there are massive gaps between four areas, split up by water, almost like it was ripped apart. Ireland is not there; it's broken into dozens of little islands that are dots on this mist map. There are the royal crests on each area, clearly showing the Fire, Water, Air, and Earth Courts. The fire kingdom, which would have been Scotland, is far bigger than the others, almost eclipsing them.

"Now you've seen what our world looks like, you must get used to the maps. Ask the castle anytime you wish to see a map. As you can see, Ayiolyn mirrors Earth in a way, and this is why we call the other worlds mirror worlds. They are all similar. Over time, we have adapted our world with modern facilities from yours, like machines and toilets. This should make your lives easier."

Arty puts a hand straight up in the air. "So, these are the four courts, but what about the rest of the world? Is there much more land like on Earth? I mean, the UK's only a very small part of Earth."

Desmerda looks pissed off, only for a second, but I catch it. "Yes, but Lost Lands are controlled by wild dragons who do not have magic and cannot shift into human form. The lands are uninhabitable and dangerous, filled with dragons who will not hesitate before eating you like you're a sheep. They are not aware of the differences and their riders are worse."

"So, we don't go there," Arty mutters with wide eyes.

"Not unless you wish for a very painful death," Desmerda agrees. "We do not go there. Do you have any more questions that aren't ridiculous?"

No one says a word, and Arty's cheeks are bright red. I thought her question was a good one, even if Desmerda didn't want to answer it. "Good. Your next lesson in two days will be in general combat. As I take a look around at many of you, I am quite sure that you have no idea about that, given how weak most of you appear." Ouch. "Today's lesson will be cut short, but I do wish you good luck."

With that, she walks out of the room, and we all watch her in confused silence. Do we get the first day off then? When the door shuts behind her, it disappears into stone. Seconds later, all the desks and chairs disappear too until the room is empty of furniture. I fall on my arse with a thud, like everyone else, and crawl to my feet. "Hey, alive castle thing, what was that for?!"

Of course, the castle doesn't answer me, but instead, a single flame drops from the ceiling, right in front of me, burning right through the floorboards. Suddenly, flames start falling from the ceiling. Droplets of it sprinkle everywhere, and the smell of smoke fills the space. I stamp out a flame in front of me, but it doesn't go out. I frown, a little fear trickling into my chest and freezing my blood as Arty comes close to my side. "This must be the fire test from the fire dragon king, Arden."

"Great," I mutter, looking around for a way out, but there are no doors anymore, nothing but tall grey stone walls and that stained glass window.

"Ellelin!" Katherine shouts, and I turn to look at her as she runs to me. Flames pour through the ceiling on either side of her, and suddenly she is shoved into one of them, burning so quickly she didn't get to scream. Hope looks bored as she lowers her arm and tilts her head as she finds my furious gaze. I take a step towards her, my heart screaming, but flames spread across the floorboards in front of me.

"She just killed her. She just killed her," Arty keeps repeating, her voice shocked. Sickness rises in my throat, reminding me of how Finley died. It's the same. This is just like how Finley died. Rapidly, more flames appear around the room, burning the floor slowly away. The ones left all move away from it, backing towards the edges of the room. We go to the window nearby, and I press my back against it as my heart pounds. Some of the walls nearby begin burning from the top, thick smoke filling my lungs, and I choke on it, coughing as I duck down low with Arty. I catch Livia's eyes across the room, and she is pulling a girl with black hair out of the flames as she screams.

"How on earth did we survive this?!" I shout at Arty, just as two more people scream as they are burnt to ash, and another two incinerate moments after that. We are all going to die. The smell of smoke and burning is overwhelming, and I can't think straight as I press my hand on the glass. I slowly look at my hand on the window, the fresh air waiting outside, along with the sheer drop.

No, that's crazy. Crazy. There must be another way. I glance behind me at the flames, coughing and sputtering. There's only a small gap in the flames, but it's big enough for me to get enough traction to break through the window with my body. I'm pretty sure I'd rather risk dying by being flattened out there than burning to death in here. This is mad.

"I've got a crazy plan, but follow me and be brave," I tell Arty, who looks at me with wide eyes as I begin crawling as far away from the window as I can get. Her eyes follow me as I stand up, flames licking and hissing around me as I look at the window. She follows my gaze.

"No! Don't do it! That's insane and you'll die!" Arty screams at me, beginning to crawl my way.

The truth is, I'd rather fly than burn.

With all the strength I have, I run straight into the window with a jump. I smash through it, bits of glass cutting into my skin as I fall. My stomach twists and turns as I scream, air whipping fast by and taking all the air in my lungs.

But I don't fall for long. I slam on something hard, clutching onto a ledge that's warm. I open my eyes, looking right down at scales. I lift my head as my landing pad moves slightly, almost knocking me off, and I look around to see I'm on the back of a dragon. It has black rippling scales tinted with red on the ends, almost like flames, and it is so warm. Large wings are spread out on either side of its huge body, and it has a long neck leading to a huge head with two horns curled up around its ears. The dragon—holy shit, I'm riding a dragon—its long tail is covered in red spikes. The dragon roars loud and I cover my ears until it stops. It turns its head to me, and its eyes are familiar. The pure, blood red belongs to a dragon king I wish I didn't know.

"Arden," I say breathlessly, only now feeling drops of my warm blood dripping down my arms and legs from the glass, and I wince, holding on tightly to one of Arden's scales. Arty lands with a loud thump next to me, followed by Hope, others I don't know, and Livia not long after with the black-haired girl she saved whose leg is badly burnt. I count fifteen, and I look up, waiting for more to come. Nine people couldn't have just died then.

Arden sweeps low, and I barely manage to hold onto the scales as he flies around the castle, his wings reflecting the bright sunlight. His dragon swoops down to the field below, landing on a grassy field. I look up at the broken window of the tower, seeing the outline of at least three girls standing there. They don't jump. They don't move as flames suddenly engulf the room, leaving nothing but ash flickering into the wind from where they stood. I close my eyes.

Arden's dragon tilts to the side, letting all of us roll off his wing onto the grass. Only it's not silent; there are people loudly cheering. I look around us to realise the edges of the field are full of people. So many people in dresses, in cloaks, and some normally dressed. They're cheering so loudly that it's all I can hear, and it cuts into my heart. People just died. Katherine died and they're cheering like that is something to be celebrated.

Arden's dragon is smothered in mist, which fades to leave him standing on the grass in a blood red cloak, tight black trousers, and a black shirt.

"Congratulations on winning my test. Fire is fast and deadly, and even the smallest flame can destroy. This was the lesson of the Fire Court," Arden declares, his voice smug. I flinch as my wrist burns, and I pull up my sleeve to see a red dragon mark on my wrist near my hand.

Males in dark blue cloaks run over to us from the crowd, and a man comes to Arty and me, bowing his head of short red hair. "We are healers from the Water Court. My name is Prince Kian. Will you allow me to heal you both?"

"She needs it more than me," Arty says, rubbing her wrist. Kian meets her gaze for a moment, and they both stare at each other before he clears his throat and turns to me. He offers me his hand, and despite the anger coursing through me, I take it. I feel like every inch of my skin is suddenly underwater, and it only lasts a moment, but when he lets my hand go, every little burn and cut from the glass is replaced with smooth skin. Even the blood is gone.

"Impressive. Thank you."

Kian bows his head once more and then turns to Arty. "May I?"

I leave them to it as I hear Arden laugh. He is laughing. You have to be kidding me. Anger fills me, uncontrollably, and I don't even think of the consequences as I storm over to him. He turns to face me, and the others he was with back away. "Nine people just died and you're laughing? You heartless fucking monster! Nine families are going to search for those girls. Nine fucking lives were just lost just so you can find a wife! How dare you laugh?!"

Silence. Everyone is silent after my rant, but I don't care. He needed to hear it. Arden meets my eyes, and I don't look away. I don't so much as blink. "Would you care if you knew their names? One of them was called Katherine, who liked to go to the arcades and was going to university soon. She could have had a whole life, and she was innocent, but she died up there. She was murdered by you and Hope. Why are your people cheering? It's disgusting. It's barbaric!"

He takes one step, his arms crossed as he stands over me. "Get over it. They're just mortals. This isn't a fun competition. You win or you die. What do you think that meant? That you weren't going to see people die? Grow up, princess. This isn't Earth. We don't have rules here for mortals like you. You're sheep to us."

I don't back down. I refuse to back down. He lowers his hands and reaches out, touching my cheek. "You jumped first, Elle. You're impressive and fiery. Just like my queen will need to be."

"I will never be your queen," I snarl at him.

He smirks before walking away into the crowds that happily cheer for him. I watch him go, only to find Lysander watching me. He flashes me an unfriendly smile before walking to Arden's side. Fuck, I was meant to get close to Arden, not tell him to fuck off. Lysander claps Arden on the back, both of them laughing together like they are close friends and he's not stabbing him in the back. I don't know what the story is or why he wants Arden dead, but I know that killing any of the dragon kings is not something I'm going to be able to walk away from. I don't think I could take anyone's life, even a monster like Arden's.

The crowd starts walking towards us, but I back away until I turn and leave. I need to get out of here. I don't want to talk to them. Most of us are standing in silence. Traumatised silence. I turn around just as the food that was in my stomach comes up, and I puke all over the floor. A few people laugh around me, including Hope, but Arty comes to my side, rubbing my back. She helps me stand. "Come on, let's go back to the room. Ignore them. There is something wrong with them if they don't feel sick after that."

I nod, words escaping me for a moment. "Thank you. I've been really mean to you. Why are you helping me?"

"Because we're friends," she says as I wipe my mouth. "And you just saved my life up there. I wouldn't have jumped. I was just planning to die, but you somehow found the answer."

A tunnel appears in the rock, and we head inside, trusting the castle to take us back to the rooms, or we're just too tired from everything to care either way. The stone tunnel leads into a room in the castle with a staircase, which we head up, and it leads into the main room where we had breakfast. Now, it's back to sofas, and the archway to the bedrooms is open.

"She said the castle is alive. It knew you needed to go back to your room, so it took us back to the rooms. It's pretty smart," Arty comments. I swear the room gets a little warmer with her compliment.

I'm still in shock, still seeing Katherine burnt alive right in front of me. There is nothing but ash and death in this world, and I'm trapped here competing to be the queen. We go back into our room to see another kind of hell waiting on our beds. Dresses. Ball gowns, to be exact. There is a note with our names clearly marked on the hangers, along with another note.

"Tonight, be ready after dinner."

"Wow, how pretty!" Arty sighs. "I love dressing up!"

My dress is all black, sparkling like it's made of a thousand stars. It's tight, low cut, and there's little fabric pieces hanging off the arms. Arty's is different. Hers is a silver princess-style dress, while Hope's is the colour of water, almost see-through and silky. Livia's is a suit dress in a dark brown shade with vines laced into the fabric.

"Oh, I get it. Each dress is for a court. You're fire, I'm clearly air."

I chuck the dress on the floor and climb into bed, still smelling ash and fire. Will I ever be able to close my eyes without seeing them burning?

CHAPTER 5

*A*rty finishes tying the laces at my back for me, and my dress is so blooming tight that I can barely breathe in this thing. This is why I don't wear dresses, and leggings are the best inventions ever. I wasn't going to get ready at all, but Arty reminded me of Desmerda. The thought of punishments from Desmerda makes me put the dress on. On the back of the note was a warning of punishments if we do not comply and get dressed after dinner. I didn't go to dinner. The thought of eating after today made me feel sick.

"It looks like we're the only group that got offered dresses," Arty tells me as she touches up her hair that is braided down her back. "I went and peeped in all the other rooms, and it's just us. Maybe we are special?"

"I hope not," I mutter, looking at Livia, who is reading a book on her bed, already dressed. Hope is still in the bathroom, hogging it like she has done all day. Hope and Livia came back a few hours after the test, and I asked Livia how her friend was, who apparently is fully healed thanks to the Water Court healers. Hope looked as smug as anything as she grabbed the dress, got dressed, and went to dinner. I don't think I'll ever forgive her for what she did. She killed Katherine. She probably killed others there, too. Hope comes out of the bathroom, her hair curled perfectly, and she meets my eyes.

"Are you ever going to stop glaring at me?" she questions, tilting her head to the side.

"You killed her," I snap, stepping up into her face. Her hand flickers to her thigh, where I can see the outline of some kind of weapon.

"Hey, let's calm down. Why don't we try—" Arty tries to squeeze between us, but I don't let her and neither does Hope.

Hope laughs, looking me up and down. "You're so innocent, like Bambi. Have you not realised you're not on Earth anymore? Everyone here has to die, and I will make sure they do because they are in my way. I want the throne, and anyone in my path will die. I don't care if you are feeling hurt or upset. I don't care which three of the idiots here are left standing at the end, but I will be one of the final four. I have a plan, and I'm determined to get what I want."

"So, you're just going to kill everybody that's in your way, huh?" I question. "Are you going to try to kill me?"

She smirks. "Do you think you could stop me? I've trained for this my entire life, and you've stumbled here because of your blood alone. Killing you would be easy."

I curl my fist. I want to punch her. I want to punch her so, so fucking bad. I don't think there are rules around here, and as the thought drifts across my mind, an amused voice makes me jump. "If you're going to fight, I'd recommend taking the dresses off. They were expensive."

I look over to see all four of the kings watching us, Arden in front of them, leaning on the door, his thick arms crossed, and he's looking far too amused. I want to punch him more than Hope. But dammit, they are impressively built and very intimidating as they all look at me.

They're all wearing suits that seem like they're more from our world than theirs, but different coloured cloaks hang off their backs, clipped to their shoulders by silver dragons. Their crowns match their cloaks, but each the same shape. Arden's is a dark red, Lysander's is a deep ocean blue. Grayson has a dark green crown, and Emrys has a crown that's so clear, silver almost, but I can see through it. Emrys and Grayson stay at the back, Grayson frowning at me and Emrys smiling. Lysander watches me, looking me up and down in a way that makes my cheeks burn, before turning his eyes to Hope. She all but runs over to him, flinging her arms around his neck, and they passionately kiss. I'm surprised enough to turn away. So not only is she going to kill her way to the top, but she's also fucking her way up too. I don't know why it annoys me, but it really, really does. Arty and I share a look that says everything.

Arden walks straight up to me, crowding my space with the sort of smug smile I want to punch off his very handsome face. God, why do they have to look like this? They are literal gods. "I see my dress choice was spot on."

"You picked this dress?" I question. "Well, at least I know who's got bad taste."

Arden glares at me, looking royally pissed off. I don't think pretty boy has ever not had a girl trip over her feet for him before.

Arty clears her throat, and I peel my eyes from Arden's. "So, you must be Emrys? I know we only briefly met. Did you pick my dress? I really love it."

Emrys shakes his head. "No, the castle did. Arden's the only one who went the extra mile."

"Oh, well, I love it," she says with a bright smile. Emrys just looks downright uncomfortable. Like we all feel. He smiles at her, offering his arm, which she takes. "Are you ready to leave?"

She nods, looking over at me. Arden offers me his arm, and I back away. I'm not touching him.

Livia goes up to Grayson, and he backs away from her when she offers him her hand. He growls at her. "We don't touch."

"Sounds good to me," she replies.

"Let's walk," he grunts, his voice cold. His eyes flicker to me for only a second before he leaves with Livia. I frown at that, wondering why he doesn't like to be touched.

Arden wraps his arm around my waist, pulling me to his side. I push against his chest. "No, we're not doing that. I'm not your date."

"Actually, technically, you are. Every night this week, we take four of you out to meet everyone that's here in the castle to see you. You get to mingle, enjoy talking to them about all of the boring shit, while I get drunk. Fun times," he deadpans, digging his fingers into my hip. "Let's go, princess."

"I can walk on my own, thanks." I push away from him, and he lets me. Hope is all over Lysander in the corridor, his hands cupping her ass and holding her to him. He kisses her shoulder, meeting my gaze as I step out. I wrinkle my nose in disgust, even as my cheeks burn, and look away. In the corner of my eye, I see him put Hope down and slap her on the ass once before they walk on ahead of us as Arden comes to my side. Hope looks over her shoulder and winks at me. I really, really hate that girl.

Arden leans down, walking at my side, far too closely. For a moment, I swear he sniffs me. "You don't like Hope. Don't worry, I don't believe she has ever been able to keep a friend before."

"Do you know her? Or has she just somehow managed to sleep her way to the top already?"

He laughs, the sound echoing and vaguely nice to my ears. "Yeah, we all know her. She is the ward of Emrys's mother. She is mortal, but she grew up in this world. She and Lysander have been a thing since they were fifteen. Toxic, if you ask me. Half the time, they're not together. Half the time, they are, but I'm pretty sure her end goal has been to sit on the water throne. I'm sure Lysander won't mind. She is epic in bed."

Men.

"So, you and Hope too?"

He leans down to my ear. "We like to share a woman sometimes. You should try being shared between us, princess."

I shiver at the thought of them—all four of them —like that, but I step away from him. "You're such a flirt."

"Only for the pretty girls that take my breath away," he smoothly replies. I shake my head at him. We walk in silence for a while. "I really need a drink."

"Why? Burning nine women today took it out of you?" I sarcastically question.

He grabs my arms and pushes me against the wall of the corridor. "Don't, for a moment, think I like killing them. I'm not a psychopath, and I'm tired of your judgment. You don't have a fucking clue about the games you're in, and trust me, princess, dying was a mercy."

He pushes away from me, my heart pounding, and he carries on walking like nothing happened. Lysander's the only one to look over his shoulder, meeting my gaze, and the look alone is threatening. I swallow around the distaste of saying anything nice about Arden, but I say it anyway. "You look nice."

"Nice?" He bursts into deep laughter. "I usually have women throwing themselves at me in this suit, and *nice* is not a word I've been called before. Gorgeous, handsome, sexy as fuck. All those things, but nice? Yeah. I'm not sure that's exactly something I was aiming for."

He runs his eyes over me, an appreciative smirk on his lips. "If it helps, you look exquisite."

"You're only getting *nice* from me," I mutter, which only makes him laugh more. "Between being an asshole or flirting, is there any other side of you? Is there any actual real person beneath the smugness, arrogant assholeness?"

He deeply laughs again. "You're making me like you, princess. Best stop that or I'll want you as my queen." I snort and he ignores me. "Where exactly are you from again? I can't remember."

"You don't remember where you kidnapped me from?"

He rubs the back of his neck. "We just opened portals to where we were told you girls would be.

We don't exactly have time to look around the area unless the girl's not there. You were in the house, so didn't get much time. It was by the sea, right?"

We head into a long hallway off the main room. "Yes."

"I don't understand the logic of living by the cold sea. Where I'm from, it's pretty much mountains with volcanoes, lava rivers, boiling hot sun, and it's perfect," he says, his voice dreamy. "The women of the court walk around in barely anything. I usually don't wear a shirt, and here everyone is trapped in their clothes. It's too damn cold here. Lysander would like it where you're from, I'd guess. His kingdom is full of water, and his home is by the sea."

I'm more puzzled than ever before as to why Lysander wants him dead. Worse than dead. He wants me to break his heart, too. "So, your court land reflects your powers?"

"Yes." He taps me on the head. "Aren't you a smart cookie?"

He's so patronising that I stomp on his front foot with my heel without thinking it through. He grimaces with a shout, hopping away from me. "You're so violent, princess. First with the toilet, now with the heels. This test isn't meant to be dangerous for us, but with you around, it damn well is."

The entire group has stopped, looking at us and laughing. Well, not Hope. I don't think she knows how to laugh. Lysander glares at me before putting all that thunder in Arden's direction. "Do you need someone to heal you?"

Arden straightens, glaring at him. "You're hardly one to talk. She actually knocked you out with a toilet."

"A toilet?" Hope questions, arching an eyebrow at me.

Lysander grumbles. "It was a toilet seat, and she surprised me."

Hope leans up to his ear. "I can surprise you, too."

He looks at me far too long before kissing her and carrying on down the hallway. Arden keeps his distance from me, making my lips twitch as I carry on walking. "Don't do that again," he warns.

I look over at Arden. "Don't be an arrogant asshole again. Oh wait, that's pretty much your entire personality."

"Ha-ha, you're very funny," he dryly replies. Several girls from the race walk past us down the hallway. So many of their faces are strangers, but there's one familiar thing that we all have in common, and it shines darkly in their eyes. Trauma. Trauma from this race that none of us asked for. I'm not sure any of them want to be here, not even Arty, and if we could leave, we would. Arty's still pretending to be happy, but I can see it in her eyes. I can see it in all their eyes. They're as terrified as I am, and they don't want this. What's the point in winning this race if you see loads of people die and you're too trauma-tised to be a queen? Unless you're Hope and enjoy killing? She won't make a good ruler either.

Maybe that's what they want. Queens who are speechless, traumatised, and do nothing other than sit next to them on a throne and pop out pretty little royal babies. That's not going to be me, but maybe that's what they want. I look at the dragon kings... Do they even want this?

There is a staircase leading off the end of the hallway, which we go down. I have to hold the end of my dress up as the steps loop around in a circle before coming out to a massive ballroom. It's a gorgeous room—even I can admit that—with tall ceilings and arched panels, and each of the walls is filled with a window panel. Each panel is a different kind of element in stained glass, and all the stained glass casts deep rainbows across the entire room, which has about fifty people in it. All of them turn when we walk in, and Arden gently grabs my arm to stop me before I carry on further down the steps, not noticing all the others have stopped.

"Bow for your kings of Ayiolyn."

The voice echoes around the room from a courtier at the bottom of the steps. Everyone bows low. It's a weird thing to see, and I don't like it. I want to turn and run away. Arden's arm wraps around my waist. "Don't even think about running. They will see you as weak and try to use or kill you. Stand straight at my side, princess, and let me show you how to be queen."

"I don't want to be your queen," I whisper back, lifting my head to look at him. His red eyes meet mine, and this close up, I can see black specs within them. His eyes are like lava pouring down a mountain, hot, terrifying but beautiful.

"They don't need to be aware of that."

I know he has a point, but a deep part of me can't accept his help. I don't trust him. I go to pull away when I find Lysander looking at me and looking damn pleased. I know how this must look. Like I'm doing exactly what Lysander wants. My head spins and my heart pounds. I can't do this. I can't do this. I let Arden guide me down the steps, and after making a brief appearance, Lysander quickly leaves with Hope. I'm pretty sure I know what they're doing.

Two people come right up to us, their mouths moving, but I don't hear them. I can't hear anything over the pounding in my ears. I mumble a quick apology before slipping away from Arden. I pass Livia and Grayson, who is like a shadow in this room, but his eyes find mine through it all. For a moment, the world settles, and then it's gone. I can't breathe. I run through the crowd, looking for a way out. I need to get out. I can't do this.

I slip into the shadows of the room behind the staircase, pressing my hands against the stone wall. I gasp. "I'd love a way out of here. Please."

I have no interest in mingling with this crowd, and I suddenly see Arden looking for me. "Please. Get me out of here right now."

Suddenly, a door appears behind me, and I quickly grab the metal handle, turning it and slipping inside. I blow out a breath as I look around the small hallway, so thankful there is no one here. I slip down to the ground, covering my face with my hands. "Thank you so much."

In response, the room gets warmer and a door creaks open. I look down the corridor, seeing another open door waiting for me. I don't know how long I sit on the stone, calming myself down and focusing on clearing my thoughts. I think of my grandmother, of seeing her again. I think of anything other than where I am right now. When my legs feel like they can work, I climb to my feet and head out of the door, which leads outside. A small pathway wraps around the side of the castle, overlooking the mountains, with a long white railing and one white metal bench. I'm not alone. Sitting on the bench is Emrys, and he's not alone.

"It's happened once more. Twelve dead and ten missing this time. I think—"

Thanks, castle. I was trying to escape the dragons, not find them. An older woman sits next to him, her hand on his arm. They're clearly related. They have the same white-blondish hair, and her eyes are the exact same shade of green as Emrys. They both turn to look at me, stopping their conversation.

The woman rises to her feet. "Who is this, then?"

Emrys rises too. "This is one of the contestants. Her name is Ellelin. Ellelin, this is my mother, Queen Dorothy of the Air Court."

Dorothy waves me over. "Please come and sit with us. The castle clearly wanted you to find us, and it is a smart beast."

"I would say another word. I wanted to be alone," I reply, crossing my arms. I'm not sitting with them.

Dorothy doesn't push and instead walks over to me. Emrys goes to lean on the rail, watching us. Watching me. "I remember well your position, as I was once in the same. I'm so sorry this has happened to you."

I frown but lower my arms. "You are?"

"Of course. You didn't ask for this race, and you will need to fight hard to survive like I did and wear the scars forever. I lost friends in my race, and I barely survived myself, but I met the love of my life. Emrys's father. We had hundreds of years together, and I don't regret a day of them," she tells me.

She is sweet. "Why are you both not at the party?"

"Ah, you're quite forward, demanding to know why the king is not at his own party. Emrys never liked parties, even as a child. The boys all refused to go to them, and it was a handful dragging them all along with me," she answers. So, they grew up together?

Emrys keeps his eyes on me. "My dear mother always seems to find me when I try to escape the castles. Her friend, the castle, always seems to help. It clearly likes you too, because it let you escape."

"Well, I saw Arden coming over and decided to run. The castle was lovely enough to help."

"I'm pretty sure a lot of girls do that," Emrys laughs. They both laugh and I find myself smiling.

Queen Dorothy places her hand on my arm. She searches my face for a moment. "You look familiar. Maybe I knew one of your ancestors. I am going to go back to the party to make up an excuse for my son's absence. It was lovely to meet you, and I wish you luck in the race. If you need to find me again, just ask the castle. It will always bring you to your friends."

She bows her head, and I find myself copying her. I've never bowed to anyone before. She goes over and kisses her son's cheek, whispering something I cannot hear before leaving through a door that just appears for her. The silence left in her wake is awkward, and I walk over to the rails, leaning against them. The snow-capped mountains tower around and above the castle—they're gorgeous. I've seen the hills of the Lake District, but this is something else. I may be trapped here, but from what I can see, this world is beautiful.

I clear my throat, tucking a strand of my hair behind my ear. "So, where is this in the world? Whose court is it in?"

"No one rules here," Emrys answers. "It's on one of the small islands, nearest to the Water Court lands. Which in your world, I believe, is Ireland, but it's broken into dozens of small islands including this one. This is the biggest of all the islands off the land, and no one comes onto it until it's time for the race. It doesn't exist, or we cannot see it until then. There were people who lived here but no anymore."

"It's beautiful here. Even if I am trapped in this place, at least it would be a pretty place to die."

"You may think this is beautiful, but the rest of our world is truly something else," he explains. "Earth is a shadow compared to here, and I do not think you would die without a fight. We are all going to die in the end. Why not fight for a life worth living? Humans die so easily, but in our world, dragon queens do not."

We barely know each other, and it's easy enough to fall into another silence when I don't agree with everything he has said. He keeps looking at me though, and I can't read his gaze. "Is it your test next, or is it random and no one knows?"

"I believe water is next," he says softly, keeping his soft green gaze on me. "And by the way, you look absolutely stunning tonight. Arden was not wrong in his dress choice. I believe silver would be a better colour for you, though."

Silver must be the colour of his court, judging by his silver cloak. I shake my head. "Do you dragon kings ever stop flirting?"

"Why should we? And if it helps, I've only flirted with you."

I mess with the fabric. "I don't usually wear dresses. In fact, I hate this thing. It's itchy and annoying."

He laughs. "I would offer to help you out of it, but I'm pretty sure that would come off as an innuendo and not a very good one."

I chuckle. He's gorgeous and funny. Absolutely gorgeous. It's hard not to notice when he's this close. There isn't a bit of his skin that isn't flaw-less. He's one of the most handsome men I've ever seen. The way his body fills out the suit only makes me curious about what he would look like without it on. I clear my throat and look away. "So, air. What exactly can you do with that power?"

He offers me his hand. "Would you like me to show you?"

I look at his hand for far too long. Awkwardly long. "Yes."

I must be completely insane because this mother-fucker kidnapped me and he's making me compete to be one of their wives, and I'm pretty sure I'm crushing on him. I've lost it. But I still take his hand. I scream as suddenly my feet leave the ground, and we float into the air. He laughs as I hold onto his hand for dear life. I'm floating. Almost like I'm swimming through the air. He never lets go of my hand but lets me float along-side with him. "I'm flying."

"It's the best feeling in the world," Emrys tells me. "Let's go above the castle. I won't let you fall. I promise, Ellelin."

Every inch of my mind screams no, tells me not to be stupid, but I don't listen. I let Emrys pull me through the air, out of the balcony, and send us flying high up above the castle, leaving us floating in the stars. All I can see is mountains, rich forests, and fields. Sea surrounds the edges of the island, which is smaller than I thought, and there is nothing else but stars.

"I feel like Wendy from *Peter Pan*," I laugh.

Emrys pulls me to him, our bodies flush, and he holds me close. Surprisingly, I like it. "So, if I pretend to be Peter Pan, do I get a kiss?"

I burst into laughter, and he laughs with me, both of us unable to stop for a long time. "That's the worst pickup line I've ever heard."

He laughs. "Can you tell I'm not good at this?"

I shake my head as he swirls us around in the air. "Tell me something real."

He frowns for a moment. "This is why air is the best power to have in this world. The others, they're trapped down there on land. Water, fire, earth. They need something that's down there.

Air, it's everywhere. It's freedom." He takes a deep breath. "I never feel as free as I do when I'm up here. This is freedom."

"Even in your dragon form?" I question.

"Even then. In our dragon form, we are still the same person, but it's different. We're more aggressive and out of control. Our baser instincts take over, and it means we are at the mercy of our dragon but they will listen to us. They have similar, if not the same, feelings as we do. If I decided not to hurt someone, my dragon would not hurt them."

We don't say another word, we just float in the stars for a while until I realise I feel so much better. So less trapped. "I'll take you back down before an angry fire dragon comes looking."

He takes my other hand, and we fly back down to the balcony. He takes my hand and lifts it to his mouth, brushing his lips against the back of my hand, never taking his eyes off mine. Maybe he isn't that bad at this. When he doesn't talk, that is. "Thank you. I needed—well, I wasn't sure what, but I found it tonight."

Where he touches my hand, it feels like it's on fire before he lets go and walks away. He jumps onto the balcony rail, looking over his shoulder. "Meet me here next week, Ellelin."

He doesn't wait for my answer before he jumps off the balcony, mist surrounding him. I run to the railing, watching as a massive silver dragon bursts out of the mist, its long tail whipping past the castle as its thick wings spread out. It moves so quickly that it's gone in seconds, into the sky, leaving me with my heart pounding.

Another door bangs open behind me on the wall, next to the bench. I guess that's my cue to get back to the ballroom. I pick up the skirts of my dress and head through the door, expecting to come out into the ballroom, but I don't. I step into a small, dark room with a jail cell on the other side and a single flame floating on the ceiling, flickering flame droplets onto the ground in front of me. I back away, but the door disappears, and I realise I'm not alone. Inside the jail cell is a young woman. She reminds me of someone, but I can't quite picture it. She has long black hair that falls in waves to her stomach. She's completely naked, except for vines that are wrapped around her legs and arms, holding her to the ground. She tilts her head to the side and looks at me with empty dark eyes.

"Hello. It's been a long time since anyone came, and it's you," she breathes out, her voice cracking and it almost changes as she speaks. "Help me. Help me please!"

She keeps repeating her cries for help as I back away. She tries to move forward, but the vines tighten, refusing to let her move. "Ellelin Ilroth. Have you come to be my friend? I could use a friend, as they keep me trapped down here. You could save me. Please save me. They destroyed everything!"

I back away, searching the wall behind me for a door. How does she know my name? "We don't know each other. I can't help you. I don't know why you're here."

"Because I—" She pauses, her eyes widening. "Go, they are coming. Go!"

A door appears and I fall back through it, tripping and falling on my ass behind the staircase in the ballroom. The door slams shut and disappears. I barely get to my feet before Arden finds me. "Where have you been?"

I don't answer as he drags me out, so many eyes looking at me, but all I can think about is the woman in the jail cell. How did she know me?

CHAPTER 6

*H*ope slams her fist straight into my chest, and I go flying across the room, landing in a heap on the floor. I straighten up, wincing from the pain. Fuck, that hurt. That hurt a lot. Hope laughs, barely sweating as she strolls over to me. The sadist loves these combat lessons, where she gets to beat the shit out of everyone. Thankfully, Desmerda blows the whistle on the lesson, and nearly everyone sighs in relief, while Hope looks annoyed.

"I look forward to our next lesson," she purrs, walking past me as I wipe sweat off my forehead. Arty comes over to me, hobbling and holding her one arm to her chest. "That's unfair. She was trained her entire life in this world for the race and knows how to fight. The rest of us got British high school, and the most we learnt is how to climb a big rope like a monkey."

I laugh, taking her offered hand and climbing to my feet. "I'm going to keep doing these lessons until I can beat her. She learnt, so can I."

Arty shakes her head. "I don't think I've ever met someone as stubborn as you."

Livia runs past us, looking far too happy. I don't know where she's been getting her private lessons from, but she's certainly learning how to fight quicker than any of us. I was partnered with Hope for our lessons in combat, which happen every other day. It's been six weeks since I was kidnapped. Six, long, pathetic weeks. Hope beats my ass every single lesson, and Desmerda boringly has been teaching us about Ayiolyn. But nothing interesting. I now know about the land, the many cities' names, and how they were built over the centuries. I've learned nothing that would be actually useful against the current dragon kings. We only really learned about their ancestors who met the sorcerer and got played, by the sounds of it.

We head back to our room, where a bottle of silver water tonic is waiting on the pillow like it always is after these lessons. I quickly down the tonic, feeling perfect afterwards. I don't know what magic's in it, but as we've learnt, the water kingdom are masters at healing, and this tonic comes from them. The Fire Court is known for its army, the best in the world. Air and Earth are more known for magic, creativity, and peace, or so I gathered. We did a whole lesson on the Water Court and how the rivers are meant to glisten like diamonds.

It's a shame their king is a murderous bastard who's sleeping with my psychotic roommate. Hope barely sleeps in this room anymore, which is a bonus. She just sneaks out all the time, no doubt sleeping in Lysander's bed. I haven't really seen much of the kings, except for when they come to get their dates and take them out for the many, many ball evenings. I'm glad it's not me going, as it was so boring. Being dragged around by Arden at the ball was dreadful. I've snuck out to see Emrys a few times at the rails, but he's never there, so I gave up a few days ago.

I pull my legs up to my chest and wrap my arms around them, dropping my head to my knees. I could sleep like this.

"Good afternoon," Matron's voice fills the air. My head whips up. I see her sometimes around the castle, but she never talks to anyone. She seems to just be watching us. Always watching us. Matron stands in the doorway, her walking stick in front of her. "Come with me now."

I spot Hope and Livia in the corridor, already waiting. Arty and I share a glance as I get out of the bed and follow after her into the corridor. All of us are sweaty, still wearing black shorts that stop at my thighs and a tight black crop top given to us by the castle on our first combat training lesson. I don't know who washes the clothes or whether the castle somehow magically gets rid of them and replaces them, but there are always freshly washed clothes at the end of the bed every morning. There are always three meals a day too, with varied options. The castle is looking after us, and it would almost be sweet if I weren't a prisoner. Livia leans close. "What if it's another test?"

Goose bumps litter down my spine. I know without a doubt that another test is coming up soon. It's got to be soon. It's been six weeks since the last one. I can't do this right now. I'm tired and I just don't want to. I don't have any words to give Livia to make her feel better, as fear swallows up anything I could say. I can't even tell myself everything is going to be okay. I know it won't be.

They said that all of this takes a hundred days. We're running out of time to avoid tests. Not that I want the water test to be anytime soon. I told Arty about the next test being water, trying to give her a heads-up, knowing she would do the same for me. Arty stays close to my side, and weirdly, I'm happy she does. Over the weeks, she has become my friend. She may never stop talking and is sickeningly bubbly, but I like her. I've never really had a good friend. But somehow, here we are.

Matron hobbles along, and I have to move quicker to keep up. Even though she's got a walking stick, she does move fast for an old lady. We go through the dome area, a new door appearing for us. Matron opens the door with just a wave of her hand, and we follow her through a small, green-walled hallway, which leads out to a brick archway at the end. The archway leads to a small, intimate room, the space taken up by a long dining table made of a gold crystal stone.

As I step through the archway, my clothes transform into a long, elegant silver dress. In fact, all of us are left in the same silver dresses when we step through. The dress drapes in back, pooling at my lower back and showing off the tattoo I didn't want. I'm not wearing a bra or panties by the feel of it, and for some insane reason, that makes me want to laugh. This castle has definitely got a sense of humour.

My good mood disappears when I see who is sitting at the table. The dragon kings and two guests. Arden smirks at me, his long black hair tied at the back of his neck, matching his black suit. I brush a strand of my hair away from my face, realising most of my hair is now in a bun with only a few strands falling down. Arty's hair is dead straight down her back, covering up her tattoo, and her dress isn't as low cut as mine. None of them are. What's up with this dress, castle?

The four dragon kings stand as we enter, and I recognise one of the two women as Emrys's mother. Next to her is a woman with greying red hair, whose very short, tight curls stop just below her ears in front of her fringe and are clipped back with blue dragon-shaped slides. I would guess she's about Dorothy's age, but I wouldn't know. They're immortal around here. They live for a very long time and apparently don't age all that much. When her green eyes meet mine, she reminds me of Lysander. This must be his mum. I wonder if she knows her son is a psychopath. Thankfully, there are a bunch of empty seats away from them on the other side of the table, and I head right to them, only for the chairs to disappear. I glare at the walls nearby. "Not funny," I hiss.

Arden smirks, running his eyes over my dress. Grayson barely looks at me. Lysander doesn't take his eyes off me, but in a way that sends shivers down my spine. They're all watching me, like it's just us in the room, and I'm not sure what to make of it. The only seat left is opposite him, next to his mother and Emrys. Hope, Livia and Arty found their seats right away, and the castle let them sit anywhere they like.

Lysander's mother, or my guess she is, smiles at us all. "Welcome. We asked the castle to bring you. I hope you don't mind. For those who don't know me here, I'm Queen Consort Meredith of the Water Court and mother to King Lysander. This is my dear friend Queen Consort Dorothy of the Air Court. We are taking turns meeting everyone, as we would like to get to know you in an informal setting."

"We don't mind at all," Hope says, her voice sickly sweet. I raise an eyebrow at that, but she is busy smiling at Meredith while stroking her son's arm. Lysander is still watching me and not pretending he isn't. I resist the urge to glare right back at him. "As we are going to be family soon, after all, isn't it best we have regular meals like this so I know you better? I've met you, of course, but it is lovely to see you more."

"That's if you survive the next couple of weeks," Livia dryly comments as she crosses her arms and leans back in her chair. "If you keep running your mouth and making enemies, I'm pretty sure some-one's going to spend the entire one of these tests trying to kill you."

I put my hand up. "That will be me."

"Bite me," Hope snaps.

Lysander laughs as an awkward silence fills the room. Hope clears her throat, a pretend smile slapped on her face. "My friends can be really funny."

Hope continues to try and make small talk with Meredith, and I just look away from all of them. The quicker this meal is over, the better. Forks, knives, and a plate appear in front of me, followed by hot food. I eat a little, pushing other bits aside, feeling them watching me every now and then. I lift my eyes to find Grayson, and god dammit, I nearly choke on a potato. Intense. That's the word I'd use to describe him, and when he looks at me like this, all that intensity slams into my soul.

Grayson is sitting at the head of the table, his arms crossed, not saying a word or touching his food. I glance at the people who come to take away our plates, their heads bowed, but they have imperfections that give away they aren't dragon shifters. It's easy to see the difference now.

"Are these your slaves?" I snap, my tone saying everything about how I feel, and I don't hide it. Everyone goes quiet.

Lysander's mum clears her throat. "No, they're not our slaves. They work for us, and willingly so. We don't have slaves here. Many of them have families they wish to feed and house, and we pay well. They came with us when we travelled here. They have been loyal servants for many years, and they're free to leave if they wish to."

"Lucky them. I wasn't given that option."

My reply to the queen leaves everyone silent for a moment. "I didn't want to leave either." Meredith's response surprises me. "In fact, I remember kicking and screaming and fighting the entire way here. I had no interest whatsoever in being a dragon queen." Dorothy shakes her head. "We took the test together," she says, pointing at Dorothy. "The other two humans who survived, I didn't know them until the end. They weren't the people we roomed with, but Dorothy and I, we shared a room like you've all done. Unfortunately, in the trial, the other two that we shared a room with died. We barely survived towards the end. Truth be told, the tests got worse and worse as they went on. The fire was the easiest of all of them. I heard that you jumped first, and that was recklessly brave. I admire that you also speak your mind and don't seem to be frightened. You remind me of myself."

I nod, meeting her eyes. "Could you tell me what happens in the tests if they are all the same?"

"No, but they all have similar themes, of course. Falling, flying, fire. These are all themes of the fire test. There's always reckless, dangerous courage that needs to be taken. To be brave is to be a fire queen. You'll need that bravery as time goes on in your rule if you win," she answers.

"Brave or stupid? That's the real question," Livia murmurs.

Arty clears her throat. "Is this all the royal family that is left, or do you guys not have any other parents around? No one will speak about the royal families here, and I was curious."

No one says a word to answer her, but we all wait. I can tell from how the guys all instantly tense that she has hit a sore subject. I'm surprised when it's Grayson who speaks. "Yes. This is the only family we have left, and I'd appreciate it if you'd be kind to them."

"No one was being unkind," I reply.

"Yes, you were," he coldly replies. "You're acting like a brat, exactly how you have been since we met."

"Since we met, we've barely spoken, so how would you know I'm a brat?"

He smirks briefly at me for a second, and then Arden laughs. He laughs and laughs. "I call her princess, but she really is a brat. I don't know if I like that nickname more."

Lysander chuckles, and I glare at him. Emrys chuckles but stops when he sees my glare. I really, really hate these arrogant asshole kings.

"There looks like there might be some competition over who gets you if you win this," Dorothy says. The guys shut up really quickly.

"I don't plan to be any of their dragon queens," I firmly state. "I want to go back home. That's it. End of story."

Meredith sighs. "I was the same. In fact, for the first year, I just tried to escape. I swam down the rivers. I jumped into the sea. I made myself a boat and tried to escape with that. Of course, my mate always brought me back. I actually found it half amusing that he let me get so far before ending my adventures. For the next year, I refused to speak to him or speak to anyone in the court. I just wanted to get back to my family, to my parents, who were missing me. So, he brought my family here. He brought my parents here, and that was the first kind thing he did. I don't think he wanted a relationship with me at the beginning, but eventually we fell in love."

"That's so sweet," Arty says with a sigh while I'm thinking about if my grandmother could come here. I wouldn't have to lose her…but this place. She would always be in danger.

Meredith nods. "It was. Sadly, he passed away."

"I'm sorry to hear that. I actually am." I meet Lysander's eyes even as I speak to his mother. "I lost my parents too, when I was six, and I have been told they deeply loved each other. My grandmother said it was a blessing they went together, as one without the other would have been a ghost."

"How did they die?" Emrys quietly asks.

"An accident. We used to travel all the time. My parents loved to explore, and they died in a boating accident, lost at sea while they left me with a nanny in the hotel. They just never came back. I don't remember any of it. I was too young, but my grandmother was my only living relative. She said she'd met me a few times, but my parents never stayed still long enough for us to actually have a bond until she took me in. She looked after me since then."

"That was very kind of her," Dorothy comments.

"Yes, we all have dead parents. Me too," Hope all but shouts. "Now, can we talk about something else?"

Meredith ignores her. "I hope you win." She puts her hand on mine. "I really do. Also, may I say, the Water Court is the best."

"The Fire Court is also quite charming," Arden sexily murmurs, leaning back in his chair and making no attempt to hide his stare. Lysander laughs, like the idea of me in his court is hilarious. I don't say a word, but quite literally, I'd rather drown than be Lysander's anything, but his mum is sweet, so I keep that thought to myself.

Hope begins to make small talk, Arty chiming in every so often. Livia and I stay quiet, so done with all this. When I'm finally given permission to leave with the others, I all but hightail it from the table to the wall, praying the castle is on board with my escape plan. A door appears for me, and I walk straight through it as it opens, watching it shut behind me. I take a deep breath, leaning on the cool stone to slow down my racing heart. "Thank you, castle, but we need to talk about the slutty dress."

I swear it gets warmer in here for a second, almost like the castle is amused. I jump when the door opens behind me and Grayson steps in. He frowns and reaches for the handle of the door, only for it to disappear. He slams his fist on the stone wall. "Interfering fucking castle."

He turns on me, and I shiver, flattening my palms on the wall. "You're a problem, Ellelin."

"Nope, I'm not, and it's time I leave," I quickly say, turning away and walking down the hallway, desperately looking for a door. His steps follow me, right before vines shoot out of the ground, wrapping around my wrists and slamming my back harshly on the wall. I grunt, struggling to get free as he leisurely walks towards me, a dragon hunting an easy prey.

"You've got issues, buddy, and I'm not playing this game. Let me the fuck go!"

He steps close, but I notice he never actually quite touches me. Just a hair's breadth away. I realise, even when he kidnapped me, he was touching the vines, never actually touching me, and all the things I've heard about him flash through my mind. "You don't like to be touched, do you? This is why you are restraining me—just to talk to me? What are you so scared of, dragon king?"

His growl is animal-like and, fucking hell, scares me. I shake all over. A vine slides up my chest, wrapping around my throat. Grayson's eyes are like hardened chunks of ice. "Why do I keep finding myself looking at you? Searching for you? Why the fuck can't I keep you out of my head?"

"That's your problem with me?" I pathetically question, my heart pounding. The vines tighten slightly. "I haven't done anything!"

"And yet you haunt me. You're the first human, dragon, or fucking anyone I've wanted to touch. Why is that?" he demands, and I think he is actually confused.

I blow out a breath. "I don't know, but maybe we can make a deal?"

He cocks his head to the side. "What deal?"

"I need someone to train me in combat so I don't keep getting beaten up every other day in lessons, and you need to learn to be touched, and maybe how to chill out. I can do that for you," I suggest, my heart racing. I don't mention I might use those skills to kick them all in the balls and escape later on. "And then when you choose a bride, at least you'll be able to stand having her close."

His eyes darken, and he leans that inch closer, so close I can smell him. He reminds me of the forest I visited as a kid, earthy and rich. Grayson's nose flares and he steps back, the vines disappearing. "We have a deal. I will come to you for an hour every other morning. Our lessons will be brutal."

"For whom?" I ask with a smile.

He looks back before leaving. "Goodnight, brat."

A door appears near me, and I quickly open it, stepping outside into a field with a tunnel on the other side. I walk across the field for a while, looking up at the millions of stars that are so much freer than me, before I sit down and cross my legs, resting back. I'm not surprised when Arden plops down next to me on the grass, lying back, resting his head on his thick arms. I am surprised that at some point, I've found him less frightening than the others. Or at least on the same level as Emrys. Lysander and Grayson scare the shit out of me.

"Well, that was an awkward-as-shit dinner, and there was no alcohol to make it better," he groans. "Sorry about that. Emrys's and Lysander's mums brought all of us up, and we can't tell them no. When they tell us to do an awkward meal, we do it."

I turn my head to face him. "Where are your parents, then?"

He sighs. "Dead like most of yours. I'm all that's left of the Fire Court royalty. You can call me one of a kind."

He winks at me, but I can see through it, just for a second. "You killed my ex-boyfriend. You can't try to be my friend now."

"He deserved it. I'll die on that hill, princess."

I sigh. He might be a little right. I don't think I can fully admit to myself what Finley, a man I knew for years, was going to do to me, without having a nervous breakdown. I shake my head, climbing to my feet. "I'm going to bed. Thanks for the weird meal thing."

He climbs to his feet, touching my arm. He is burning hot where he touches me. "I would like to get to know you. I know I'm a flirt. I talk a lot, which most people find charming, but you don't seem to. We met when I kidnapped you and killed your ex-boyfriend, but I still see potential between us. Someone I could imagine at my side at the end of all this. Maybe we could talk? Just hang out sometimes."

Lysander's threat floats into my mind. My grand-mother, drowning deep underwater, a dragon's mouth wrapped around her legs and pulling her down. That dream plays over and over in my mind as I look at Arden and see the vulnerability in his eyes. He is lonely. Even if every inch of me wants to shout no, to tell him that I have no interest in being his queen, I force myself to smile, for my grandmother. "I'd like that. We can talk now if you have time? Maybe you could show me around parts of the castle I haven't seen?"

His smile is so big, bright, and playful that I almost feel guilty. I let him put an arm around my waist, pulling me against his side. I'm a terrible person for this...but I'll be anything to save my only remaining family. Arden leans down closer to my ear as we walk. "Don't say a word, but the water test will happen in the middle of the night tonight. Be ready."

CHAPTER 7

I lie in bed, completely still and paralysed with unrelenting fear that feels like it's wrapped around my throat like one of Grayson's vines. Arden's warning plays over and over in my mind, and every second seems to go by slower than the next as I wait for the Water Court test to begin. I woke Arty up and told her that the water test was tonight, and I wanted to tell Livia, but Hope was in the room when she came back late. Arty barely believed it anyway, especially when I told her it was a warning given from Arden. She said that we probably shouldn't trust him.

Arty could be right, but I have the gut feeling he was telling me the truth. That he was warning me about what's going to happen tonight because he likes me for some insane reason. Or just wants to fuck me before I die. Either one of those two reasons—most likely the second one. For those reasons alone, I can't close my eyes. I can't sleep. I stare up at the bed boards in front of me, staring at them but not seeing anything.

My own racing heart is distraction enough.

Softly, like a lullaby, I hear a creaking noise below me, and I sit up, digging my hands into the soft bedding. The gentle creaking changes into loud creaking, right before the bed underneath me disappears, and my scream rips out of my throat as I slam down into cold water, slipping and sliding down a tunnel. The tunnel spins me around in darkness, in circles as I slide down the walls, and I hear Arty's scream above me, knowing she's not far behind. Water sprays into my mouth, the rock walls rip at my top right before I'm suddenly falling, and I land hard on a stone floor, smacking my cheek on the stones in shallow water.

I lift my head, rubbing my sore cheek and looking around at the dim room. Every wall is thick stone, high and covered in glowing green moss, which is the only light. The ice-cold water is up to my wrist before I crawl to my feet.

Arty comes sliding down the whole tunnel after me, sliding to a stop, landing and not smacking her face like me. The tunnel we came out of disappears, leaving mossy walls in its place. The walls are too high to climb by the looks of it, but I walk over, touching the wet moss, which falls apart in my hands. We can't climb out of here. The walls themselves are smooth underneath the moss too. I turn and help a shocked Arty to her feet. She wipes water out of her eyes. "I guess your dragon was right."

"He isn't mine," I mutter, but it feels like a weak answer that neither one of us wants to argue about at this point. My boots clap in the water as I walk around the room, touching all the walls for some kind of clue.

"Look," Arty whispers, and I turn to see her standing in front of two metal levers that have appeared on the wall in front of her. I don't like this.

I blow out a breath as I walk over to her side. "I'm guessing we have a choice. Left or right?"

Arty glances at me, her face pale. "I'm not choosing. You choose."

"Why do I have to be the one to choose? For all I know, this whole room could flood with water and drown us if I choose the wrong one," I mutter, still rubbing my cheek. "In fact, I'd bet that's exactly what is going to happen if we choose wrong. It's the water test, after all."

Arty is silent as I continue. "I thought this one would be easier because I'm a good swimmer, but now my decision-making skills are being tested. I'm screwed. I can't even decide on my favourite pizza flavour."

"Mine is pepperoni with pineapple," Arty nervously replies, her cheeks brightening so she has some colour to her other than her hair. "At least you can swim. I've actually always had quite a bit of crazy fear of water, so I'm probably going to die here. If I do die here, then I'm really glad that we were friends for the short time that we got to be friends, and that you didn't kill me for my endless chatter. Like now. I seriously can't stop talking when I'm frightened or excited or—"

"Just being you," I sigh. "Arty, come on. I'm not going to let you drown."

"Really?" she questions, her eyes wide.

I shake my head at her, not answering that one. I look back at the levers. "Let's go for the right. I don't know why, but it's a fifty-fifty chance, right?"

"Together?" she asks, picking up my hand and linking our fingers together before placing them on the right lever.

I nod and together we pull it down. The same soft creaking echoes around the room before the floor and walls begin to shake. The walls rapidly slip down, and there's nothing on the other side except for more walls—and more water that fills the ground halfway up my boots. Two more levers appear on the other side of the room.

We walk over, silently agreeing to get this over and done with as soon as possible. "Left?"

"What if it's always right?" Arty nervously replies as we stop in front of the lever. We both put a hand around the left without another word. My heart feels like it is beating a musical as time slows down to a stop as we pull the left lever. This time the wall doesn't go down. Instead, the floor underneath us disappears and we fly down into a water tunnel, plunged deep into cold water, my hand slipping from Arty's. I gasp, only to have a mouthful of water threaten to drown me, and I search for the light above. I spin in the water, looking for Arty. She can't swim. Oh my god, she can't swim. I look around desperately, twisting in the water, feeling my lungs burn, but I can't see her. I swim up to the surface, knowing I need to get some air before I dive again. Gasping, I scream. "Arty!"

"I've got her!" Livia screams back at me. I twist in the water again, following her voice, barely making out two figures in the water nearby.

"I'm going to drown! I'm going to drown!" Arty screams over and over, and Livia tries to calm her down. When I get closer, I see Arty's arms waving about in the water as Livia is struggling to hold her afloat.

Hope is swimming nearby. "She's going to drown you, dumbass. Let her go."

I'm glad Livia doesn't respond to Hope as I swim towards them all, hooking my arm under Arty's, and she instantly calms, bursting into tears. Livia nods at me from her other side, and together we start swimming, pulling Arty between us. Hope is long gone, swimming straight ahead in the distance towards the only light source in the room. We both swim faster towards it, even pulling Arty between us, who is still crying. It takes us a while before we find a way out, a stone ledge with a tunnel behind it. We pull ourselves up onto the stone ledge, and Arty lies on the ground, breathing heavily.

Livia meets my gaze. "Thank you for saving her," I say.

She looks away. "It was the right thing to do. I'm guessing you picked the wrong lever like us?"

"Left was wrong. It must have always been right," Arty coughs out.

Hope is pacing behind us, but she stops, sneering down at Arty. "Can you not swim? Seriously? You knew this test was coming. Your parents never thought to teach you to swim? Did they hate you or something?"

I stand up to get between them as Arty sits up. "They did try once, but I have a fear of water."

Hope rolls her eyes. "Aren't you scared of heights, too? What's wrong with you?"

I step between them and shove Hope's shoulder, making her stumble back. "Don't pick on her, you bitch. I get it, you're as annoyed as we all are, but I'm not letting you speak to her like that."

Hope sneers at me before turning away. "She isn't worth bothering, anyway. The pair of you are weak."

Livia steps to my side. "We need to figure out how to get out of here. The water is rising."

We all look down to see the stone ledge we're on has disappeared underneath our feet, and we all stand up, looking down the tunnel behind us, knowing it's our only chance out of here. We're all soaking wet, scared, still in our pyjamas and royally pissed off, but somehow Hope makes it a million times worse by just being here as she glares at us all and storms off down the tunnel.

Arty is shaking as I hook my arm through hers and guide her down the tunnel. I lower my voice. "Don't let her beat you down. Shine brighter than her. I know you can."

She gives me a shaky nod, but she goes silent as our makeshift group heads down the dirt tunnel, Hope leading the way. It spirals around into another large stone room with mossy walls. This one is also filled with water, but this time it's up to our waist. Two more levers appear on the opposite wall, moss wrapped around the handles. I get the feeling, if we fail at this one, the water is going to be up to our shoulders or higher, or another drop we might not survive.

"We can't pick the wrong lever," I say. "Maybe we should pick right this time."

"It'll be too obvious for them all to be rights," Hope mutters like we are stupid.

"Maybe it's as simple as water can be," Livia comments, looking between the levers and back to us. "I don't know, but we need to pick before we drown."

"We should vote," Arty quietly suggests.

Hope rolls her eyes. "Fine. I pick left."

"Right," Arty and Livia say at the same time.

"Right," I breathe out, hating that a decision so simple could kill us all, but we have no choice but to take it.

"I swear to the dragons, if you all get me killed, I'm haunting you all," Hope snarls. "Especially you, purple."

I narrow my eyes at her, but she turns and pulls the right lever. A large creaking noise echoes before the wall drops away and water floods into the room, pushing us back a few steps. Arty cries out, clinging to my arm, and I barely manage to stay standing upright as the cold sea water fills the room right up to our shoulders. The water doesn't stop coming.

I look up at the ceiling, noticing it's not far away and the tunnel behind us is completely gone. It's so dark in here I can barely see the edges of the walls anymore. Yet the moss glows brightly, shining green light around the room. We all swim to the nearest wall, Arty letting me tug her along. The vines are thicker here, easier to hold onto as the water rises slowly. Slowly but deadly. It only takes a trickle of water, built over time, to kill us all. I desperately look around for a way out, but there is nothing. Just nothing.

Arty latches onto my arm tightly, and even though her nails are hurting me, I can't feel anything but terror. Hope shouts over the sound of running water. "Leave her and swim with us. She's just dead weight at this point, and we need to find a way out."

I'm surprised she gives a shit if I'm coming with her or not. "Just go and find something. I'll look after her."

Livia gives me a sympathetic look, but part of me wonders if she agrees with Hope. I look at Arty. "I'm not leaving without you."

I watched Katherine die in front of me. I watched Finley die in front of me. I'm not having anybody else I know die. Especially not Arty. She's too bright, too nice, too lovely to die here like this. The dark, fucked-up world definitely needs her as one of its queens, even if the idea of her being with any of the dragon kings makes me feel sick to my stomach. The current picks up, threatening to tug us from the wall.

The fear that I see shining in even Hope's eyes tells me enough. We are screwed. I search the room again and I pause, seeing something deep in the water. A glowing white light. "I see a light. It's right at the bottom!"

They all look. Hope shakes her head. "There's nothing but darkness."

The light gets brighter…but they can't see it. I wonder if this is Lysander helping me in this test. He said he would help me, and it would make sense that they can't see the light that I suddenly can. It has to be the way out. I wonder for a second why his girlfriend can't see it. Talk about being a douchebag. "It's there. You're going to have to trust me."

I look at each one of my roommates, searching their faces.

"I think we have to swim down to the bottom," I carry on. "They are always saying the dragon queens need to be brave and good with the elements of the court they're in. They want us to be good swimmers and brave."

"Okay, I'm with you, purple," Hope states.

"Me too," Livia agrees. "Better than drowning up here."

"I can't—I can't," Arty cries. "I can't do that. I can't swim down there. I can't even open my eyes underwater."

She starts panicking, clawing at the moss edges of the wall like she can crawl out of here. The water is so high now; it is tipping into my mouth with every word, and I can barely hold onto the moss wall to hold myself up. We don't have time for this. I grab hold of her chin with my one hand, turning her face to me. "Look at me. I'm your friend and I'm not going to let you die. So, you're going to be brave and you're going to let me pull you down. I can do it. I can pull you down with me, and you only need to kick your legs."

"But—"

"I'm a damn good swimmer. I've always been a good swimmer. My grandmother was adamant about mastering the skill of swimming. We lived so close to the sea, and she was always worried about me falling in and drowning. She probably had a point, and now all those lessons that I detested growing up, now they might actually be useful. Trust me, okay?"

Her eyes meet mine. Something I can't read flashes in them. "I trust you."

"We're following you," Livia states.

Hope is staring at the water. "Why can't I see a light?"

I don't say a word. Lysander must not like her all that much, and I don't know why I feel a mixture of happiness and disgust at the thought. Surely, he'd want to save his girlfriend rather than letting her drown if he had any intention of her becoming a queen at the end of all this. But then again, he is a psychopath. So perhaps he was actually quite happy with her drowning. I take hold of Arty's hand.

"On a count of three," I shout. "One, two, three!"

I dive into the water, pulling Arty with me as I hold my breath. She struggles for a moment before latching onto my arm, keeping at my side, kicking her legs as hard as they can go, but she doesn't open her eyes. The salt stings, and I briefly look back to see Livia and Hope following, swimming as fast as I am. I turn back, focusing on the light right at the bottom, getting closer and closer to me. The current is stronger with every inch I swim down, pushing against me, making it difficult to swim through it. I push through, swimming down towards the light with everything I have, feeling my lungs burn and itch with the desire to open my mouth and breathe.

Finally, the light is close, and I stop, pulling Arty closer. Hope swims past me, reaching for where I point, and she disappears through the light. Livia goes next and I'm still weighed down by Arty, but I don't give up. My lungs burn. Every inch of my body hurts from the exertion of pulling her through the water. I'm just about to push her into the light when she suddenly lets go of my hand.

My eyes widen in panic as she disappears, not into the light, but pulled in the current. I spin in the water, looking for her. She can't die. God, no. I shouldn't have let her go. It's so dark down here. I can barely see her outline, but I see her struggling in the water not too far away. I swim hard, pushing off the ground to get to her, and I grab her hands, making her stop, and her eyes open.

Sheer panic. That's all I see. I nod at her, hoping she can hold on a little longer. I yank her down roughly with me towards the light, knowing I don't have long left before I need air.

I barely manage to push her through the light, watching her disappear, when a current of water slams me to the side and pulls me up, away from the light. I gasp, letting too much cold water into my lungs, and my body shakes. I could seriously die just trying to save Arty's life. What the hell am I doing? I need to survive. I can't die here. The edges of my vision tip with darkness as I swim towards the light, desperately pushing against the current that seems to be getting stronger and stronger with every second, pushing me away like it wants me to sink into its depths and never come out again.

Lysander said he would help me. That didn't mean that he was going to save me from this.

"Swim! Don't you fucking dare stop. You're Ellelin Ilroth and water cannot drown you." Lysander's voice shouts in my head, over and over. I'm sure it's the lack of oxygen, but his commands make me swim harder as I listen to his voice. "Swim! Swim!"

No one can save me unless I fight for myself with everything I have. I keep swimming towards the light, desperately, pathetically swimming towards it. Everything in my body starts to shake, convulse, and die as I run out of air. I stop. I swear my fingertip just touches the light before everything turns black.

I wake up with a gasp, looking up at a ceiling made of light. No, not light, but yellow stained glass. It's a domed glass ceiling with a spiky point at the top, and the yellow glass is covered in swirls of yellow mist making the room so bright it hurts to open my eyes. But I'm alive. Hell, I survived! I'm lying on a soft, massive bed with white silk sheets. I sit up, wincing at the burning feeling in my lungs and the general burning of my muscles throughout my body.

"Careful. They healed you, but you might be sore. You technically died for a few minutes there." I turn my eyes to Emrys, who's sitting on a chair by the bed. "But I was worried about you being alone, so I brought you back here until you woke up in case you needed more help. I can heal some minor injuries."

My jaw drops. He does look worried. The air dragon king is worried about me, the girl he kidnapped and danced with under the stars. He leans back in the chair, his shoulders relaxing. "You're glaring at me. You must be okay."

I chuckle. "I'm surprised I'm alive."

"Me too," he admits, rubbing his chin. "You fell through the portal just in time, but you weren't breathing, and your heart had stopped. I don't know how long you haven't been breathing. Lysander's brother worked hard to heal you, and I swear even Lysander himself helped. Not that the stubborn bastard admitted to helping. Lysander's brother isn't anywhere near as powerful as Lysander, and you needed a lot of magic to be saved."

Lysander saved me. So did his brother. I need to thank his brother. For a moment, I want to thank Lysander for saving my life, but then I remember the only reason he would have saved me would have been to make sure I continue with his sick deal. "Artemis was a howling mess over you, claiming you saved them all. Quite heroic. My entire court will be talking of you now. First test, you jumped before anyone else and saved many lives. Second test, you risked your own life to save your friends."

I sigh. "I think I'm just dumb and keep getting into bad situations. All I want is to go home, not be some hero."

He laughs. "May I?" He points to the side of the bed next to me. I nod. He comes and sits on what must be his bed. It smells like him, and it's weirdly comforting. He leans back, stretching his legs out, his arm brushing against mine. I'm still in my pyjamas top and shorts, but I'm not soaking wet anymore, at least. "The water test is always the most barbaric, especially if you're not a good swimmer. Six died today. Nine are left. How did you know to swim down?"

I don't say a word. He just smiles at me. "Ah, so you have your secrets then, don't you?"

"Of course," I sweetly reply. Shitty, murderous deals, the kind of secrets that would make him hate me.

He tucks some of my damp hair behind my ear, and he pauses, resting his fingertips on my cheek. "I think the biggest secret I have right now is how much I want to kiss you. You want to leave, and I secretly wish you never do."

My heart pounds as I stare into his eyes, my body feeling like it's on fire. It would be so easy to kiss him, to imagine he isn't a dragon king. To imagine I was free and not trapped. "I have no interest in kissing you."

He leans a little closer. "Your racing heart is saying something different. I could listen to it beat for me all night."

"Is that why you brought me here? To keep me in your bed all night?" I ask. Fuck, I'm flirting with him.

He doesn't move; he doesn't back away. "These are our private rooms. The others will kill me for bringing you here. We share these rooms, and the girls are banned, except Hope." He lifts my chin up with his finger. "But I wanted to make sure you were okay. That's the only reason I brought you here. I promise, Ellelin."

The way he says my name...fuck. It's sexy. I want him to say it over and over. What is wrong with me?

I keep telling myself to not go any closer, to step away, to remind myself who he is. He's so gorgeous, so breathtakingly gorgeous, and charming, and he's looking after me. And for some reason, I just need——

I kiss him. He looks surprised for a second, startled, like he was being playful before and didn't actually expect me to kiss him. But that only lasts for a second before he's sliding his hand into my hair, with a low growl, tightening his grip. He deepens our kiss, taking my breath away. I've never been kissed like this before. It's passionate, and he sends shivers throughout my entire body from just one kiss.

"Fucking excuse me. Since when are we allowed to bring them back here to fuck?" Arden growls, an animal-like sound echoing from him. Dragon-like sound.

I break away from Emrys, flinching as I turn to see Arden leaning by the door, his red eyes glowing like pools of lava. Well, there goes my ruse of pretending to like him. He's certainly going to know I'm not that interested now. Burning jealousy shines in his red eyes like the flames.

Emrys holds his hands up. "Cool the fire, friend. Ellelin was injured and I wanted to make sure she was okay."

Arden doesn't move, and the way he looks at Emrys makes fear snake down my spine. "Did that involve sticking your tongue down her throat?"

"Chill the fuck out," Emrys growls back at him, moving slightly in front of me. The air in the room seems to pause, tense. "You need to stop. You don't want to start this now. You've changed since this began."

"Can you blame me?" Arden replies. They both have a silent conversation, and whatever they communicate is passed between them with just a look. They both seem to pause, and the mood seems to lighten when they look away. Arden moves his eyes to me, no longer glowing red. "Are you okay, princess?"

I clear my throat. "Yep. I didn't drown and I'm alive."

"I didn't see the test, but I heard about you," he laughs. "You're fucking crazy brave and I love it."

My cheeks burn as Emrys helps me off the bed. I'm still a bit dizzy, woozy almost, and everything from my lungs to my legs hurts. Arden reaches for me, but I put my hand up. "I'm fine. Is this still part of the castle? Can I ask it to take me back to my room? I think I need a nap, and I want to check if Arty is okay. Livia too."

"Your friends are fine, and yes, this is the castle, but there is only one exit," Arden explains. "Come. I'll take you back. If it makes you feel better, I promise not to stick my tongue down your throat on the way. Unless you ask me to… which I'd be highly amenable to."

"Sleep well," Emrys says, touching my arm, and I swear I feel his touch even as I walk away from him to Arden.

Arden whispers. "You're blushing." I weakly shove Arden's thick arm, barely even making him budge a little. They both laugh, the jackasses.

When I get to the door, I turn back to Emrys. "Thank you."

"Anytime."

Arden begins to lead me down a spiral staircase, and I briefly notice three more doors next to Emrys's room. The staircase goes down into a cushy living room. There's even a TV in here, several games, consoles—all very expensive—and rows of DVDs. I bet they don't get Netflix here. Arden follows my gaze. "We found a way to make fire magic into a power system for Earth technologies. The dragons in my court spend a great deal of time working out how to adapt to many parts of Earth. They are ahead of us, in my opinion. The other worlds, we can't get to anymore, not since the sorcerer came here, so I enjoy studying Earth."

"They don't have magic or dragons," I reply. There's an expensive espresso machine in the corner. I look at it longingly. "That espresso machine looks far nicer than the one they have for us. Have I told you I'm a huge fan of coffee?"

"Do you want a coffee before we go back?" he asks. "It's Grayson's machine and I'm sure it would piss him off for us to use it. So we should use it."

I grin at him. "No, but maybe another time. I'm tired."

"So, you've made a friend with Emrys," he murmurs, leading me to a wall with a white dragon painted on the stone. "Air queen. Is that what you want? Who you want?"

My lips part. "I want to go home."

"Maybe you could make friends with me and make a new home," he murmurs, touching my hand.

I shake my head. "You make it sound like we're leaving this test together at the end if I don't die. You literally just saw me kissing someone else. Doesn't that put you off?"

He leans an arm on the wall behind me, his firewood scent wrapping around my mind and not budging. "No. If we're being honest, it turns me on. But I don't think you're ready for that conversation yet."

My cheeks burn as I just even think about what he's implying. A door appears where his hand was, and he steps back. "You can come back anytime. Lysander might get pissy. Grayson definitely will. But you should come back. It's good having you around."

"Is that invite for all the girls?" I ask.

He crosses his thick arms. "No, just you, princess."

What the hell am I getting myself into with these dragon kings?

CHAPTER 8

"*I* still can't believe you saved me. I'm going to say it a hundred times over until it feels real. I still can't believe it!"

Hope looks at Arty, rolling her eyes as she stands up off the table. "If I hear you say *believe* one more time, I'm going to throw you out the nearest window."

Arty just sighs, leaning her head on her hand and smiling. "I still cannot believe it."

"You've said that a hundred times since yesterday," Livia mutters, watching Hope walk out, her black hair flowing around her back. I don't even know why Hope decided to sit with us for breakfast this morning. After the test, she didn't come back to our room. But I swear she almost looked at me with something akin to being thankful.

Arty's eyes widen. "But it's true! We would have died without her."

Livia just shakes her head as I chuckle, sliding out of my seat. I was surprised to find a very nice coffee on my table waiting for me this morning, with a note from Arden. He made me a coffee with Grayson's machine and left it for me. The gesture was surprisingly…sweet.

The moment I stand, my plate and coffee cup disappear like usual, and I smile at the castle. That's one thing I'll miss about this place when I go home to Earth—the magic washing up a castle. I underestimated how much I hated washing up until I came here.

Arty carries on, yammering on and on about how I saved her, just like she has done since I came back last night, and Livia just groans. My body is still aching, and I'm still absolutely shattered from the water test when Grayson storms into the room. Everyone goes quiet. All the girls are completely silent as he stomps in front of me, glaring down. "Come with me. Now."

"Yes, sir," I joke. He turns around, storming off with big strides that I struggle to keep up with. I almost forgot about our deal. After the water test, it doesn't seem as important to me to learn how to beat Hope in combat. I'm most likely going to die in one of the tests before I ever get a chance.

I chase after him, looking down at my wrist, at the new dragon marking. This one is on my other wrist, and the dragon is a dark sea blue in colour. The exact same shape and size as the one on my other wrist. I rub it, knowing that these markings will always be reminders of the many, many women who died, not the fact I won. These marks are their deaths, and I'll be forever reminded of the dragon kings.

I follow Grayson through a door, into a slim stone corridor, and out into another room. This room is large, some sort of training room, I'd guess. The walls are littered with several antique-looking weapons, and the floor itself is spongy as I walk across it. Warm sunlight blasts in from several windows all around, which overlook the mountains and hills for miles ahead. I think this is the back of the castle. I'm starting to get to know this place.

Grayson pauses in the middle of the room, and he turns around to face me. His dark brown hair is brushed to the side, matching his long-sleeved brown shirt tucked into loose joggers. He lifts his hands into the air at his side, slowly raising them. Vines snap and creak out of the ground, cracking through the spongy stone before rising up and making a structure of a man made of vines. Grayson steps to the left, and the vine man does the same.

My mouth parts. "That's so cool. Could you make an army of these?"

"I could," he responds coldly, suctioning the rest of the warmth from this room.

I clear my throat. This is awkward. More awkward than I thought it would be. "Right. So, you haven't warmed up to me at all over the idea of us helping each other?"

His lips thin. "No. You will do exactly as I tell you, and you'll have a chance of surviving the race."

I nod. "Yes, good. I need to get through to the end of this test, and then I'm going home."

His lips seem to twitch with amusement. Just for a second, but I see it. He doesn't think I'm going home, and he has no problem being an absolute dick about it, like his friends. He may not say much, but he doesn't have to. Grayson is easier to read up close.

I want to call him out on why he thinks it is funny, the idea of me going home, but he begins his training, and his face tells me not to do anything but listen. I see Hope's smug look every time she beats me, and I use it as inspiration. His commands are clear, and I think he must have taught someone before. I do everything he asks as he tells me where to stand, how to stand, what stance to be in. I'm tired even before he uses the vine man to attack me. It slams into my chest hard, and I rocket across the floor, landing in a thump on the jelly-like floor below me.

"Ouch," I groan.

Grayson doesn't give a shit. What a surprise. I look over at the asshole, his arms crossed against his tight chest. He could at least attempt to look less like a friggin' god as he beats me up. "Get up and shake it off."

It doesn't really hurt that much. I'm just winded, but I still wince as I stand up, rubbing my chest. Grayson doesn't look remotely sympathetic or actually seem to even give a tiny bit of a shit. "Again."

For an hour, or what I suspect is about that, Grayson uses his vine man to throw me across the room while barking out commands on how I'm meant to block the attacks. After I've been attacked. I just fall on my ass. Again. Again, and again. I'm pretty sure I'm covered in bruises head to toe by the end of Grayson's lesson, and he comes over, throwing a vial at me.

I down it quickly, feeling healing magic wash throughout my body. "So, if the Water Court are healers and the Fire Court is good with technology and has the smart ones, what does your court do?"

He looks down at me, his silver eyes so clear. "We keep our secrets within our mountains and lands."

I stand up, brushing off my legs. "Okay, it's my part of the deal now. The touching."

Wow, that sounded dirty.

Grayson doesn't seem to notice, and he steps away from me like I'm on fire. I continue anyway. "I need you to talk to me. About anything mundane. I think talking sometimes distracts you from overthinking things, or it does for me. I've always been a chronic overthinker. Maybe it'll stop you from overthinking the whole me-touching-you thing. I wanted to start with your hands."

He looks worried.

I think that's the easiest way to describe the look in his eyes as he stares at me. This big, fierce dragon king looks worried about me touching his hands. A part of me, some deep part of my heart, shudders at the thought of whatever happened to him to make him hate people touching him so much. What must have happened to make him this way? I can see it. Fear. Pure fear in his eyes. I didn't know fear like that until I came here. Something about it absolutely terrifies me, right down to my bones, about what must have happened to him. His hands are shaking slightly as I gently touch the back of his hand with my finger. "Come on, the Earth Court must be known for something else. It can't just be keeping secrets."

He grits his teeth, his whole body tense. "I'm not going to hurt you, Grayson. I'm just a small human, remember? I'm also trying to be your friend. You want me to be part of this world?"

"I never said that," he snaps. "What part of you thinks I want a bride? I'm here because, without magic, my people would suffer, and they have been through enough. I'm here for my people."

My lips part. I never thought about it from his side. He doesn't want this either. I'm not sure any of them do. "Tell me about your court."

I have no intention of being part of his world—I'm sure he knows that—but I do want to know more, even if the main reason is to distract him. I'm sure he also knows that I'm trying to distract him. He's too smart, far too intelligent to fall for it.

I'm surprised when he actually does talk. "Mines. We mine iron, stone, rare jewels, and everything this world needs. Every house, structure, town, and city built in this world comes from the Earth Court mines. That's what we're known for. We are a tough court, much like our nature."

"What about the Air Court?" I ask next.

His lips twitch…and my god, he is handsome. My heart flutters, the betraying thing. "Fun. They are laid back, as relaxed as the element they worship."

Grayson hasn't noticed that I've wrapped my hands around his. His palms are rough, way too rough, and my hands are so small compared to his. In fact, every inch of his hand is rough, like the skin has grown back over and over. I don't comment on it as I run my finger across the top of his wrist and feel a scar. I quickly look down and notice many light pink scars slipping out of the edge of his sleeve. "How?"

He rips away from me with a feral growl that sends shivers down my spine. "I asked you to help me, not to question me. That wasn't part of our deal."

"I didn't mean—"

"Enough," he growls, moving away like an injured animal. His eyes flash green, the silver melting away. "This was a stupid fucking idea."

"No, it wasn't, Gray," I protest.

His eyes narrow. "Gray? My name is King Grayson, and I'm not your friend."

I want to tell him it's all going to be okay, but I feel like my words would be completely fruitless right now in this state that he's in. He shakes his head and turns away, walking out the door at the back of the room and slamming it behind him, hard enough that the ground underneath shakes with his power. I blow out a breath. I shouldn't be feeling bad for my kidnapper. I shouldn't want to fix him. He literally kidnapped me. I wrap my arms around my chest, looking at the castle around me. The walls are glowing slightly, and I get the sense the castle is listening. "Any chance you know the answer to what happened to Grayson?"

The room just goes slightly colder, right before another door appears to my left. I walk over and open it, stepping out into the prison. "Wait, no!"

I look behind me as the door slams shut of its own accord and disappears. Not this shit again.

I turn to look at the woman in the cage, and a deep part of me knows I shouldn't be here. Something in my chest feels so wrong. Feels completely wrong. The woman is crying, weeping loudly, vines still wrapped tightly around her limbs. Her dirty, muddy hands are covering her face as she weeps on her knees, weeping so loudly, so violently that I don't think she even notices I'm here until I take a step forward, causing a small rock to roll from my foot across the floor and clink on the bars.

Her head whips up, her eyes, red, puffed and swollen, meet mine. "Are you going to help me? Release me from here. Please. I can tell you how. It'd be so easy. Just come in here and let me out."

I'm not that stupid. "Those vines. Is it the earth king that keeps you bound down here? Did you do something to him?"

I wonder if that's the reason the castle brought me here. To give me the answer. She shakes her head "No. Yes, I am bound here by earth magic, but it was not the king that bound me here. I've never met those kings."

Something makes me believe her. "Why would you want *me* to get you out? I haven't got any magic. I wouldn't even know where to begin. There's no lock on these bars." I cross my arms.

"Plus, I don't know you. I don't know why you've been trapped in here. You are most likely dangerous."

"Yes, I am, like all creatures in this world. The dragon kings' fathers locked me in here a long time ago. They were cruel to me and wanted to trap me forever because I was a threat to their thrones. The dragon kings you know now were only children when I was brought here. I was falsely imprisoned. All I was ever trying to do was save this world and be free. They punished me for it. Punished me dearly. I've lost everything, just like you did. But you can help me, and I will restore what you lost. I didn't lie before. You're special."

I'm confused. "What I lost?"

Her eyes sparkle. "You don't know? Oh, how sad."

Silence drifts between us before she giggles like a child. "I need one drop of your blood. That's all it would take for you to release me. I can tell you everything. I can get you back to your home and tell you all the secrets you don't know."

I don't answer her, stepping away. Her eyes are so bright, and she looks at me greedily. "There's potential stirring in your blood. You could differ from the rest. You just have to listen to me and let me out of here."

Suddenly a door opens, and I don't willingly go into it as a rush of air pushes me through, and the door slams shut behind me. I fall straight on my ass on the other side, only to be somewhere new. I stand up, looking at five crowns on cushions in the middle of the dusty, cobweb-filled room. Each of the crowns are elements, but the one in the middle is black, shiny, and spiked. I walk over to it, gently raise it, and I swear I feel something rush through my blood as a song plays in the air. A familiar song. I drop the crown, backing away and falling through an open door, my heart racing. This time, I land on my ass outside my classroom door, and it takes everything in me to stand up, calm my racing heart, and go inside.

CHAPTER 9

"Where are you from then?" I question, leaning back in my chair. Livia and I have been left alone in the dining room after dinner, and it's quiet, way too quiet. Arty was tired, and she went to sleep easily, and Hope was gone early. I don't feel like sleeping early. I'm too restless, and Livia just stayed.

She's usually with that dark-haired girl who she saved from the first test, and I've got to learn her name. She didn't die in the last test, but there's only a few of us remaining, and the room seems emptier than usual now that they're all sleeping. We should be sleeping, I know that, but every time I close my eyes, I find it hard to not remember everything that's happened recently. I wonder if I ever will be able to just live without these memories. Without seeing Finley, Katherine, and the nameless others die in front of me.

Livia spins a fork on the table. "London. Can't you tell from my accent?"

"I guessed south," I respond, "but I never really left North West England, so I've not heard all the accents. Are your family missing you?"

She snorts. "No. I have six siblings, and I was the oldest. My mother got pregnant with me when she was a teenager, and my dad, who's not my biological dad, took me in as his own because he loved her. He tried, but it was clear I wasn't like the others, not like their children together. I always felt different, out of place," she admits. "I was planning on leaving myself, getting a job somewhere else, just far away from where I was brought up. I love my mum. She tries her best, but I have a lot of siblings, and one person can only be stretched so thin. Plus, I think I remind her of my biological dad, who left her pregnant as a teenager. My grandparents kicked her out because of me and never spoke to her again. She didn't have it easy."

She puts the fork down. "I don't particularly look like my siblings." She raises a hand, gesturing towards her face. "I'm slightly Korean, and that all comes from my father's side. I didn't know about this race, and I bet it's my father's blood who got me stuck here. One more thing to never thank him for."

"What about your siblings? Surely, they would miss you?"

She blows out a breath. "Maybe." Livia looks down and then says, "I'm going to find Florence. The rest of her room died in the last test, and she hasn't been taking it well."

"You seem awfully close to her," I suggest.

She grins and winks at me. "She's gorgeous and kind. Of course I'm trying to get close to her."

I chuckle as she walks off to find Florence, and I shake my head, watching her go. The dragon kings really, really didn't think this whole race through. What if nobody here actually likes guys? I don't think Livia does. I think she's half in love with Florence already. That's going to be interesting when she wins this. Not that I care who wins. I'm not going to be here for long to witness the fallout. Lysander will take me home…even if there is a high price for my freedom. Arden.

I've stupidly grown to like the bastard over the last two months here. He is funny, charming, and has a morbid sense of humour. But more than that, there is a sadness in his eyes that I want to know more about. It doesn't help that he is goddamn gorgeous. I'm so stupid. I can't grow feelings for him. I push my chair back and walk down the corridor to find some fresh air. To find an escape.

The castle leads me into the main hall, the several staircases drifting in different directions are empty, and everything is so silent. A reckless part of me wants to go and see the kings, to see what they're doing on this Saturday night, like we are friends. It's been several weeks since the water test, since I nearly died, and I've seen all of them way too many times.

Emrys meets me on the balcony some nights, and we talk for hours, and I've had countless mornings with Grayson. He never lets me touch more than his hands, and he certainly doesn't speak to me anymore. He just comes in, takes me for training, and barks orders at me like I've personally insulted him. I would tell him to fuck his lessons with his attitude, but I'm getting better, quicker, faster at all of this. I can feel my muscles burning, getting stronger, and I need the training. My body feels like it's exhausted after every training lesson before I even go to my tutoring lesson. Hope still systematically beats me, but Grayson is teaching me how to dodge her moves and how she would fight me. She would have been taught to fight like them, and he knows her. Though I wish he would talk more. It's kind of boring most mornings.

Matron walks down the steps, seeing me, and pauses. "Are you lost?"

I shake my head. "No…"

She lifts her head higher. "You are lost, Ellelin. Perhaps you should ask the castle to find yourself."

I frown at her cryptic words as she turns, walking back the way she came. She looks back at me once, almost like she is going to say something more, but she changes her mind and keeps going.

A door appears to my left, and I frown at it. Hopefully, no one hears me. "If you're taking me back to see the prison woman again, I'm not interested. It's creepy. Find someone else to keep her entertained."

The door creaks open slightly. I sigh, knowing that I don't have much of a choice. I have a feeling that if I tried to walk away, the castle would just send me where it wants me to go anyway. It seems to have a bit of a sassy personality like that. I walk through the door, down a slim corridor, and turn the handle of the door on the other side. I step out into the dragon kings' living room, and all four of them are here. Hope too. Crap.

Hope is sitting on Lysander's lap, and he is missing a shirt—and he is toned. Fit, not a tiny bit of anything but muscle on his chest and stomach, even sitting. Now I'm jealous. Hope's hand is wrapped around a glass of red wine, and her laugh dies off as she follows Lysander's green gaze to me.

"How is she allowed in here?" Hope snaps, narrowing her eyes at me. "Are you guys seriously letting *her* in here? This is our space."

Arden ignores her, rising off the couch, his white shirt pressing against his muscles. He has a beer in his hand. "Don't get jealous, Hope. It doesn't look good on you. Welcome, princess. I was hoping you'd come back."

He comes over to wrap his arm around my shoulders, and he pulls me down to sit on the sofa between him and Grayson. Grayson makes sure not an inch of our bodies is touching. Lysander just glares at me, Hope draped over him in a small black dress that is not uniform. How'd she get the castle to give her that to wear? I mostly get black leggings and matching short crop tops, with a cloak to cover me up. Grayson looks down at me with annoyance flashing in his eyes, his hands resting on his long legs. He is dressed casually, like he does in our training, but his tone is anything but. "Why is she here? Who showed her our place?"

The other three look warningly at Grayson. Hope is too busy trying to distract Lysander to care if Grayson is going to lose it. He is a ticking time bomb at the best of times, and I don't think he takes change well. I take the beer out of Arden's hand. "Maybe I just wanted to drink, and you should, too. Being serious twenty-four seven is going to give you a heart attack."

Grayson coldly looks down at me. "Dragons don't die from heart attacks."

"Really?" I sarcastically reply, taking a deep sip. Arden and Emrys chuckle. "It was a joke. Look, I told the castle I was bored, or I thought it, and here we are."

"My question was, how do you know how to get here? You have to be invited," Grayson slowly asks.

I shrug. "Emrys brought me here. He's nice like that. Not like you."

Grayson turns his glare on Emrys. Problem solved. Arden leans down close to my ear. "You're causing trouble between us, princess. Tut, tut."

I glance at Lysander. Trouble was already there.

Emrys winks at me. "I'm going to get more beer. Chill, Grayson. She's here now and a tiny mortal. How much trouble could she cause?"

I chuckle. The beer is downright disgusting, but I don't comment on that as I drink some more before handing it back to Arden. Hope possessively attaches herself to Lysander, leaving her drink on the side to kiss his neck, stroking her hands down his chest. Lysander doesn't seem to notice her efforts as he watches me. My cheeks burn as I look away. Emrys comes back a few moments later, this time with a glass of red wine, and he hands it to me. "This is better than Arden's terrible beer."

"Hey! I made it myself, and it's not bad," Arden protests.

"It definitely is bad," I say with a grin. I take a long drink of the wine and accidentally moan in appreciation. The wine is absolutely delicious, and when I open my eyes, I find all of them watching me to the point it gets awkward. I can't read their gazes. "So, is this what you do on a Saturday night? Sit here and drink?"

"It's almost a tradition for our weekends," Arden murmurs. "But I enjoy having you here with us more."

"Stop flirting with the poor girl," Emrys tells him.

Arden only grins at me. "She loves it, really."

Arden's arm is wrapped around the back of the sofa, his fingertips brushing my shoulder every now and then. Even through my clothing, the soft touch sends shivers down my spine. Lysander's eyes flicker to Arden's fingertips on my shoulder, darkening slightly before he smirks at me. I'm doing what he wants, and for a moment, it makes me sick to my stomach. He finally stops looking at me, drifting his eyes to Hope.

"You two should get a room," Grayson dryly comments.

Hope lifts her head. "We will. You three can join if you want?"

I choke on my wine, and Hope laughs. "Prude. I bet you're still a virgin."

"I'm not," I tightly reply. "I can think of a word for you, though. It begins with a *B*."

Lysander growls, picking Hope up and taking her with him up the stairs after she clearly tries to climb off him to attack me. After a few minutes, her soft moans echo from upstairs, and not long after, the sound of banging furniture.

Arden laughs. "Lysander is always in a hurry with his women. I prefer to take longer before racing to the best part."

I rub my face. "Are they always this loud?"

"Always," all three of them say at the same time. I chuckle, taking a deep drink until half the massive glass is gone.

Arden's eyes widen. "Careful with the wine, princess. That's dragon wine. Unless you're brought up here, you'll get drunk on it pretty quickly."

"Maybe I want to get drunk. It's so serious here," I blurt out. Wow, I feel good. "You dragon kings are mean and serious. It's like you were born with sticks up your asses along with the crowns."

I hiccup, and they all laugh, even Grayson. I blink at him in surprise. He has a very sexy laugh. Arden tries to take the glass from me, but I slip off the couch. "She's drunk."

Arden pulls me back to the sofa as I quickly down the rest of the wine. He peels the glass from my hands. "The room is spinning. It's pretty, like you three. Even Lysander is a pretty psychopath."

They are all laughing. Oh, fuck. Maybe this wine *is* strong. I pat Grayson's hand and link our fingers. The laughter stops and Grayson stares at our hands, along with Arden and Emrys, who look ready to fight to save me. The tension in the room is uncomfortable, but I snort out a giggle. "My hand is so tiny in yours. It's like I'm a little bug."

"She's drunk. We should take her back," Grayson comments, but he doesn't pull his hand away.

I ignore them. "Shh, moody dragon. Wait a minute, I have the BEST idea."

"Oh, yeah?" Arden questions, leaning forward. He's so cute. Cute big dragon king.

I grin at him. "I want to see Grayson's dragon! I've seen Arden's and Emrys's. What's yours like? Is it grey? Is that why you have that name?"

Grayson doesn't answer me, but he still doesn't move his hand away either. His hand is so warm. I hiccup again and turn my eyes to Arden. "You'll tell me, what's his dragon like? Pleeeease?"

"Big," Arden answers with a laugh, taking a long drink. "Not as big as mine. I'm definitely the biggest out of all of us."

"You'd like to think that," Emrys interrupts. "But it's not true."

"I can prove it is," Arden suggests.

"Are you talking about your dicks or dragons?" I question.

Grayson coughs on his beer, barking out a laugh. "Dicks, brat."

I giggle, leaning my head on his shoulder. Emrys and Arden look at me in shock. What's up with that?

The sound of Lysander and Hope having very loud sex above finally stops. I'm pretty sure she was moaning that loud just to piss me off. Sex is *never* that good. Emrys gives me more wine, while Arden tells him that's a bad idea. I keep drinking and drinking, hoping to wash away any thoughts of the race, of where I am, or who I'm with. I can just pretend I'm home. I don't take my hand off Grayson's, and somehow, he becomes an anchor for me. He doesn't seem to mind me holding his hand, either. He is mysterious, an asshole, but I don't think he would hurt me.

"Did you grow up together, then? You seem like friends."

Emrys leans back in his seat, his unbuttoned shirt revealing the muscles of his chest. Damn. I'm not sure which one of them is hotter, but it would be a close contest in looks alone. It's a shame they are spoilt, entitled douchebags who kidnapped me. "We did. Well, our summers were spent together travelling the courts. Hope was with us as well. The rest of the time we spent in our own courts, training and learning to be kings. Our childhood was designed to build a bond between us and make us brothers in everything but blood. Then we might have some peace. Our people need it after—"

Emrys stops when Grayson clears his throat. "After what?"

"Nothing," Emrys quickly answers. "Somehow, these jackasses became my brothers."

I stand up, putting my hands on my hips. "I want to ride a dragon." I stumble a little on my feet, and Grayson's hand comes to my lower back to stop me from falling. I grin at him. "Thank you. Now can I ride you?"

His eyes darken, but he doesn't answer me. "I mean, I've ridden Arden's dragon for a bit, but I was terrified. So it doesn't really count, and I want to ride one of yours now. Can we do that?"

Arden's husky laugh makes me look at him as he spreads his arms out on the back of the sofa, parting his thick legs, too. Something about that pose makes him unbelievably attractive, and I want to crawl onto his lap like a puppy. Wow, I think I've drunk too much. I don't even attempt to hide how much I find him attractive as I meet his eyes. He runs his eyes slowly up at me. Appreciatively. "You can ride my dragon any time you like, but not when you're drunk, princess."

He rises to his feet. "You can ride all three of us if you wish. Well, maybe not Grayson. He never really does allow anyone that close. He much prefers to watch."

My cheeks heat as I think about the possibilities of that. Of them.

Emrys's arm wraps around my waist. "Stop with the flirting, asshole." He looks down at me. "Come with me. My dragon is the best."

"Hey, no, that's not true!" Arden disagrees, climbing to his feet after us as Emrys leads me away. Grayson doesn't move from the couch, so I'm guessing he's not coming with us. Part of me wishes that he would. I'm really curious about what his dragon looks like. Emrys leads me through a door that goes to a massive open archway of the tower, with nothing but a ledge balcony to stop me from falling.

Emrys kisses my cheek quickly before he jumps out of the arch, my lungs stopping for a second, right before he transforms mid-air like he did before, mist spreading around him like smoke. Arden runs past me, jumping after Emrys, mist spreading around him too, until two massive dragons fill the air. They take my breath away with how magnificent they are. Dragons are real and they are better than I ever could have imagined.

Their colours contrast with each other. Arden's dragon is all black with red-tipped scales that shine like rubies in the moonlight. Emrys's dragon is pure silver like I'd imagine air to be, and he matches the moonlight above. Night and day, black and silver. Emrys's dragon flies closer to the castle before landing on a ledge just below where I am, making it easy for me to jump down. Even as drunk as I am, I'm still nervous about jumping. I lean over the edge, feeling my heart thump in my chest before I jump down onto his back, almost rolling up onto his wing. I grab hold of his scales and pull myself back on his back. Fuck.

This close, his scales seem to glitter under the moonlight, and I stroke my hand over his back. Emrys lifts his head, letting out a long roar that hurts my ears before he jumps off the castle and into the air. A part of me knows I should be absolutely terrified of this. I'm riding a fucking dragon! A dragon! But it feels…right. Like I've always meant to do this. Or I've lost my mind in the race, with all the death and hot dragon shifters stuff. I laugh, holding on tight as Emrys swoops down into the mountains, the cold air biting against my cheeks. Arden flies just behind us, just as swiftly as Emrys.

Their dragons are nearly the same size, but Emrys's scales are smoother, and he doesn't have any spikes like Arden's. Arden's dragon moves to fly above us, tilting upside down. I chuckle as he spins in a circle around Emrys, who snaps at his tail as it narrowly passes his mouth. I scream as Emrys suddenly dives into the mountain, swinging us around it, and we come face to face with a dragon I've never seen before on the other side.

But I know him.

I know those eyes.

Grayson's dragon is massive, far bigger than Emrys and Arden. He's a deep, forest green with a grey-tipped tail and grey feet. He's absolutely gorgeous. His wings are covered in tiny little scars that make them glisten like snow, and I wonder what the hell happened to him once more. Grayson's dragon roars, echoed by Arden and Emrys. I laugh and wave to Grayson as Emrys turns us back to fly around the mountain range. Grayson jumps off the cliff and flies with us through the mountains. I let go of Emrys's scales for a minute and hold my hands at the side and scream at the top of my lungs.

I may have been kidnapped. I may not want to be here, but riding dragons is so fucking cool.

CHAPTER 10

My mouth is dry as I wake up, and my head is pounding. Absolutely pounding. Everything comes back to me as I rub my forehead, looking around the kings' room where I got shitface drunk last night.

Oh, my god. I asked to ride their dragons. Oh, my god, I did ride their dragons. We flew around the island for hours and hours until I passed out on Emrys's back, and he must have brought me back here. I barely remember passing out, but someone has given me a pillow and a blanket, taken my boots off, and tucked me. The blanket smells like a put-out fire. Arden.

I climb to my feet and look around the room, noting the clock and the window showing the sun high in the sky. Crap, ten o'clock! I've definitely missed my training with Grayson, and I'm going to be late for my tutor lesson. Shit. I quickly pull my boots on and run my fingers through my messy, wind-swept hair before running out the door that appears for me. "Thank you, castle!"

I run down the corridor, grab the banister of the staircase, and rush up. I get all the way to the top, breathless, and halt. Desmerda is already waiting for me, her arms crossed, her white cloak pooling at her feet. The door behind her is shut tightly. I don't know how long she has been waiting, but I doubt saying sorry is going to help. "Come with me."

I pause, a bad feeling nagging at my chest as her eyes shine with anger. "I'm so sorry I'm late. I overslept."

"Follow," she purrs, turning from me, the feeling in my chest smacking like a drum, telling me that I shouldn't ignore this feeling. My hands are clammy as I follow her against my better instincts. The castle feels like it gets colder by every second as I walk behind her down two corridors. Something in me tells me to run, but I don't. I stupidly walk with her. She leads me around the main classroom and to another oak door, which leads into a smaller room.

The moment I step into the room, icy mist surrounds me like a vice, and I scream in unbearable pain as it attacks every inch of my skin. I fall to the floor with a thump, sucking in a deep breath. The mist tightens itself into ropes around my body, pulling me upright. Desmerda walks over to me, her eyes like rubies. My feet lift off the ground, so I'm floating in front of her, at the same level. "You are late for my lesson, and I warned you there would be punishments. I am your tutor, and you will learn a lesson."

"Wait—"

Mist wraps around my mouth, gagging me. I try to scream as I panic, struggling against her magic, but nothing comes out. I can't scream. I can't move. Tears fall down my eyes as she rips the back of my shirt. Something like a whip lashes against my skin, and I mentally scream in pain, crying against the gag. The mist pain was like a bee sting, but the whipping…it's worse. I cry, weep, and beg through the terrible pain, but no sound comes out around the gag. I feel trapped, bound, powerless as she hits me over and over again until I feel my back wet with my blood. Until the room spins. Until I can't smell anything but my own blood in her vicious attack.

She doesn't stop hitting me until everything goes fuzzy, and time seems like it fades. My body feels weak, and the mist disappears. I slam hard on the floor, gasping for air, crying out. Desmerda kicks me onto my side, looking down at me. My blood is sprayed across her white clothes and face, but she smiles.

She enjoyed hurting me.

She almost looks drunk on the pleasure of hurting me. "Do not be late for my lesson again. Tell your friends what the punishment is, and don't try to heal yourself with tonics. I've made sure they won't work. Good luck surviving the next test in this state."

"No...no...," I breathe out through gritted teeth. She walks out of the room, leaving the door open. I don't know how long I lie in a pool of my own blood before I manage to find some strength to rise to my feet. Every step is painful as I get to the door, clinging to the wall to hold me up. The door leads me straight into the corridor that leads to my room. "Thank you."

The corridor seems to get warmer as I limp down to my room. I don't get to my bed before everything goes black and I smack my face on the floor.

* * *

"**E**llelin, wake up!"

Cold hands shake my shoulders as I blink my eyes open a few times, smelling smoke in the air. Is my room on fire? I cough, covering my mouth, and my mummy looks down at me. Her black hair is messy, like she just woke up. She scares me. "Mummy, why are you scared?"

"Ellelin," she breathes out, pulling on my hand, and I climb out of my bed, leaving behind my teddy. I reach for it, but she is pulling me with her too fast, my bare feet slipping on the stone as we rush down the corridor outside our rooms. Suddenly, she pushes me behind her, black shadows ripping out of the corners of the corridor and smothering us both in a bubble. This is mummy's power, and I love when she does this. We float around as shadows and scare people. I giggle but stop as she turns, her eyes glowing black as she kneels in front of me. She is crying. I touch her cheek, but she grabs my hands and holds them in front of her. I hear screams in the distance and the sound of things breaking. "Ellelin, you won't remember this. You're too young. Dragon above, you're just six. You might not even remember me and your daddy, but we love you so much. I will make sure you escape. You *have* to live. You're all we have left. Castle, please, please save her. Send her to my mother, and don't let him see her go."

"Mummy, I don't want to go," I wail, clutching her hands. She pulls me into a strong hug, and I relax in her arms. Mummy isn't going to let me go. She loves me, and this must be a silly game. She kisses the side of my head, whispering softly. "Ellelin, Ayiolyn will always fight for you, but not yet. Live, and save our people one day. Remember, Ayiolyn is yours if you claim it."

I wake up warm. Far too warm and in far too much pain. I cry out as I try to remember a weird dream about my mother. I swear she said something about Ayiolyn, but the more I think about the dream, the more it slips from my mind. "Breathe, I've got you."

"Lysander?" I breathlessly question, turning my head to the side. I'm lying on my bed face down, and I have to open and shut my eyes a few times to believe I'm seeing Lysander in front of me, kneeling by my bed. He's frowning at me like he usually is, but it's more than that. He is concentrating. It takes me a minute to realise that the water is wrapped around my back as I lie on my front, and he's crouching by the side of my bed. His hands are covered in my blood, and water flows freely from his fingertips. "Are you healing me?"

"Yes. Don't look so surprised," he growls. He's furious. Absolutely furious. "I'm asking you once, Elle. Who the fuck did this to you?"

I don't answer him. What's the point? It's not like he really cares, and I don't even understand why he is healing me. How did he find me? "Did Hope tell you to come? Did she find me?"

"They are all still in lessons," Lysander tightly replies. "I smelt your blood and came."

I meet his clear green eyes, his red locks of hair falling into his forehead. There's so much anger in his eyes. "Why are you healing me? Tell me that first."

He smirks. "Can't have you dying on me quite yet. My plan won't work with anybody else. If you die, then every plan I've got goes flying out the window."

I gulp. Of course he needs me alive to kill Arden. I don't know why I was thinking there might be another reason. "Desmerda. Our tutor."

The pain finally fades into a low ache on my back. "Why?"

"It was a punishment for being late to class. I woke up on the sofa at yours this morning and overslept," I admit. "She did warn me. This is my fault."

His eyes tighten. "This is not your fault. No one deserves to hurt you like this. You're mine to destroy."

A strange claim. I don't argue with the psychopath, not when his power is making me feel so much better.

"Why do you want Arden dead?" I whisper. "You grew up together. If he's your friend, why do you want him dead?"

For a long time, I don't think he is going to answer me. "His family destroyed mine. It doesn't matter if we're friends. He betrayed me and he knows it. Arden thinks I forgave him for it, and I haven't. Water always remembers."

My heart pounds. "How exactly did he betray you?"

"Don't ask any more questions, and stay still while I heal you, Elle. These are magic-tipped injuries, and she made it so that it's nearly impossible for you to be healed. You would have died, plain and simple, if I hadn't gotten here," he growls.

"Anyone might think you care about me with how protective you're being right now, Lysander," I murmur.

He chuckles. "You're not dying until you finish your part of the test. That's all you are to me."

"I thought...when I was drowning towards the end of your test...that I heard your voice in my head telling me to swim. Telling me not to give up because I was too damn strong to die like this. Was that real? Can you talk in my mind?"

"No. You must have been hallucinating," he snaps at me. "I wouldn't tell anyone else that unless you want them to think you're insane."

I don't know why, but I think he's lying to me. In fact, I'm nearly certain he is. He sort of gives it away with how he looks at my back, refusing to look at me. I stay quiet as he finishes healing me until I feel almost like I'm drugged. Woozy. "You've lost a lot of blood, Elle, but you will live." He covers me with a blanket and heads to the door. "Sleep it off."

"Lysander."

He pauses, looking back at me. "Yes?"

"Why are you trying so hard to be the villain?" I ask. "Villains don't heal people."

His eyes are darker than before, and a cruel smirk tilts his lips up. "Anyone can be your villain, Elle. It just depends on whose side you're on."

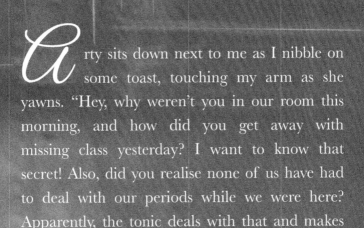

CHAPTER 11

*A*rty sits down next to me as I nibble on some toast, touching my arm as she yawns. "Hey, why weren't you in our room this morning, and how did you get away with missing class yesterday? I want to know that secret! Also, did you realise none of us have had to deal with our periods while we were here? Apparently, the tonic deals with that and makes sure we don't get sick with colds either. I found this out yesterday. I wonder if I'm still allergic to—"

I still feel woozy after everything that happened yesterday, and it takes me a minute to even focus on the fact she is talking to me. I left early this morning, and the castle led me to a room with a big bathtub that I spent a good hour in. "Desmerda was—"

I blanch away from Arty at the sound of her name. I know it's not Arty's fault, it's not like she's the one who hurt me, but even though the scars are gone on my back, even though the blood was all washed away, I can still feel everything that happened to my body. Some scars cannot be healed so easily. I slept well and woke up to fresh sheets, which I'm guessing was Lysander. I have to thank him. Even though the thought of thanking Lysander for anything is sickening. I'm still surprised he healed me.

Desmerda is still in this castle. She could still do that to me again, and no one would stop her. I couldn't stop her. Any of them could do that to me. I realise that threat now. Yesterday made me realise that I am human, and they have magic that I can't even fathom. I'm easy to kill. I've never felt so weak. At least on Earth, everyone else was human. Yes, we can murder each other, but it takes a great deal of strength to do that, and it's uncommon there. It's just a normality here. It was a punishment. A punishment will give me nightmares for the rest of my life, along with pretty much everything that's happened since I got here. Arty touches my hand, but I sharply pull away from her. "Talk to me. I can see you're not okay."

"It's nothing," I bite out, pushing off the table.

"Elle, wait!" she shouts after me, but I quickly leave. I'm storming down the corridor, only to come face to face with Grayson.

He crosses his thick arms, and my heart races for another reason. "Good. You're on your way to me this time. Come on."

He turns around and I frown, realising that we've got training this morning. I'd almost forgotten. After a few steps, he pauses in the corridor, turning back to me, tilting his head to the side. His eyes are almost animalistic, the way he looks at me. "Why do you smell like old blood and fear? Are you injured?"

"No," I say because it's true. I'm not injured anymore. I'm a bit woozy, but not injured. He knows I'm lying, or at least not telling him the whole truth. I can see it in his eyes.

"Fine. I will find out myself," he coolly responds and turns around. He all but jogs down into the training room, and I struggle to keep up. The second we are in the training room, he makes the vine man appear out of the cracks in the ground. He instantly jumps at me, and I scream, falling onto the floor in a heap, covering my face with my hands.

I know how to fight. I know how to defend myself, but I can't move.

I can't breathe. It feels like the world suddenly gets too small for me. There's too much of everything, and I can't breathe. All I can hear is the sound of my skin ripping on my back. All I can smell is my blood. Her laughs echo in my mind as she hurts me over and over. All I can hear is Finley burning, Katherine dying, everyone dying. I cover my face with my hands, shaking from head to toe. I can't breathe. I can't breathe. Sobs echo from the back of my throat.

Warm, rough hands pull my own away from my face, and I blink in surprise. I never expected Grayson to be in front of me. He is kneeling in front of me, his eyes a calming, protective storm bringing me back. He gently lowers my hands before cupping my face. His hands are shaking, all of him is. He's terrified to touch me. But he is anyway because he knows that I'm losing it. "Whatever happened, brat, you don't have to tell me as long as you're okay. You're having a panic attack. Breathe with me and let the memories, the thoughts that frighten you, wash away with the air."

I breathe in a shaky, cold breath, listening to Grayson's soft commands. "Breathe. You're going to be fine because I'm with you and I am not leaving. I'm your rock, Ellelin. Hold on to me and don't you dare let go."

The panic fades slowly as I listen to his breathing, until I can't focus on anything but my pounding heart. "Breathe with me." I copy his breathing, long breaths in and out, until the room stops spinning, until I feel less dizzy, and everything isn't so terrifying anymore. My eyes widen when I realise that both his hands are on my face, his thumb resting against the hollow of my neck. His gaze drifts over my face, searching my eyes, drifting to my lips. I carefully look at him, wondering what he would taste like. Is he thinking the same thing?

He leans into me, sucking in a deep, raspy breath. "Tell me to let go."

My mouth parts. "No." He leans a slight bit closer to me, and I know every single inch between us is a mountain to him. Our lips are a breath away, and my heart is pounding so hard for a new reason. I want him to kiss me; I want it so badly it actually hurts.

He suddenly leaps away from me, holding his hand up between us as he climbs to his feet, like I'm the real threat here. The ground literally shakes and rumbles beneath our feet with his power. "No."

What the hell happened to him?

"Gray—"

"King Grayson," he growls as he corrects me. "Leave."

"I'm sorry," I whisper.

His eyes lock onto mine as I stand. "Don't apologise for the fact that I am fucked up and can't be touched. That's my problem, and the only person who should apologise for it is not in this room."

"Still, I'm sorry," I whisper. "I'm sorry you're hurting, and I don't know how to fix it. I'm sorry that I even care when I shouldn't. I'm sorry about all of this, as it's fucked up. If you want me to leave, I will."

"That's the problem," he growls. "All I want is to be closer to you. I never want you to leave."

My heart warms, and he clears his throat. "Now, do you want to continue training, or would you like to leave early?"

I'm selfish, as I know it would be easier for him if I left early. If I'm being honest, I don't want training, but I want more time with him. I feel safe here. I feel like nothing, and no one can hurt me. My mouth feels dry as I reply, "Training. We have a deal, after all."

"Fine," he tightly responds. "I don't know what happened with you, but I'm surprised it doesn't happen more often with the girls here. You've been dragged from your world and forced to compete in a murderous task to become one of our brides."

I snort. "True. Do you even want this? A bride?"

"What do you think?" he asks, spreading out his arms. "I hate most people, and here I'm forced to socialise more than I'd like. The idea of a bride…"

He looks at me. "Well, the thought was abhorrent to me. It's not anymore."

I try to ignore his unsaid words that make my heart pound faster. "Isn't there another way for you to keep your power rather than this barbaric test?"

"No. It's this or our courts lose our power. We'd be at risk of war with the wild dragons of the West," he answers me. "And they would invade us, rip our people apart, if we lost our power."

Grayson doesn't answer any more questions and begins training, but this time, he is softer with me. Every time the vine man pins me to the mat, he makes sure that he doesn't leave me pinned too long this time. The hits aren't as harsh, not as brutal as usual. I think he feels sorry for me, and that…I don't know why I feel more embarrassed about that than what Desmerda did to me yesterday. Lysander healing me, and me blurting out random things to them when I was drunk, and now a panic attack. I really want to bury my head in a sandpit. I don't even want to think back to the riding-a-dragon comments. So embarrassing. Arden and Emrys are bad influences.

The vine man disappears into leaves that blow away in the wind as a door appears. Grayson crosses his arms. "You should go. If you have a breakdown again…tell the castle to find me. Go, you don't want to be late."

Pure fear stakes through my chest, and Grayson frowns, clearly picking up on my fear. He takes a step forward, but I leave before he can ask anything. I rush out of the room through the open door and head down the corridor. My whole body is shaking, and I clasp my hands tightly shut into a fist as I get to the staircase with the rest of the group to wait for Desmerda. Arty comes over to my side, all smiles, but her eyes are worried. "Are you okay?"

I don't have the strength to speak. I turn away, noticing Hope and Livia are nearby, leaning against the wall and talking quietly. The rest of the group are chattering, and yet I can't focus. Everyone goes silent, and I look up, surprised to see Matron hobbling down the stairs. Gasps echo around the room, and I realise that she's dragging a body behind her. She leaves the body on the steps, moving aside so everyone can see. The white, blood-soaked cloak is all I see at first, and then her silver hair…Desmerda. She is dead. There are cuts across her neck, arms, and stomach, and she is soaking wet, some bits of her frozen. A few girls throw up, and Arty covers her face with her hands. I can't look away from Desmerda's unseeing eyes, and I smile, my shoulders relaxing. I shouldn't be happy she is dead, but I am.

I'm so fucking relieved.

Matron looks over her shoulder as a young man walks down the stairs. He's wearing the same cloak as Desmerda's, but a white suit underneath instead. Clearly, he is from wherever she came from. His hair is black, spiked to the side with gel, and his eyes are pure red, too, but not as creepy as Desmerda's were. All over his skin is more of the markings that we have, but in a pearly purple colour. He stops at the side of Matron. "This is your new tutor, Xandry. As you can see, Desmerda suffered a terrible accident."

She pauses, looking directly at me. Several eyes turn my way too, following her gaze. "Therefore, she will be buried instead of teaching you today."

She clicks her fingers, and the body disappears. Arty sighs. "So gross."

My hand flies to my neck as I realise something. Did Lysander kill her? Did he kill her because she hurt me? It's the only explanation for it, but it makes no sense that he'd care enough to do that. There were little bits of ice I saw on her, all the cuts like mine on my back. He's a psychopath, so I know he has it in him. But to do that for me... that's insane. He hates me as much as I hate him. I know he only healed me so I wouldn't die and mess up his plan. Matron walks back up the steps. "I will leave you in his tutorage."

Xandry takes her place on the steps, closing his hands in front of him. "Welcome. I am originally from the Water Court, and I joined the Twilight many years ago."

"What's the Twilight?" someone asks.

Xandry frowns. "I see my colleague was not teaching you very appropriately. The Twilight is a religious part of our community, dating back thousands of years. We are called to announce births, lead mating ceremonies, guide young drag-ons, and perform funeral rites in all the courts. We are neutral in court wars. Anyone from any court can enter it. We take many vows, and our lives are in service of the mighty dragon gods."

"Mighty dragon gods?" I ask.

Xandry frowns. "You really don't know this?"

No one says yes. "Right, the mighty dragon gods made this world. There were five of them, each representing an element."

"There are only four elemental courts," Livia questions.

Xandry doesn't answer her. "I'm here to teach you. I understand you're mostly doing combat training and a few lessons on history here and there. I don't see the point in teaching you too much of the histories, considering that most of you will die, and the ones who are left will be taught by historians in their own courts as they become queen. I do believe in teaching you to defend yourself." He looks around the room, pausing on Hope. They stare at each other for a second too long, a hint of recognition between them, like maybe they knew each other. "Defending yourself will be vital because there are many threats within this world. Threats that will always be there for royals. You'll need to know how to defend yourself well and how to defend any children that you might have. So, I will take you two at a time and watch your individual skills so I can best judge how to help."

He picks two girls at the front. "The rest of you wait here."

They follow him up the stairs and into the classroom, and most of the girls burst out into whispers. I walk to the side, around them and to the back. I sit on the bottom step of a staircase. Arty follows me over, sitting close. "I'm your friend," she tells me softly, quietly. "I know you've got a lot going on. You've been disappearing some nights. But you're the best of us. If you die, if you break down, then the rest of us have no chance. So please talk to me. I can help you, and I will keep your secrets."

I look into her eyes. "I was late for Desmerda's lesson yesterday, so she whipped my back until it was a bloody mess and I passed out."

She gasps in horror, covering her mouth, her eyes filling with tears. I gulp and continue. "I barely made it back to my room with the castle's help. When I woke up, Lysander was healing me."

"King Lysander?"

I nod. "Yes, he healed me. He was furious about what happened when I told him."

We both look at the steps where Desmerda's body just was. "Do you think he killed her for you? Why would he do that?"

I shrug. "I don't know. Why the hell would he do that for me? That's insane."

"Maybe because he likes you and wants you as his queen," she blurts out. "I mean, I've noticed he is always looking at you. They all are always looking at you. Dragons can be quite protective of things they consider theirs."

"What the fuck did you just say, you stupid bitch?" Hope shouts, stomping towards us from the shadows at the side of the staircase.

I step in front of Arty. "No, you don't get to take your anger out on her. Maybe you shouldn't have been eavesdropping."

She steps right up into my face. "Maybe you should stay the fuck away from men that aren't yours. He. Is. Mine." She sneers at me. "I'm warning you now, princess," she hisses, mimicking Arden's nickname for me. "I don't care which one of the dragon kings you're fucking, but it will not be Lysander. That throne is mine. He is mine. You stay the fuck away from him, or I will kill you. Do you understand?"

"Crystal. I don't want him. You have nothing to worry about!" I shout back at her. "You're welcome to him! Now stay away from my friend."

"Your friend?" She laughs, looking over my shoulder at Arty, who is silent. "You're so clueless. So fucking clueless. It's pathetic. You're right, I shouldn't be worried about you. You're going to die soon."

She storms off and I watch her go, wondering what the hell she meant by that.

CHAPTER 12

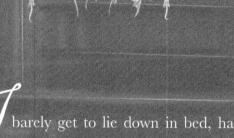

I barely get to lie down in bed, hardly closing my eyes, before I sense magic around me. At first, I didn't recognise magic, the salt-like taste that surrounds me, but I do now. When I open my eyes, there's nothing but mist, and I'm floating within it like it's a cloud. It only lasts seconds before I slam hard onto a rock floor that's freezing cold, making me flinch as my bare legs and arms touch it. They took us to another test in our sleep, and my shorts and thin top are doing nothing to keep me warm against the bitter cold wind that blows around me. I shiver from head to toe while I force my stiff, cold hands to work as I climb to my feet.

"Oh, my fucking god," I whisper in horror. I'm on some kind of island of red rocks with whirlwinds and channels of air above making such a loud noise that I can't think straight. I crawl forwards, looking down to see I'm on a ledge and I'm very, very high in the sky. The island is floating in the clouds, and distantly below, I can see mountains and maybe the outline of the castle. My breaths come out in harsh pants as I crawl back, sweat trickling down my spine. The air test. The third test of the race.

I look up and around, seeing the remaining girls are all on ledges at the bottom of this place. It's a giant circle, with tall, thick stone walls stretching up around all the edges. Swirls of wind are blowing in different directions, and they almost look like they're tunnels. Right at the very top is a rock shaped like a star, and within it, something glimmers like water. A portal. That's the way out. It's really, really high up. I look around for Arty, and I see her waving at me, but she's four ledges away, and getting to her is out of the question. I'm on my own.

For a moment, I meet the eyes of several of the other girls, and they all look absolutely petrified. I feel the same. The fire test was more of a puzzle, the water test was pure instinct, and this…it's a test of bravery and guts. They want their queen to reach for the stars and get there no matter what. I should have listened to them when they said the tests just get worse.

Rocks break off below me, crumbling into the air. The island is breaking away. Great, I'm on a timer too. My body feels like it's locked in place, and I find it hard to move. Hard to breathe. How the fuck am I to get out of here? I look back at the wall, realising I can definitely climb it, as it has several deep holes. I rub my face, standing up and shaking as I touch the ice-cold stone, my purple hair whipping around my shoulders in the wind.

My dragon markings seem to glow as I glance at them, almost like the dragons behind the marks are telling me to get fucking moving. I can't die here. I won't die here. They might see me as weak, as someone who they can throw into this test and watch to see if I can make it, but I'll show them. I will make it. I blow out a breath, rolling my shoulders before finding my first space in the rock to pull myself up, and begin to make a plan.

The rock ledge shakes slightly from side to side, and my time is running out.

My heart is racing hard in my chest. I need to move. Now. The ledges are going to go soon. I look up the wall, seeing another ledge above, but it's far from the wall, and I'll have to jump for it. It's my best chance. I can't see any other way. But first of all, I need to climb. My hands are sweaty, far too sweaty, and I'm nervous as I begin climbing. The last time I did rock climbing, I was eleven and my grandmother took me to a place in Maryport. I fell off and gave up, and we went to the aquarium instead and had chips for dinner. At eleven, I knew I wouldn't enjoy rock climbing, despite my grandmother's suggestions of learning it as a fun skill.

Digging my feet into the gaps, I pull myself up. Three more times, I climb until I'm too far away from the ledge for my fall to not hurt. Until there is no other way but up. The other girls start to climb, clearly having the same idea as me. I look over at the girl next to me, her black hair short and curly, just as she grabs the wrong spot. The rock gives way, and time seems to slow as she falls backwards, desperately reaching out with her hands for anything to save her. Her scream echoes into silence as she falls. Sickness rises in my throat as I imagine her splattered across the mountain range below, but I push down the image, push down the fear of that ending for me, knowing that I can't lose focus. I need to keep going.

I keep climbing upwards. I climb up using all my strength, pushing myself until my body burns with the strength I need to hold on. I get as close to the ledge as I possibly can, a bit higher than it so there's more chance of this working, but even then, jumping is risky. There is nothing below to catch me if I miss. It's all or nothing. I blow out a breath and jump, slamming hard onto the rock, digging my hands into anything that I can find. The rock is pretty smooth, but it tilts towards the ground, making it a bit easier for me to climb, pushing my body on top of it as it flattens out. I roll onto my back, panting, looking up and realising there are no other ledges around, and I don't know how I'm meant to go any further.

With a groan, I climb to my feet and look for the others. Arty has somehow gotten higher than me, on a thick ledge, and she is waving down at me. No, not waving. She's pointing at something, and I look around, my stomach dropping when I realise what the hell she's thinking. There's a current of air moving really fast nearby, a jump away, and it makes a spiralling tunnel that would take me high up straight up to another ledge. At least halfway to the star. But I would need to fly in it. Oh, my fuck. I'm going to die. I'm definitely going to die. There's no way I'm surviving this. I have to just stay here on this ledge and maybe—

I hear another scream, someone else falling, and I gulp. I can't stay here. I see Livia on the ledge above and Hope not far behind her. She runs and fearlessly jumps into one of the tunnels of air nearby her ledge, spreading her arms out. The air current pulls her up fast, spinning her around in circles, and she throws her arms back, leaping out of the air current and flawlessly landing with a thump on a high-up ledge. She looks down at me with a smirk before running and jumping across several of the ledges, getting higher and closer to the star.

If she can do it, I definitely can. Maybe not as perfectly and flawlessly as she made it look. I look at Arty, meeting her hazel eyes shining. I nod once at my friend. We have got to be brave, as my grandmother would tell me. She would tell me to jump rather than die pathetically when this ledge falls. I look down. Everything is falling away into the air. The whole place is going to go soon. I lift my head and, with a scream, I jump.

The air current picks me up in a sheer, cold embrace, the wind whistling down my ears and taking the air from my lungs. I spin over and over in the current, throwing my hands out to the side, smoothing myself out. This reminds me of flying with Emrys above the castle. This is no different, except for it lacks Emrys's magic holding me up. It's just a current of air. The air is so biting cold, so fast, that it's hard to see where I am. I see the outline of the ledge, and I throw my arms back like Hope did, sending myself right out of the current into the air.

I scream, barely reaching my hands out in time to grip the rock before my body slips off the ledge. The sharp rocky edge cuts deep into my hands, making it slippery as I hold on, my legs dangling in the air. With a grunt, I barely manage to get enough traction to pull myself up on the ledge, sucking in air. Lifting my cut hands and realising I've just made everything a lot harder for climbing, I stand and look around for anyone else, Arty or Livia, even Hope, but I'm alone. I've lost them in this massive place. I hope they survived. Well, maybe not Hope. Finally, I spot Livia and her friend Florence a few ledges below, using the walls and jumping off them before trying to get to a current nearby.

I see three ledges above me, and I begin to jump up them one by one, not pausing as I hear more rocks crumbling and falling. The walls of the island are falling too, revealing bright blue skies. The sun just rose in the distance, the daylight bright. My ledges soon run out, leaving me with another risky current of air. Hope passes me in this air current, flying up quite high. I watch her go past before jumping in myself, following right behind her. I scream again, unable to help the fear response, and concentrate on where she is getting out. She certainly knows what she's doing, and I'm following her.

The air current is harsher than the last, and it feels like it's ripping my skin apart with every second, sucking the air out of my lungs, too. I can barely look down, but when I do, my heart leaps in my chest. It is such a long way down. The current swirls around in circles, almost like it's a tornado, and I blink, almost missing Hope jumping out. I wait, counting the seconds until I'm where she was, before jumping and landing on a large rock.

I lift my head, seeing two small, narrow rock paths that lead to the star on the other side. It clearly has a portal within it. Now I'm this close. Through the portal, I can see the dragon kings waiting in front of a busy crowd. Emrys pats Arden's shoulder, and Arden's whole face lights up when he sees me. He grins and I find my stupid face actually smiling back.

Hope rolls her eyes at me. "I should push you off just for that stupid look on your face. You know they don't actually care about you."

Ignoring her, I climb to my feet and look at the thin pathway that's between me and getting out of here. "We still have to get over that ledge, and arguing isn't going to help us. So back the fuck off."

"Says the bitch who followed me up here," she bites out.

I resist the urge to throw one of the stones on the ground at her stupid face. I realise something that sours my tongue. I look at Hope. "If we hold hands, we can balance each other. It'll be easier than walking that alone while this whole place is falling and shaking.

She purses her lips and narrows her eyes. "I don't trust you. You might push me off. I'm not holding your hand and definitely not helping you."

I narrow my eyes at her stubborn ass. "Fine. I don't trust you either, but I know we both don't want to die, and I'm willing to trust that. I'll just wait for Arty to get up here, and we will watch you fall."

"You think she's getting up here?" she asks with a laugh. "She's terrified of heights. She's not going to survive that long without you holding her hand."

"I wouldn't bet against her," I snap.

Hope rolls her eyes at me, looking across at the platform. I look around and down, minutes passing as I am looking for Arty, for Livia, for anyone but Hope to come. But I don't see anyone near us. There's another way in from the portal from the back, and she might have gone that way. It's probably easier, but I can't get back down to it.

Hope is tapping her foot on the stone, and she barks out, "Fine." She holds out her hand. "For future reference, I will never trust you. If you push me, I'm taking you down with me."

"Aw, you want us to die together. How sweet," I sarcastically tease, taking her sweaty hand. We both step onto the pathway at the same time, and I don't look down, knowing it will make my legs shake and make me freeze. Her hand tightens in mine, almost painfully, and the blood from my cut pools in our joined hands. I realise it's not just my hands bleeding, but hers are too.

My heart is in my throat with every step we take across. The wind is blowing harshly against my body. Hope wobbles and I pause, waiting for her to straighten up. She nods at me when she is ready, and we move again. I focus on the dragon kings waiting, watching intently. Arden looks ready to jump through. Emrys is the closest.

Grayson and Lysander are pacing behind them but watching. The rocky pathway gets smaller and smaller the further we get towards the end. So close. We are so close.

Suddenly the ground shakes, and I jump, landing on the ledge, but I crawl to the edge as Hope falls off, missing the landing. She screams, clinging onto my hand, and I throw my other arm to grab hers, pulling with everything I have. I dig my feet into the stone as I pull her up, crying in pain. She finally hooks her leg on the rock and makes it easier for us to get her up. I fall back with her on the ledge, the portal by our heads. I look over at her. "Why didn't you let go?" she asks, panting.

"Because despite everything you think about me, I'm not a killer," I bite out. She doesn't say a word as I let go of her hand and stand up. I walk straight out through the portal and onto the grass on the other side, where it's far warmer. Within seconds, Emrys picks me up and swings me about. I let myself relax in his grip, just for a moment, and he kisses my cheek. "Fuck, I was scared for you then. You're alive."

Cheering bursts out of the crowds, and for a second, I actually feel good about winning. Good, that I somehow survived the impossible. Then I remember that not everyone has survived, and I still have friends in there. Livia, Florence, and one other girl whose name I don't know are behind the kings. But Arty isn't with them. She's still there. I climb out of Emrys's arms and turn around, watching the portal.

Hope is already out and with Lysander, who is talking quietly to her. Arden comes to my side, Grayson following. All four of us stare at the portal, the seconds ticking by. "I should go back in and—"

"No, you won't," Arden coolly interrupts. "Your friend will make it if it is fated to be."

"How is any of this fate?" I demand. "It's just messed up. It's insane!"

"Calm down, Elle," Lysander commands. I narrow my eyes at him for a moment, but he is ripped from my glare by Hope, who kisses him, turning his head with her hands. I'm guessing she somehow thinks there's something going on between us. There is definitely not. He's my enemy. He may have healed me, but that doesn't make things okay between us. He literally threatened to kill my grandmother and is blackmailing me into getting close to Arden and then killing him. He's always going to be my enemy for that, and he can be nothing more. I watch the portal, every second feeling like years. Nobody else comes for such a long time that I almost give up and cry for my friend. I almost burst into tears, because at some point, I really started to care about Arty.

Then I see her. A flash of blonde hair in the wind right before she runs across the pathway. Why is she running? She is going to fall! Only when I move as close as I can get do I see the ledge and pathway is cracking, breaking away as she runs. My heart is beating a mile a minute as her wide, panicked eyes meet mine. She jumps at the last second, falling through the portal and slamming into me. We both tumble to the floor, and I laugh as she cries, hugging her tightly.

My wrist burns and I lift it up, seeing a white dragon appear under the red one on my wrist. As I stand up, Grayson walks over to me. He stands close, and for a moment it's just us. Arty is talking nonstop, Emrys and Arden are cheering with the crowds, and the world seems hell-bent on being overwhelming. "Well done, brat, but that was easy compared to what I have planned."

The earth dragon king walks away with a cruel smile, and I have a feeling the worst is yet to come.

CHAPTER 13

*a*s I'm finishing mermaid-braiding my hair after my shower, a sound makes me pause. I look over my shoulder to see a new door in the bathroom open, creaking slowly enough to sound creepy and make me jump. I narrow my eyes, seeing the prison on the other side. At least the castle isn't trying to hide where I'm going this time. I glare at the walls around me and reach for the door back to my shared room, only for it to disappear.

"For fuck's sake, I don't want to see her!" I say out loud. Thankfully, I'm already dressed, as it would be awkward as I'm left with no choice but to go visit the prisoner, who I wish I never met. The woman isn't sitting on the floor, and this time, rainwater drips in from outside, thunder vibrating through the air above. This time, she's not weeping; she's happily twirling one strand of her black hair around her finger. Her massive dark eyes watch me like a hawk. "You smell like them. The new dragon kings. Now they have their claim on you. All but one, and the puzzle is done." Her voice is sweet, sickly, almost as if she sings her words to me.

"I don't ask to come here."

"I'm aware," she coos, with a look in her eyes that chills my bones. She looks familiar though. The more I come here, the more I can't shake the feeling I've seen her somewhere before. I just can't think where. "But did you know that you never needed to be claimed in this world?"

"You act like you know something more about me than I do. Which is impossible. I know everything about my life. I know my parents. I know my grandmother. I didn't know I had some weird ancestor who came from this place, but now I do. Stop being cryptic," I snap.

The door I came through angrily slams shut beside me, and I jump. The woman laughs. "Yet the castle keeps bringing you here again and again to see me. How interesting." She intently watches me. "Do you know about the fifth court yet? Have you heard about it? Are you curious?"

I vaguely remember Arty saying something on my first day here that there was a fifth court, but I brushed it off as nothing, as something she must have misheard. "They haven't told us about it, but I've heard here and there that there might have been a fifth court."

"There are five elements," she states, holding her head high. "So, of course, there were five courts in the beginning. The fifth element was the strongest."

I might be stupid, but I find my feet moving closer. I find myself wanting to know more. Something about the fifth court...bothers me. I don't know why. "What was it?"

"Spirit, young one," she replies, her voice luring me in. "Spirit is all around you and can be found in the light, darkness, and shadows. The fifth court could control death. They could make and decide when someone died. They could bring shadows to life. Shadows would worship them, follow their every command like baby dragons' kits following their mothers." She rises to her feet, her tattered dress falling off her shoulders as she continues.

"They were deadly, far worse than anyone here. They didn't shift into dragons. They didn't need to. The shadows would make dragons for them to ride. They could fly into war, and no one could ever escape the fifth court. That was the fifth court's famous saying. 'Challenge us and everywhere you go, our shadows will follow until we claim your death.' Every court in this world has shadows. Every corner. Every inch, and they could attack from anywhere. That's what made them the most dangerous court. The court would not only attack you, but they could control your death. They could slow time towards the end, turn the last seconds that it would take to die into hours. They could kill you with one touch and also, for those they were bonded to, they could bring them back from the dead. The royals of the court were particularly dangerous. They had power like no one had ever seen."

My jaw drops. To control death…that is an insane power. "What happened to them?"

She dramatically plops onto the ground. "Dead. All of them. The sorcerer killed them. He was smart," she continues with a sigh. "To go after them first. He knew they were the most powerful threat in this world, and if he could get them out of the way, then the other courts would fall in time. And they all did. They all fell so hard that even now, the remains are weak. True power has been lost, and getting it back will take far stronger dragons than the ones ruling. Only when all five courts are one will the stars bestow their power."

"I think they are pretty powerful," I point out.

She smiles. "You're so…foolish. They have an inch of the power they were born with. They are trapped in his curse that you're living out now. Everything's connected, Ellelin. Even you."

It's still creepy she knows my name, but this is the most I've heard of this world. I'm curious about this place, even if I do want to go home. "The dragon shifters will go extinct. They are being hunted even now. Every day is a ticking clock, with no one to wind it, and no one will be able to stop it from dying."

"What's hunting them?"

Why do I even care?

"I'll give you the answer in exchange for one drop of blood on this door," she replies, her tone greedy. "One drop of blood. It will free me, and I will answer every single one of those burning questions in your mind. I'll explain to you why you don't need to be in the race. I'll explain to you how you can choose your own future. I'm your ticket out of here. The castle knows it. It's why it keeps bringing you here."

The castle walls groan, getting colder, and thunder bangs outside alongside the clinking rain on the stone. "I don't trust you."

She pushes her hair over her shoulder. "Go and ask them about it. Ask them about the fifth court and see how much they value you over their secrets. See if they don't kill you on the spot for knowing more than you should."

She starts laughing. "So many secrets. So many lies. On and on and on it goes. No matter the world, the secrets are the same. The undying love is the same. How sad everyone dies for the same thing in the end."

She laughs. I put my hand on the wall without realising I even moved, and thankfully, a door appears. I twist the handle, looking back at the crazy woman as she laughs and laughs. "I still don't know your name."

She grins at me, showing all her broken and black teeth. "I'll tell you when you free me, and let's be honest with each other, you're one test away from finishing the race, and you don't want to be any of their queens. There is only one ticket to freedom, because they're never going to let you go. You know it, I know it."

My heart races as I turn from her, and she keeps laughing as I rush through the door and slam it behind me, leading me out to the main corridor. Matron is standing on the stairs, talking quietly with Arty, and I'm surprised. They both go quiet. Matron turns back to look over at me. Her eyes wander across my face before she turns around and carries up the stairs. Arty hops over with a big grin on her face. "I was just looking for you!"

"What did she want?" I ask as Arty hooks her arm through mine.

"Oh." Arty pauses. "I was just asking Matron about food choices and if we could choose something nice for our last meal here. Before I came here, I much preferred to eat far more vegetables than there are offered, and there never seems to be a great selection. Plus, do you think they know about pizza yet? Because they really need to know about pizza—"

I cut off her rambling. "When we first met Matron, you said there was a fifth court."

She pauses mid-sentence, stumbling over her words a bit until she stops. She unhooks her arm from mine. "No, I didn't."

"Yes, you did."

She frowns at me as she takes a step back. "No, I didn't. I don't know what you're talking about. Anyway, I have to go—"

"Wait, Arty." I reach for her arm, but she moves out of the way. "On our first day here, you said there was a fifth court, and I need to—"

"No, I didn't," she bites out, angrier than I've ever seen her before she storms off up the staircase, all but running from me. I watch her go, wondering what the hell that was about. I've never seen Arty so cagey. I've never seen her like that at all.

A thick arm falls over my shoulder. "Ah, just the beautiful woman I've been looking for. Have I ever told you purple is my favourite colour?"

I chuckle, looking up at Arden. I've gotten used to this constant need for touching that he seems to have. "Hello to you too."

"Come on. I want to show you something." He tugs on me.

"Should I be concerned?" I ask. Part of me wants to ask him about the fifth court, but at the same time, if I ask him, then I'd have to explain about the crazy lady in the prison that the castle keeps taking me to, and something in my gut tells me not to do that. I mean, I don't know them. I don't trust them completely, and I know nothing about this world. I could be killed, like the prison woman said, for knowing too much. Arden might like me, but he will hate me in the future when he finds out I've only spent time with him and flirted with him because of a deal with Lysander, which ends with his death. If I can do it, that is.

Asking him about the fifth court seems reckless. I can't be reckless. I need to survive here. Arden's going to hate me either way, and something in my chest stings at the thought of him hating me. When he finds out the truth about Lysander, and he will have to find out at some point, he might kill me first. I can't stay here, and I can't kill him. I don't think I even have it in me to kill someone. But if it's between leaving here and killing him, I don't know. Because staying here means I'd have to be someone's queen. It means I'd be trapped for the rest of my life, and I might as well kill myself with that option. It will be between me and him.

I look up at Arden and really look at him. His black hair is cut to his shoulders, but shaping his handsome face, and the darkness of his hair makes his tanned skin look like honey. Somehow, he makes long hair look attractive, although it's cut shorter than when we first met, and now it's styled. This close, I can see he has stubble that I want to run my hand across. He is ridiculously handsome, and if we met in any other way, his looks and humour would have made me fall hard for him. I wouldn't have been able to stop myself.

But he isn't human. He is a dragon shifter king, and I'm just the mortal he kidnapped that's trying to kill him. Arden leads me through two corridors and a door into the main room of the kings' place before leading me up the stairs. He opens a door that's clearly his bedroom, and I raise my eyebrow at him at the door. "Your room?"

"It's a surprise," he says, leaning into me so my back presses on the frame. We are close. Really close.

"Is it in your pants? Because if it is, I'm leaving."

He laughs. "I really, really like you. But even I wouldn't use a cheesy pickup line like that. That's more Emrys's style, and that's why he is single. But some girls do seem to fall for it because he has a pretty face."

Yeah, I hate that Emrys can make me laugh with his terrible pick-up lines and pretty face. Arden isn't what I'd call pretty, not like Emrys, but he is more ruggedly handsome.

I walk into Arden's room. His place smells like fire, not that I would have thought it could smell like anything else. There's a massive fireplace that takes up the one side of the wall, with flickering flames lit inside, and it's lovely and warm in here. He doesn't have a bed, but rather a massive couch covered in red blankets and big cushions. There are several bookcases around the room, filled up with books, but in the centre of the room is a massive table filled with all sorts of strange little bottles, rocks, crystals, insects and so much stuff that I don't know what to look at first. Thunder bangs outside, and a flash of lightning brightens the room for a second.

Arden waves me over to the table. "As I told you before, my court is good at things like this." He clicks his fingers, and a fire lights up on a Bunsen burner in front of him. His eyes light up and he looks so excited as he moves around the table, arranging things. He waves his hand over the flame, and it swirls around in the air as he picks up a bottle off the table and the flames hold it within. I watch as it burns around the bottle, the liquid inside turning from a cool pink almost to a dark blue. Arden picks the bottle out of the flames like it wouldn't hurt him. Maybe he is fireproof. It shouldn't surprise me. "I have two things for you."

He picks out a ring that has an empty oval-shaped mounting. Then he picks out a green gemstone from the flames, which glows slightly on its own, and sets it in the base. He uses his fire to melt the surrounding metal to hold it in place. "This is a stone from my court. It's a green fire gem. Green fire can heal cuts and burns, and sometimes even save lives. I want you to have one. My father invented these."

He comes over, putting the bottle on the side next to me. My heart is in my throat as he lifts my hand and slides the ring onto my middle finger. "Now when you cuss me or anyone else out for being a dickhead, I'll know you're safe with this ring."

I snort with laughter, running my finger over the stone. I think this is the first gift I've ever been given by a guy. Finley never bought me anything. "Isn't this ring considered cheating in the race?"

He shrugs. "What Matron doesn't know won't kill her."

Kill her. For a moment, my mind flickers to thoughts of Desmerda and Lysander killing her for hurting me. But Arden brings my attention back to him. He lifts the potion bottle to me. "Try some. Don't worry. I've taken the heat out of it. It won't burn you."

He drops the potion in my hand. I frown before taking a sip, and my eyes widen as the sour taste takes over. The world goes hazy for a second before everything's so intense. Every colour in the room is brighter than it was. I can see flecks of dirt and dust in the air. I can see so much more. And Arden? Wow. He's so much more like this. My mouth parts as I look at him like he is the sun. He's truly beautiful. "I invented this. This way, you can look through our eyes as shifters. I thought you might be interested in seeing the world like we do."

"It's incredible," I breathe out.

"Come," he says, taking my hand. Where his fingers touch my skin, it burns to life like there's something alive between us. I just want to touch more of his hand, so I end up grabbing his hand with my other one, linking our fingers. I feel a bit dizzy on my feet for a moment. He looks down at me. "Maybe I should have lowered the dosage. I haven't given it to a mortal as short as you. You look drunk and it's giving me flashbacks about you begging to ride our dragons."

My cheeks burn as I lift my middle finger. "Shut up."

He grins, looking at the ring, and something possessive flashes in his eyes. I lower my hand as he leads me to a wall where there's a row of half windows, showing the storm outside as it blasts against the glass. Arden opens two of them, and he leans out of one. I lean out of the other, watching over the mountains. It's so beautiful. I can see so much more. I can see for miles, even through the rain and thick grey clouds. Some of the mountains have an inch of snow on top of them. I can see villages and old ruins, woodlands and the distant sea. "I might be from a court where it never rains, but I like the storms here."

"I've always loved storms," I breathe out. "They are loud, demanding and frightening, but also calm and beautiful."

"Reminds me of someone I know," he murmurs. Looking at me. "Princess, I know you want to escape my world, but there's so much more to it. I hope you don't always want to leave," he tells me truthfully. "I know you don't want to be anyone's queen or owned by anyone, but if you came to my court, you wouldn't be owned by me. Yes, you will be my queen, but you'll be my equal at my side. I won't make you have dragon babies. I won't make you do anything you don't want to do." He looks me dead in the eye. This close with that drink in my system, I can see his eyes for what they truly are. Beautiful and intense flames. "I haven't extended that offer to anybody. I've lived in my castle on my own for a very long time. Yes, I spent my summers with the other kings, but the rest of the time it was just me, but now I'm imagining more. I'm imagining you there too, at my side. I could show you so much more than this. You'd love my court if you gave it a chance—if you gave me a real chance, Ellelin."

I turn away, feeling so many things at once. I watch the pouring rain, feeling his eyes watching me. Only me. "Where's the rest of your family? Someone said that you're the last of the Fire Court."

He is quiet for so long that I don't expect him to answer. "I lost my mother, my father, and my little brother in a dreadful accident when I was only seven years old. Lysander lost his father at the same time and his mother never recovered. Gray's family were destroyed that night too. I barely

233

remember them, to be truthful with you, and what I do remember is bits here and there, but I miss them. I miss the warmness my court was said to have when they were alive. My mother had red hair. My father had black hair, and my little brother had little bits of red hair, too. He was only a baby. I remember my mother singing to me and chasing me around the castle while she was pregnant. I remember my father locked in his laboratories, shouting and barking orders. He always had a smile for me when he saw me, but those memories are slipping away with time even now."

My heart clenches. "Arden, I'm so sorry."

He clears his throat. "They died and I don't have any cousins. I don't have any distant relatives like the other courts do. There is only me. My people have only me. If I don't make an heir for them, the royal family of the Fire Court will die with me. Truth be told, I wonder if that wouldn't be a bad thing. My family fuck everything up, always have done, and I doubt I'm much better."

What Lysander is asking of me is so, so much worse now. "I know it must have been horrible to lose them. I lost my parents when I was six," I say quietly. "And like you, I don't really remember them. My memories feel like they are lost in a fog. I vaguely remember them having black hair. I think my mother had really dark blue eyes and used to sing to me. I don't remember my father, other than a tall man that I see in my dreams sometimes. I wish I remembered more. My grandmother told me a lot about them, but she didn't have any photos, and I somehow morphed her memories into my memories."

He leans back. "I do that too. Emrys's mother told me a lot about my parents. They were best friends, and she looked after me the best she could, but she had her own court, her own children to look after. The summers with her were the best, with the others too. I'm lucky I have them."

You're not that lucky, if you knew what Lysander is doing. He isn't your friend. He is your enemy. He is my enemy, too. Arden takes two steps closer to me, placing his hands on my shoulders and very slowly drifts his fingers down the back of my arms then back up, making my whole body shudder. He leans a bit closer to me, and I find my lips parting for him. I find myself wanting him to kiss me, wanting more as my butt hits the window ledge, leaving no space between us as he presses his body into mine.

I arch my neck up to look at him, and he stares into my eyes right before he leans down and finally kisses me. God, it feels like coming home. His hands tighten on my shoulders before drifting down to my waist as I wrap my arms around his neck, letting myself fully lose myself in him. He groans, his tongue slipping into my mouth as he picks me up, pushing me against the wall, pushing himself into me. A moan escapes my throat, and he tilts my jaw and presses his warm lips on my throat, sending shivers down my spine.

I freeze as I look over Arden's shoulder, seeing Lysander watching from the door. He holds his hand out, and cold water starts to form in my hand, shaping into a dagger before hardening to ice. My blood goes cold as I realise what he wants me to do.

Stab Arden as he kisses my neck, as he is distracted by me.

Kill Arden and I can be free. My grandmother will be safe.

Lysander watches with a cruel smile. My heart pounds, the seconds feeling like minutes as Arden keeps kissing down my jaw, down my neck, lightly nibbling at my skin. He feels so big between my legs, pushing into me, and my body wants so much more.

But the dagger feels so heavy in my hand, and I realise I can't do it.

I mouth, "The deal is off."

And I drop the dagger. Lysander's eyes narrow, the dagger melting away into pure mist before it hits the ground.

"Arden, we have a problem," Lysander angrily shouts, banging his fist on the door.

Arden lifts his head, a growl ripping out of his throat. "Get the fuck out, friend."

"It can't wait, but she can," Lysander comments, sounding bored. "You can fuck her later. It's not like she has anywhere to escape to or anyone waiting for her."

He's angry with me. Fuck, that comment was for me. What have I done?

Arden kisses me softly once, putting me down. "Can we continue this later?"

I find myself nodding, not really hearing or feeling anything but dread as Arden leaves with Lysander. I should have tried to kill him rather than letting my heart win.

CHAPTER 14

KING LYSANDER OF THE WATER COURT.

*A*rden kissed her.

He was kissing her, tasting her. *Fuck*. He would have fucked her if I didn't interrupt them. Why the hell does it make me feel like drowning this entire island until there's only me and her left? Until he is drowned, dead and not fucking coming back. If I didn't hate him before, I definitely hate him now. Not that the fucker knows it. He's not once even suspected that I hate him or that Ellelin was playing him like a violin to my command. The game must have become real for her, and it pisses me right off. Arden assumed we were friends because we were forced to grow up together. He assumed that I'd forgotten everything that had happened between our families. He assumes that I can just get over it. I won't.

"What is it?" Arden angrily demands from my side. He is angry with me for interrupting his time with Elle, and I can't erase the image of her legs wrapped around his waist, her hands in his hair. How fucking turned on she smelt. She was kissing him like she was in love with him before I interrupted. She chose to save this fucker over her own family, and she's going to pay for that.

"My court was attacked by the West," I state quietly, making sure no one else hears us. "It was a big attack. They killed two hundred of my people, and another hundred are missing, mostly women."

Arden's eyes widen. I might hate the fucker, but for now, while he is alive, he has the biggest army in Ayiolyn. "Fuck."

"There's more," I continue. "At the same time, a village in your court was rumoured to be attacked. Someone from your court is here to speak to you. I think you took great losses."

"We both have," Arden murmurs quietly, his face pale.

He's too weak to protect his people. I should have protected mine better. They wiped out an entire village this morning, and my people are missing. The dragons of the West are getting ballsy, and I don't like it. The longer we stay here, the longer I can't hunt them down. The village they took out was undefended, but I've corrected that problem. "Do you need help, Lysander? I know your people still remember what my father did—"

"No," I cut him off. "We don't need any help."

I need this damn race over with so I can leave and protect my people. I need him dead for the next part of what I want to do. I will get revenge for the past, for everything I lost.

Arden storms off, leaving me alone in the corridor. I walk to the window, jumping out and shifting into my dragon. Shifting feels like freedom, and I need a moment with my wings stretched out. Flying is like swimming through the sea, the feeling unlike anything else.

My dragon's thoughts are on one person only. Ellelin. Arden kissing her. I growl, ice spitting off my wings into the air. My foolish jealousy is more intense now, and my dragon wants to rip everything apart. I fly around the castle, landing on top of it, watching as Ellelin goes back through the castle. Her purple hair falls to her ass, her tight clothes revealing how curvy her body is. I want her. Fuck, denying it is pointless, but I hate her. I'm not hate fucking my new enemy. She knows too many of my secrets, and she let me down by not stabbing Arden in the back. That would have made this night better. I watch her through the windows until she gets to her hallway. I fly around to the edge of the castle, sensing her going into the bathroom and the distinct scent of water running.

I shift back on the roof, letting the castle make a door for me. It leads me straight into the bathroom, where she's lying in the bath. I freeze the water completely around her, and she gasps, turning to face me, fear flashing in her blue eyes. I hate that her eyes are the perfect shade of ocean blue. Her skin reminds me of the warm sand outside my castle. She smells fucking fantastic, too. "Don't scream or I'll drown you."

Her eyes are panicked as she stares at me. I sit on the edge of the tub, keeping my eyes on her face. I'm not that much of an asshole. "Should I leave you frozen in here until you die? You're useless to me if you're not going to kill Arden." I sigh. "It seems I'm due to pop back to Earth and deal with your dear, sweet grandmother."

I hate being a dickhead, but I'll be one to get revenge. Arden has to die, painfully and heartbroken. If I attack him outright, then I won't get what I want. It needs to be her. Needs to be someone else to be blamed while I take over his court. The fear doubles in her eyes, and they fill with tears. She doesn't let them fall. She only holds her head as high as she can and narrows her eyes at me. "I'm not doing it, and you're not going to kill my grandmother because I'm going to tell Arden about this. What do you think your friends will do when they know you tried to blackmail me to kill Arden?"

I reach forward and wrap my hand around her throat. I hate the way she looks at me. She isn't scared, but there is just pure fucking fire in her eyes that I feel right down to my cock. I usually love women like her. Ones that are not scared of me or anything. Ones that like having my hand wrapped around their throat as I fuck them. Those are the kind of women I like, and she's definitely one of those. It doesn't help that she's goddamn fucking gorgeous. I keep my face blank. I don't show her how turned on I am. What I would do to her if she weren't my enemy. "You are going to kill him, Elle. Don't fuck with me. You won't like the consequences, and I don't give a shit about what my so-called friends think."

She looks right into my goddamned soul. "Liar."

I tighten my grip. "I'll give you more time. Perhaps you can become his queen and then stab him in the back. You're not going to say a word to anyone because that will guarantee your grand-mother's death. If you think I'm dangerous now, you should see me when I have nothing left to lose."

The ice cracks as she struggles to get free, but she's weak, mortal. Even if she drives me fucking insane, she's still those things. "Fine." She snaps. "Just fine."

"Good." I remove my hand and stand, using my power to melt the ice around her body. My cock is rock hard, and I adjust myself as I face away from her.

"Get the fuck out of my bathroom, Lysander."

"With pleasure," I growl. I leave out the door to her room, making her chatty friend gasp. I fucking hate my enemy.

"There you are. Were you looking for me?" Hope's voice makes me pause, and I see her coming towards me down the corridor. She brushes her body against mine when she is close enough, leaning up and kissing my jaw.

I push her back. "I'm not in the mood."

Another door appears for me, and I open it, heading back to my room. Hope follows and I rub my face as she begins shouting. "What the hell was with that? You come looking for me, and then you decide you don't want me?"

I lean on my desk as she rants away. "For a good year, you ignored me, and then we came here, and you've been all over me for months. Then suddenly you're cold with me again. I don't get it. I thought you wanted me to be your queen and that was why you were so into me since I got here. What's changed?"

My dragon pushes against my mind, wanting to be free again. I'm not in the mood to deal with Hope. It was a bad fucking idea, starting things with her again when I got here. I was lonely, and she was just there. She wants to be my queen, fine, but I don't want the happily ever after she has planned. My plan with Arden and Ellelin is all that matters. "Nothing. Just get out, Hope."

She walks up to me, brushing her hands up my thighs. "I can make you feel better. Whatever has you in a bad mood, I can distract you."

I'm tempted for a moment, but I'm done fucking her and thinking of only one person—who isn't her. Hope has always been desperate for attention, for me. It's becoming nothing more than annoying and unattractive. She has this imagined bond to me thanks to my dumb ass saving her life as a kid. I remember seeing her floating on a long piece of wood, not breathing. I used my power to pull the water from her lungs, and my mum decided she would love a daughter. We didn't grow up together; she was always sent off to train in various courts. My mother thought it was best she learnt to be as strong as she possibly could get before the race. The first time we were together, she told me she loved me, but I just wanted to get laid. I should have stopped this then. I remove her hands and head to the open window in my room. "Lysander!"

I jump out of the window to escape her, shifting and roaring as she screams my name. I let myself fly around the island, to the sea, before diving in deep. The ocean washes away everything, including thoughts of Ellelin fucking Ilroth.

CHAPTER 15

KING ARDEN OF THE FIRE COURT.

"*I* don't want Ellelin to enter your race."

Grayson looks up at me from the couch, stretching his legs out. I thought he'd look at me like I'm insane, but he doesn't. I swear I see understanding in his gaze.

"You know I can't." He purses his lips and I growl. This stupid fucking curse is like a noose around our necks. All of ours. We can't stop the race, only guide it and choose what parts of our magic we want to use within it. I didn't see her coming. Ellelin fucking Ilroth has taken hostage of every inch of me. In my head, I'd convinced myself I could pretend to accept some girl as my queen and then leave her alone within my court for the rest of her life. I didn't want a bride…not until I met her. Now all I can think about is having her in my court, sitting on my throne, and in my bed in the evenings. Or mornings. Or whenever we want.

We can't save any of them without losing our magic and putting our court in danger. Asking Grayson is pointless, we both know it, but he is my trusted friend, and I want him to know what is going on in my head. "I don't want her in it either," he murmurs.

"There must be a way. We could take her back and swap her for someone else," I desperately suggest.

"Arden."

Flames flicker in my hand, and I put them out before I burn our room down. Again. "I know."

"Come and spar with me," Grayson commands. If anyone else commanded me, I'd tell them to fuck off, but not Gray. He was always commanding with all of us since we were kids. He would stand apart and boss us about even in stupid games of hide-and-seek. Lysander always cheated by using his powers, and Emrys would take the time to fly around his castle and find an impossible place to hide. The fucker always won. But Grayson wanted to be with us, just from a distance. It took me years before I realised why.

I nod, following him out the doors to the sparring field. "No magic. Just spears. Make it a challenge."

I grin, picking up a spear off the rack. Grayson does the same. I rip off my shirt. It's too hot out today for it. I've only ever seen Gray take his shirt off once, and I understand why he won't, even if it gets soaked with sweat when we spar.

I sense her before I swiftly turn to see Ellelin coming out of the castle through a tunnel. I love this interfering castle. Ellelin and her talkative friend, Amy or something, are with several of the other girls, who all come to a stop when they see us. She smiles brightly at me, and I grin back. Fuck, I'm falling for this girl. The new tutor is with them, and he steps in front of Ellelin. I frown at the fucker for ruining my view. "Ah, we came to see if we can train outside, but it seems like you've taken up the area. Maybe a demonstration on how to properly fight is in order? My students could observe."

Hope laughs. "Oh, I'm down for watching."

I roll my eyes at her flirting, noticing how Ellelin glares at her for a second. Grayson nods, looking Ellelin's way for a few seconds too long. He follows her gaze to me. Elle's eyes are wandering over my chest like she can't stop looking, and when her eyes drift lower, I know I'm fucked. I'm going to lose this fight while she is watching me like that. Her eyes meet mine, and I wink. She smiles slightly. I don't know when she got under my skin, but she has, and I live for every time she looks my way. I don't think any other girl I've ever met has been able to do that.

I look at her once more, and I swear my mind goes foggy. I fuck up on everything and anything that I meant to be doing when she is around. I glance at the ring on her finger. I shouldn't have given her that. Absolutely not. It's worth a fortune, and there is only one of those rings left in the world. My father might have invented a way for it to be worn as jewellery for my mother, but the stone is thousands of years old and belongs to the ruling family of the Fire Court. It shouldn't leave the court.

Fuck it, she is going to be my queen. She deserves the ring. I lost my mind a long time ago when it comes to her. It started in a little tiny house with weird pictures of a cat on the wall, and a fiery hellcat who knocked out my friend with a toilet lid. That night, I was done for.

Grayson's playful growl snaps me out of those fond memories. I straighten my back. Grayson won't care where my thoughts are. He will literally beat the shit out of me if I'm not focused. He doesn't have any sympathy for his enemies and not much for his friends.

He's ruthless and my best mate. Grayson gives me no chance for any kind of breather before he's lashing out at me, his spear heading straight for my head. I block it with my own, spinning out of the way and twisting on my foot and turning to block his next move. Our spears clang loud, and even while we aren't using powers, I can taste magic in the air around us from our dragons. He blocks my attack, and for a while we circle each other, our spears clanging with each hit, smashing and vibrating around the field. I feel Elle's eyes on me, watching like a hawk, and I can't focus as much as I did. Sweat pours down my body, Gray's too, and we both are panting hard after half an hour of this. I fucking love sparring with him. Grayson whacks me hard on the side, sending me stumbling a bit. I huff, literal smoke coming out of my mouth, and he grins.

"No magic, asshole," he reminds me.

I chuckle and jump at him. He uses his spear by holding it with both hands, blocking my attack, and I push down my spear with all my strength. Just then, I scent Ellelin. Fuck, she is turned on by this. I can smell it in the air. My dragon roars. Grayson's just as strong as I am, and we both know it, but I'm far more easily distracted than he is. I push down with the strength from my dragon, him growling in the back of my mind, adding to the sense that we absolutely have to beat Gray to impress Ellelin. My dragon's a competitive asshole, but even now, he seems distracted by her as much as I am. I want to shout at him to focus, to push all of his strength into me, especially when Grayson manages to push me off him hard enough that I fall backwards and land on my ass.

The tip of his spear is pressed into my neck in a second.

The bastard doesn't even attempt not to look happy as he lifts his spear and brushes sweat off his face. The girls are cheering. I climb to my feet. "You win, clever bastard. Maybe we should get Emrys and Lysander down here. We haven't sparred all together for months."

"Lysander is busy and Emrys isn't going to fight with an audience. He doesn't like to show off," Grayson points out, lowering his voice. "For pretty girls he might change his mind though."

I resist the urge to smack his arm, knowing he doesn't like to be touched. Except...he let Ellelin hold his hand and lay her head on his shoulder. That shit shocked me the other night. I'd like to know how she has gotten him to trust her. Livia, I think that's her name, is talking to Elle as we walk over. "I could get used to the Magic Mike show any day. That was hot and I'm not even into men."

Ellelin nods. "I love Magic Mike shows. So hot, but maybe this was even better."

"Who the fuck is Magic Mike?" I question, crossing my arms, and Ellelin jumps out of her skin. They both giggle, and I'm pretty sure I missed the joke somewhere. Ellelin looks up at me with her beautiful, clear blue eyes. Her eyes remind me of the blue sea at Lysander's home. It's so crystal clear that there isn't anything you can't see. Fire is my element, my home, but I will admit sea blue is calling to me recently. I flick a bit of her dark purple hair. I even enjoy the purple hair. It's a strange colour to have chosen, but I like it, and I assume she doesn't like her natural hair colour for some reason I'm yet to find out.

She frowns at me as I breathe in her scent. She smells like jasmine night flowers that my mother used to have in her room. I never knew which court they came from. "You're done with training already?"

"Unless you want to spar with me," I suggest, offering her my spear.

Her cheeks go red and it's cute as fuck. "No, after watching that, I'm good."

Emrys comes out of the tunnel and walks over to us. Hope and the others are leaving, and she waves at us. I know she doesn't get along with Ellelin, but I believe it's because they are more alike than they want to admit. Lysander doesn't make it better, blowing hot and cold with Hope like he has done for years. We all know he doesn't love her, and he won't have her as his queen unless he is forced into it. The only one who never sees that is Hope. She has loved him since we were kids and he saved her from drowning. He found Hope as a kid, floating in the sea, with no parents to be found. His mother took her in as her ward, along with Emrys's mother, who had her half the year. Hope said she doesn't remember where she is from, but I think she is lying. She came from the West.

The fucker leans over and kisses Elle on the cheek, and fury burns in my chest. My dragon's all ready to rip out of my skin and tear my friend to pieces for just kissing her cheek. I have to physically hold myself still, tell myself that he's my friend and that we don't rip our friends to pieces because we're jealous over a girl. Even when she looks at him like that. She likes Emrys. I'm certain of it, but I'm not sure how he feels. Emrys has always been hard to read. I thought for maybe a moment that she likes Grayson, too. They've been having these weird private lessons together. I look between them.

Yeah, I'm wrong. He glares at her like everyone else.

Emrys touches my forearm. "I need to speak to you, mate. Alone."

I nod. What the fuck has happened now? I turn to Elle, kissing her forehead. Emrys and Grayson watch me kiss her forehead like I'm stealing her from them. We have a big fucking problem brewing here. "I'll catch up to you later, and we can have dinner together if you want?"

"I'd like that," she replies, looking at Gray. "You could join us, if you want?"

"I will," Grayson replies, moving to her side. They walk off together, and I frown at their backs. Grayson…wants to eat with her? He hates eating with people.

When we are alone, I turn to Emrys. "What's the matter?"

His voice is quiet. "My court's been attacked again. I can't stay here much longer. It's getting ridiculous. There were reports of them using lightning, and they have taken twenty of my people."

"Must be a rumour. It's impossible," I mutter, rubbing my face. The dragon riders of the West are a real fucking big problem. For years, they never had a leader, and they wouldn't dare attack our shores, but in the last three years, a new leader has appeared, and they are attacking. Our spies are dead, and we have no idea what is going on over there now. They are mortals who ride dragons that are trapped in shifter form. Since this race began, they are attacking more and more. They know we aren't there to defend our people. "I'll send more of my fighters to help your court. If any court falls, we are all fucked."

"Thank you, friend." Emrys pats my shoulder. His people are not fighters, and the dragon riders know this.

The longer we stay here, the longer it takes us to get a bride to keep our magic, and the more danger our people are in. The West is coming for us, and we are at war.

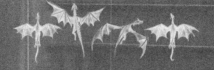

CHAPTER 16

"As you know, the rules of my training session are simple," Xandry begins, pacing in front of our group as he always does. "I'll choose two of you to come into the ring. Fighting dirty is allowed, but try not to break any bones, with the final race coming up. I would suggest no hitting between your legs, but you are all girls, and I don't think you play that dirty."

I ignore Xandry's terrible jokes as some of the girls laugh, not me though. I glance at Arty, who hasn't spoken to me since yesterday. When I got back to my room, she was sleeping, and she didn't come for breakfast. I don't know what upset her about my questions, but I want to ask more. I need to know why she is being like this. Arty looks my way and quickly looks back at the tutor.

"Can we get on with it?" Hope deadpans. It's been two weeks since the air test, and Hope still hates me, even though I saved her life. It didn't surprise me she didn't say thank you, but she's more of an ungrateful cow than I realised. It's becoming personal for me to beat her in combat, and I haven't been set against her in a few days. Now all I want to do is beat her. It's all I think about. I'm avoiding Arden like the plague after our kiss yesterday because I feel awful. I asked the castle to take me to Lysander today after Grayson didn't show for training, but the castle didn't want to help me. Maybe it knows about our deal and how much of a crappy person I am to Arden.

I need to make a new deal with Lysander. I need to make sure he doesn't hurt my grandmother. I feel terrible letting Arden that close to me, because I'm doing exactly what Lysander wanted me to do, but at some point, it was no longer about Lysander's threat. At some point, I didn't want to play his game anymore and it just became about wanting to be near Arden. I haven't felt like this before and it's confusing, as much as it scares me. Grayson and I barely talk during training anymore, but the tension is thick between us, making it worse with every lesson, and I was almost glad he didn't show this morning. He is making every lesson that we have worse. Sometimes I see Emrys around the castle, and I swear he is looking for me. He asked me to come to the balcony the last time I saw him, but I didn't trust myself to go. Because the truth is I have feelings for them, feelings for them that I shouldn't have. I can't have a life here and one back home. It doesn't work like that.

I didn't choose this, and having feelings for them isn't what I want. I refuse to admit I care about the dragon kings. Caring would be the end of my freedom.

"Fine, Hope, you're up first," Xandry bites out. Hope is the only one who seems to piss him off in class. He looks around, settling on me. "Ellelin, up you come."

Hope grins at me like she has already won as she goes to the middle of the circle. Xandry comes over to both of us. "Let's make this more interesting. Don't stab deep."

He hands Hope and me silver daggers. Fuck. I haven't trained in daggers. My hand feels sweaty around the handle of the blade as I take it from Xandry. Hope looks like she has won the lottery as she spins her dagger around in her hand. "Today is going to be a good one."

"You're as psychotic as your boyfriend," I mutter.

Hope shrugs. "I like to think of us as engaged, considering our wedding won't be that far off now. Shame you won't be around to see it."

I snort and laugh. "Aww, did he get down on one knee and everything? Did you blush as you accepted his ring?"

Her eyes angrily narrow on me. "I might not have a ring, but I'm in his bed every night. You're one to talk with a Fire Court ring on your finger. Did Arden get down on one knee too?"

There are hushed whispers around the group, who are watching intently. "It's not an engagement ring!"

She laughs. "Keep telling yourself that. One day you might believe it."

Hope launches at me, and I'm so distracted by her taunts that I barely move out of the way, the tip of her dagger cutting my arm. I wince and hear Grayson's voice in my head. "Think of something else. Calm and focus. Don't let emotions distract you."

I blow out a breath, focusing on Hope. They said the race takes one hundred days, and there are three days left. We all know that our test is coming soon, then this'll all be over, and I have to somehow figure out what I'm going to do next. Arden wants me to have a life in his court. Lysander might try to claim me to somehow work out his deal. I don't know what Emrys and Grayson want, but I can't be anything they need. I have to escape or become one of their queens and be trapped here forever. The last option does not sound like anything I am interested in.

If I tell Arden about Lysander, he is going to start a war with Lysander, and telling Arden would mean that I'd have to go with him—if he doesn't kill me for betraying him. I'm not sure I can warn him about Lysander. Part of me just wants to ask Grayson or Emrys to let me go if I become their queen. Anything but Lysander. He can go and drown in his own court for all I care.

Hope and I start circling each other, and I watch her carefully. Sometimes she moves too quickly on her left foot. She always goes for a strike in my chest before hitting my legs to get me down, and she was always fast, quick, and impossible to predict before. But now I'm starting to predict her, because Grayson has shown me how she fights. Grayson has shown me how to defend from her strikes, dagger or not.

She jumps at me, and I swiftly move out of the way, slamming my fist into her stomach as she goes past. She gasps, rolling to the side and looking at me with wide eyes. The amount of pleasure I get from her not just looking at me like I'm weak is amazing. I might have started off weak, but I've climbed up so I can be stronger. Some days, feeling weak is all I have, but I remind myself that only I can make myself stronger. Hope charges at me, and I can't block her, so we both go down in a puddle on the floor. I don't let her pin me down or knock my dagger away. I wrap my legs around her waist, flipping us both over and pushing her away. Her dagger clatters on the ground, and I kick it out of the circle.

She brushes her hair out of her eyes. "You bitch!"

"Find another insult!" I shout right back at her, leaping at her, my dagger cutting a line across her stomach through her clothes. She gasps, stepping back. Grayson showed me that move. I'm going to have to thank him. She looks so surprised. We both watch each other, but I let her move first, using all that anger up. This time she comes at me harder, more desperate, her blood pouring down her legs. I barely avoid her, but her leg goes under mine with a swoop, knocking me over. I slam my foot into her knee before she can even do anything, making her stumble back. I flip myself to my feet and swing my leg around, kicking her hard in the chest. She flies out of the circle, slamming into the wall and sliding down it.

The room pauses, right before the girls cheer. No one has beaten Hope before. Xandry blows his whistle and throws healing tonics at us both. I drink mine at the same time as Hope, handing over my dagger too. Hope storms over to me. "How the fuck did you do that?"

I shrug with a smile. She narrows her eyes. "I've ruthlessly trained, day and night, for my entire life for this race, and you just—" She stops, her mouth opening and closing, lost for words. "I trained because I'm human in a world of shifters and I would have died if I didn't. You just got here, and somehow after a couple of weeks, you magically know how to beat me? No, you're cheating somehow."

"That's enough, Hope. Lose with some honour," Xandry firmly tells her, putting his hand on her shoulder, and she pushes him off.

"No, I want to know how she did that!" Hope demands, getting in my face.

I smile at her. "You're not perfect, Hope. You've lost. Get over it."

"But how did you learn? Did Lysander teach you behind my back in private training lessons or something?" she asks, her voice filled with hurt.

I blow out a breath. "For the last time, I have no interest in Lysander! Stop being paranoid."

Her eyes tighten and she honestly looks like she's plotting the best way to kill me. "I see how you look at him."

Xandry slides in between us, making her step back. He places both his hands on her shoulders this time. "Enough, Hope. You lost at training. It's just one battle, and as for Lysander, it's been the two of you for years. Soon this will be over."

She shoves him off again. "Like you give a shit. You abandoned us all when you were a kid so you could go and be some stupid priest that can't have bonded relationships or even give a shit about anyone. Congrats on your new teaching job here, but I damn well know I'll never see you again after this, so don't pretend you suddenly care about anyone in this world. We both know you don't," she snaps.

Xandry is silent as she turns, storming out to the door, but then she pauses, taking several steps back. Grayson walks in through the door, dressed in dark greens. His court colour. A feeling of dread settles into my chest. "Grayson."

Even Hope sounds worried. Is she dreading this last race? If she is scared, then fuck, I should be peeing myself right now.

Grayson's face is blank, showing no emotions. "All of you, come with me. The earth is calling you."

Nope. Nope. Nope.

Xandry pushes me in the back when I'm the only one who doesn't leave after Grayson. My stomach seems to drop because I know what this is. The final test of the Dragon Crown Race is here. Arty comes to my side, and I give her a wary look. She gulps. "Congratulations on winning against Hope. If we both die, well, at least you have that. Look, I'm sorry about yesterday, and for what it is worth, you're the only real friend I've ever had. Thank you."

"Talk to me," I ask as we walk down the staircase. "I don't understand why you got so upset."

She touches my arm. "Thank you."

Arty walks ahead of me, and I'm left more confused than ever about her. I shake my head, focusing on what is coming next and bracing myself for this test. One more time. I have to live through just one more of these fucked-up tests. Grayson leads us through the castle, and all of us are nervous. Two of the girls are crying, and I realise there are so few of us left. Grayson leads us to the middle of the castle, and suddenly the staircases move up, leaving us in a massive, empty room. He commands the space, standing in the middle of us all. Screams ripple around me as the earth gives way, and all the girls sink down into the ground, disappearing in holes, and the holes close back up.

But not me.

My heart pounds as Grayson walks over to me, tilting my chin up with one finger. Like he needs to touch me, but he can't do more than this. I have the feeling every time he lets himself be touched or reaches out, it's a battle for him. I want to take the battle away, fix him, but I don't have time. I can't be what he needs, but I hope someone is. "What are you doing, Gray?"

His voice is husky. "I have no fucking idea, but I don't want to send you into the test. I want to kidnap you again, this time for myself, even if that would be a death sentence for my people. Even if it would fuck up my world. Tell me I'm mad. Tell me there is nothing here and these stupid feelings aren't real."

"They're not real," I breathe out. Liar. I'm such a liar. "I want to go home, but not if it kills so many. We can't be selfish."

He leans forward, pressing his cheek against mine. He's shaking slightly. I can feel it, but it's nowhere near the nerves he had when we first started our training lessons. "I saw you win against Hope. Now I know you can fight. So, you go down there, you fight this final test. Survive for me." He brushes his lips against my ear. "And you'll be my queen. Not theirs. Mine. I'll rip the earth out from under all the other courts to keep you."

"Gray—"

I barely manage to say his name before the earth gives way beneath me, and I sink down under-ground, landing with a thump in a cold dirt tunnel. It's not high in here, so I have to crouch when I stand, and I cough on the dirt and dust floating around me. It's so dark and it takes a while for my eyes to adjust. Grayson wants me as his queen, so does Arden. Lysander wants me dead, and Emrys…I have no idea what he wants.

When this is over…I have to run from them. First, I have to survive. There are flickers of light from little blue things dotted around me, but I can barely see. The light they give off is too dim. I scream as something slams hard into my back, and I look around to see vines. My blood turns cold when I see they're not vines. They're snakes —snakes that are made out of something that looks very much like vines. One of them snaps at me again, cutting my arm, and I scream, running straight down the tunnel, turning at the first left and then the right. I hear more screams echoing around me, and I jump over a massive vine snake in my path. I'm running blindly when I trip, slamming into the ground. I blink in the darkness, more of the blue things floating around me, and I look up to see a boot.

I rise to my feet, looking down at the dead body. There are vine snakes wrapped around her, biting her, repeatedly choking her. But she's already dead. Her blood is pouring down into the earth, making those blue lights.

Florence. Her eyes are wide, but she's gone, and a wave of sadness hits me. I didn't know her all that well, but she fought to survive. She shouldn't have died here. No one should have died in this castle. Livia. She is going to be heartbroken.

"I'll tell her, Florence. I'll look after her." I'm in shock, and I don't move for too long. The snakes notice me, and I turn, running fast. I turn around a corner, only to fall headfirst into a hole. The ground slips out from underneath me, and I fall with a thump into another tunnel, this one stinking like something is rotting. I turn just as a massive snake jumps straight towards me.

CHAPTER 17

KING GRAYSON OF THE EARTH COURT

I pace up and down repeatedly, like keeping still is making even an ounce of a difference to Ellelin's fate. She was born for this, so the curse claims, but I believe she was born for me.

Ellelin is in danger. I told myself that it's one more test, one more battle for her to win alone before we can face every battle together from here on out. I've never been as obsessed with anything or anyone as I am with her. I can't get her out of my head, and frankly, I don't want to anymore.

I feel through the earth with my powers to sense if she's still alive. I don't give a shit if the others survive. This test is deadly, designed by my court to find their perfect queen in the most brutal manner. The snakes are from my court, bred to be vicious. They are made of vines, their bodies filled with a deadly poison. One bite and she will suffer. She could die from it.

The other dragon kings come to stand with me. Lysander, Arden and Emrys are waiting, and I wonder if they're waiting for her, too. Ellelin has captured their attention, and I don't like it. They want her as well, but she's going to be mine. They don't know about our private training sessions, and if they do, they don't realise what's going on in them. She's the first person I've let touch me since, well, since I was a child. She may hate me when she realises that I'm covered in scars, and I'm not near as perfect and as beautiful as she is, but I can't let her go. I won't let her go. I carry on pacing when suddenly chills snake down my neck.

I can't feel the earth anymore.

I lean down, touching the ground with my hand, searching for my power, but I feel nothing. Absolutely nothing.

I meet Arden's gaze. He sensed it, too. Lysander looks lost in his head, and Emrys is frowning at his hand. "My power is gone," I tell them.

"Mine too," Emrys claims, patting Lysander on the shoulder, and he snaps out of wherever he was.

Lysander frowns. "What the fuck happened to my magic?"

I walk faster until Arden slams his hand into my chest to stop me. I growl at him as he lowers his hand. "I don't know. I can't feel them in the test anymore or the surrounding earth."

"They couldn't have all died. That would mean the test is over and broken," Arden all but whispers in horror. "She can't be dead."

"No, she isn't yet," Lysander coldly comments.

I narrow my eyes at him. How the fuck would he know that? "They were alive. Several of them were still alive, so they can't be dead. No part of the curse talks of this."

Emrys looks around the room. "Something else is going on."

Fuck it, I'll go down to the tunnels the long way. I run to the doors, but they all disappear, leaving us locked in. There's no way out. I slam my fists on the wall. "Castle, what the fuck are you doing?"

The castle wall groans in protest, and the room goes ice cold. I step back as the ground begins to shake slightly, but not with my power. Something is really fucking wrong.

"Can you hear that?" Lysander quietly asks, and it's the first time I've heard him panicked. He must be worried about Hope.

I listen, hearing a song being played from the castle walls itself, and it gets louder and louder.

Arden goes still. "I know that song." His lips part. "I haven't heard it in a very, very long time. I was a kid when I heard it last, but I'd never forget it. It's the song of the fifth court. It's the song of the shadows of spirit."

His face is ghostly white, and no one says anything. The fifth court...they were all slaughtered. They were slaughtered in this very castle they used to live in twelve years ago, but none of them were left to explain what happened that night. The test hid their people in the darkness until there was a test, and only members of the fifth court could come here. They were indestructible until that night. We all heard the explosion of the island, saw what was left of it until it disappeared. Until this test revealed everything wasn't lost, the castle somehow survived. My own parents died that night. The Spirit Court was the most powerful of all of us, but they're gone.

Why is their song playing through the castle, and why the fuck have we lost our magic?

The ground shakes once more, the song growing louder and louder by the second. Lysander meets my gaze. "We need to get out of here. Now!"

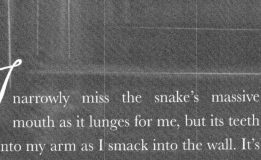

CHAPTER 18

I narrowly miss the snake's massive mouth as it lunges for me, but its teeth dig deep into my arm as I smack into the wall. It's so dark I can't see anything as I scream in pain, breathing in the smell of rotting. I reach out, seeing piles of bones…human bones in a corner near me. Sickness rises up in my throat. I can't die here. Ignoring the pain in my arm, I stand up and run. I'm blindly running, the sound of hissing filling my ears and making my heart pound with fear. Snakes. I hate snakes.

I run into another wall and gasp as the air is knocked from my lungs. Leaning on the wall, I turn on my side, feeling the wall with my hands until I find an edge. Bones crack under my feet, but I try to ignore them, and the smell too. I'll fight for my life, no matter the circumstances. I have to get back home, even if I found something here that almost makes me want to stay. The dragon kings…I can't get all of them out of my head and some of them out of my heart. It's too bad they aren't human and we didn't just meet randomly.

I blow out a shaky breath and close my eyes for one second to calm myself down. There has to be a point to this race. Snakes…what the hell do I know about them other than they should be in a zoo, behind a glass wall, and unable to eat me for dinner? I know nothing about them. This place is a maze, and maybe I just need to escape. I haven't seen anyone else alive yet, but I hope Arty and Livia are okay.

I blow out a breath before I run in the darkness, the blue lights so dim that I can only see the outline of a tunnel ahead of me. "How am I meant to escape when I can't see?"

I scream as the floor gives out from under me, and I roll down a tunnel, smacking my face on the ground and reaching out for anything to stop me. The ground just keeps falling with me, and I can't do anything but fall with it. Suddenly, I crash hard into a large rock with my leg first. I hear the break, the sickening snap of my bones in my leg, and I scream out in incredible pain. Tears fall down my cheek as I gasp, blowing out breaths through the pain. I cry, touching my leg, and everything spins as I manage to sit up on the rocks. I can't move. I'm going to die. The thought, the truth, hits me harder than the break. I've fought for months to survive, to get out of this race and win it, and I'm going to die down here.

"Get up. Don't you dare fucking die, Elle!" Lysander's voice fills my head, or at least I'm somehow imagining it does. "Get up! You're far too fucking stubborn to die like this. Get up and use the walls, use anything, and fucking walk!"

Lysander sounds frantic in my head. He can't be real. He actually sounds like he really cares if I die or not. I grab the rock, using it to pull myself as another scream rips out of my throat. I barely manage to stand when blue lights float up from the middle of the room, and the smell of fresh blood hits me. There's another body in the middle of the room, one of the girls, but her throat has been cut with a blade. The snakes are biting her, but she wasn't killed by them. What the hell is going on? The snakes, no doubt smelling my blood, turn my way. So many green flashing eyes face me, and I flinch. My mind is filled with Lysander's voice, shouting one word over and over. "RUN!"

Dozens of snakes head towards me, slithering and hissing. I hop back to the wall, trying desperately to get away and failing as they keep getting closer and closer. I fall over within moments, and I crawl backwards until my back hits the wall. I'm trapped. The room feels fuzzy and my arm burns, and I feel hot. Too hot, I'm burning up. I look down at my arm to see something black spreading down my skin, out of where the snake bit me, mixing with my blood. That's why I'm hearing things. I'm poisoned.

The snakes are moving so fast, and I close my eyes. "I'm going to die."

I don't know how Lysander hears me. Or if, in my final moments, I've lost my mind and I'm talking to myself. "No, get the fuck up, Elle! Don't you dare give up!"

My heart is pounding in my chest as I refuse to open my eyes. I'm going to die in this place. I'm not surviving this. I can't survive this. Suddenly the ground gives way underneath me again, and I fall through dirt, coughing, choking on it as I scream in pain from my leg as it knocks into everything. My stomach is filled with butterflies as I float in the darkness, right before I slam onto cold stone with my head. I groan, touching my head, feeling myself bleeding from the fall. It's brighter here, and it's cold as I lift my head. The room is spinning. I blink my eyes a few times to focus, and everything slowly comes into focus.

"Arty?" I quietly ask with a smile. Arty leans down in front of me, not meeting my eyes. Blood is all over her cloak and clothes, but she doesn't look injured. "What happened to you? Are you okay? Where is the blood from? Arty, I need some help and—"

She puts her hand on my head, and I wince. She smothers her palm in my blood, and I helplessly watch as she rises up and goes to the cage bars behind her. We're in the prisons…and she has my blood.

"Wait! Don't—"

Arty presses her hand against the bars. The whole castle shakes. It shakes hard enough to make cracks in the walls as the bars slowly melt in the middle, darkness and shadows swirling around them before there is a big gap. I look at Arty's back as she bows her head low and doesn't move. Why would she do that? The woman steps out, dramatically stretching her arms to the side. Her body morphs in the mist, changing. She gets taller, slimmer, until a thin man stands in front of me, with a long black cloak falling from his shoulders. His hair is dark red, blood red, and his eyes look like black sapphires with stars within them.

Everything about him feels wrong.

The strange black marks curl around his cheeks, made of symbols, and they spread down his neck. On his hands are rings, literally on every finger, glittering in the light. He runs his fingers across the bars before stopping in front of Arty and proudly smiling at her. Something in my stomach drops.

I'm too weak to even rise up, to even stand on my feet, but I manage to sit up and press my back against the nearby wall, clutching my arm to my chest. My leg is definitely broken, and the pain is so bad that every breath hurts. Everything inside me is screaming, but not just in pain.

I still hear what the man says. "Well done, my daughter. Tell me, have you done what I asked?"

Daughter?

Her head stays bowed. "Daughter?" I ask loudly. She doesn't answer me. She doesn't even look my way. Neither does he.

"Yes, I killed all the others except for Hope and Livia. They escaped me and passed the race before I could get to them. I'm sorry."

The man smacks her hard across the cheek, but she still doesn't lift her head. She doesn't make a sound. He walks close to his daughter. "Don't worry." He puts his hand on her shoulder, squeezing tightly enough that she winces. "We will hunt them together, and I will fix your incompetence."

"Yes, father," she quietly replies, keeping her head bowed.

"Arty! What the fuck are you saying?" I pause, looking at the blood all over her and remembering the girl I saw with her neck cut. I gasp, covering my mouth. She killed her...and Florence. Hope and Livia, she would have killed them too. My heart goes cold. "Arty, you're a treacherous bitch! Who the hell is your father?"

The man finally looks at me. "Don't go insulting my daughter, Ellelin. She is going to be one of the rulers of this world one day. My name is the Sorcerer, and thank you for releasing me. I've been trapped in there for twelve long years and been trapped in this world for far longer than that. But thanks to you, I'm free."

The sorcerer?

He coldly smiles down at me. "I told you, if you got me out, I would tell you everything. I will, as I keep my word. This castle is all that's left of the Spirit Court. This massive island was blown to pieces by me. I blew it up twelve years ago. I managed to escape my prison twelve years ago after being imprisoned for thousands of years, along with my trusted wards and wife, and child. I knew the fifth court was the most powerful of this world and if I took them down first, the rest would fall. They battled so strong to fight to win, and I destroyed all of them. Except *you*."

"What?" I whisper, everything becoming so hazy. I swear I hear echoes of Lysander in my mind, screaming at me.

He walks over, leaning down and touching my chin with a long black nail. "You're from this world. You are the princess of the Spirit Court, the last living heir." He says it with disgust in his tone, and I can't believe him. I don't...but—"The magic that locked me in here was from your family; therefore, it was only your blood that could get me out. I sent my daughter into the test. I wanted to make sure that she could get close to you, and she did. She told me you even called her your friend. How pathetic and how easily you trust someone. You're a long way off the great spirit dragon king and queen. They would be ashamed of you."

I feel sick. "You're lying!"

"I'm not and you know it." He pulls his nail off my chin. "Arty was tricking you! This whole time, you had a snake at your side. You don't have friends here."

I look at her and my heart hurts. Everything hurts. The sorcerer picks up my bad arm, and I scream in pain as he digs his fingers into my bite. "You're not going to live long. Not with that poison in your system, not as injured as you are. Even the healers of the Water Court would struggle to save you now. Oh, how fun it is to watch the Spirit Court dying with you."

"Fuck you!" I growl out, his face spinning in front of my eyes.

"You would have died in that test. I should have just left you there and got your blood later, but I wanted to look at you. I want to watch you die. The last hope of the Spirit Court burning out before my eyes. It gives me great pleasure after they locked me in here for twelve years."

My heart pounds and everything feels fuzzy as I see him open a portal. The water-like portal is shimmering nearby us as he picks me up by my bad arm, and I scream as he drags me across the room. "Good luck surviving in the West. You won't be forced to come back here, because there'll be nothing left when I'm done. You can die alone, far from home."

"Father, no! You said she—"

I hear Arty's protest as he roughly throws me through the portal, magic washing over me like a wave as I roll out the other side and land in hot sand. I gasp from the pain, my body feeling so weak. I'm from the fifth court. He has to be lying.

It's hot, boiling hot as I lie here, my clothes sticking to me as I lift my head, looking up at the burning sun above. "Where am I?" I whisper.

My grandmother might have lied. My parents might have never died in a tragic accident on Earth. They might have been the king and queen of the fifth court, and all these months…I've been home. But I've lost everything. I'm going to die here, alone, and I won't be able to save anyone. I hear wings, large wings blowing the sand around me up into the air. All I see is dark black scales and dark greenish black eyes as a dragon sweeps down towards me before picking me up in its long claws and flying us away.

EPILOGUE

THE SORCERER

"No, where did you send her! Bring her back! NO! Ellelin! Baby!"

I turn to face the cell next to me, removing the old magic hiding it from the world. On the floor, in vine chains, is a woman crying. Her crown might be gone, but she has all the elegance of a queen even as she begs in a ruined black dress.

The queen of the fifth court.

Ellelin's mother.

I lean down, tilting my head to the side as I watch her strange emotions. She loves her child more than her own life; I am proof of that. I've been wearing her face for months, hoping her stupid daughter would trust me more with the face of the mother she can't remember. We've been down here twelve years together, kept alive with her magic. What was left of it. It's gone now, and her daughter hasn't got a clue how to tap into her powers. She is dead, or at least, she will be soon. The fifth court was never cursed; they chose their own queens, and the dead king chose this weak mortal-turned-queen.

It was a pleasure to see her court, how great it once was, burn down to the ground while its royal family defended their people so they could escape. I slaughtered them all before they could get off the island. All except that small princess. I don't know how she escaped, but I am impressed. It's a shame she was kept alive just to die so easily. It's been twelve years since I escaped the last imprisonment of this world and tried to take over. This queen used the last of her magic to lock us both down here, setting the spell with her blood so it could only be broken by her bloodline. Her daughter got away to Earth with the help of someone while her father fought me. He paid for that fight in his blood. I enjoyed his screams, and I can taste his blood even now. He was so powerful, and Ellelin had the potential to be as powerful as her mother and father. No one could have fought against the fifth court if the princess had her power.

Such a terrible, terrible shame.

I look into her eyes, almost the same colour as her daughter's as I smile. Winning feels good. "You should thank me. You got to see your daughter again. Her father isn't so lucky. I still have his bones hidden away in your home."

She tries to rise, that stubborn fifth court trait showing. She might be weak and locked within her own magic, but she still tries to fight to escape for her child. It would be sweet if it weren't so annoying.

I glance at my own daughter. She was useless most of her life, but I have to admit, she did well. I might let her live and help me with taking over the courts. Without their magic, it will be easy. Too easy. I will need an heir, and my daughter isn't male as I'd hoped, but she is smart. I can make a new heir when the time is right.

Finally, I win. I came to this world so long ago, and I was surprised by the dragon kings, who stopped me in my tracks with their magic. They died making the spell to hold me, but I cursed them before I was locked away. I escaped with the help of my wife until this dragon queen outsmarted me. She was the last powerful dragon queen that stood in the way of claiming this world, and her power tricked my own, locking us both down here.

The new dragon kings fell for the fifth court princess, and they didn't see what was going on right under their noses. Stupid children.

Love blinds all. This is the second world I've been to, and the other fell all too quickly. This world was smarter, but they all will fall in the end until I'm the only ruler of the worlds.

The dragon queen is stubborn, the vines cracking. I send a wave of magic to force her to her knees where she belongs. This world will bow to me, or I will bend their bodies to make them. The dragon queen's eyes are like diamonds, tough and endless as she glares at me. "Wherever you sent her, she will survive. We always survive."

I sigh, bored of this woman and her company. I'd kill her, but I might need her yet. "I sent her to the dragon riders of the West. She will be tested and die like all mortals do."

"Father!" Artemis gasps. "You said she wouldn't be killed! She'll never live through—"

I ignore my silly child's protests and cut her off. We have to find her mother and bring her here to be at my side. Matron is stuck in this castle, and she won't be a threat anymore, but I might kill her just to make sure. "Come, we have lands to take over and command. The dragon riders will be next. As a present to you, you can pick which court to take over first."

The fifth court queen screams her daughter's name as we leave, but no one can hear her.

 KEEP **R**EADING HERE WITH BOOK TWO...

AFTERWORD

Thank you for reading about my dragons! For those who guessed from the hints throughout this book, this is in the same world as Fall Mountain Shifters (Her Wolves) and there will be crossovers in future books. There are five books planned in this series and the next is on pre-order now.

I wrote this book with my beautiful rainbow baby lying on my chest and I told her all about the dragons I wanted to write about.
This book is for my family and for my readers.

PART I

A monster has stalked me my entire life.

But now I'm hunting him.

My job is to hunt monsters, and I'm damn good
at it—until a monster breaks into my apartment
in the middle of the night and kidnaps me.

Turns out he isn't just a monster.

He's the Wyern King.

Wyerns, a race feared by everyone, are known to
be stronger than the fae who rule my world, and
no one has seen them in years until now.

The king needs my help to track down his missing
sister from within a city his race is banished from,
and I'm the best he can find.

Only, he isn't the only one looking for monsters in
Ethereal City.

The Fae Queen's grandson is missing.
Working for fae, monster or not, is risky. Most who are hired end up dead, and I have too much to lose to end up as one of them.

I'm going to find the missing royals and be careful about it, especially with my grumpy boss breathing down my neck and watching my every move.

The Wyern King is cruel, cold, and unbelievably beautiful for a male… and my new enemy.

Heir of Monsters is a full-length paranormal Monster Romance with mature themes. This is a spicy enemies-to-lovers romance and is recommended for 17+.

Monsters are real.

If I needed any more proof than the thing in front of me, then I might be the one going mad in this world. The monster twists its grotesque head back to me, assessing me with its red eyes and mottled skin. It stands at over seven feet, two feet taller than me, and its once mortal-like body is a mixture of wolf and gods know what else. I risk taking my eyes off it for a second to look for my partner, and I catch a flash of red in the darkness behind the monster. I block out the awful stench of the creature and the rattling noise of its bones as it moves while I look for a safe way to take it down without getting us killed.

Clenching my magically blessed dagger in my hand, I whistle loudly. The monster roars loud enough to shake the derelict walls of the ruins before barrelling for me, each step shaking the ground. Like the dumbass that I am, I don't run but charge right back at it to meet it halfway. This plan better work, or I'm so fired. Or dead. I'm not sure which is worse.

"Calliophe! To your left!"

I barely hear my partner's warning shout before something hard rams into the side of me, shooting me into the air. I crash into the stone wall, all the air leaving my lungs as I roll to the floor and gasp in pain.

That hurt.

Blood fills my mouth as I push myself up and pause as I get a look at the giant cat-like thing in front of me. It might have once been a cat, even an exotic and expensive breed, but now it's been warped and changed like the monster behind it. It might even have been his pet. Once.

It lunges for me, snapping a row of sharp yellow teeth, and I narrowly jump to the side before kicking it with my boot. It hisses as I grapple for my dagger in the dust and slash the air between us as a warning as I crouch down. Its eyes are like yellow puddles of water, and I can see my reflection. Despite being covered in dust and dirt, my pink eyes glow slightly, and I look tiny in comparison. Even tiny, with a dagger, can be deadly. If the main monster runs, we might not get another chance to catch it for days, so I call to it, "Over here!"

The strange cat hisses once more, and the hair on its back rises. It straightens with its five strange legs that make it almost as tall as a dog.

A pain-filled female grunt echoes to me, and I clench my teeth. "I need a little help over here, Calli! Or I'm singing and screwing us both over!"

Dammit. I'm going to be the one buying the drinks tonight if she sings. Or worse, explaining this messed up mission to our boss. I'd rather buy the whole entire bar drinks and be poor. I jump on the cat, surprising it and slamming my dagger into its throat as it scratches and bites me before it goes still in my arms. I gently lower it to the ground, closing my eyes for a moment. I love animals, but whatever that was, death was a mercy for it. I pull my dagger out of it, yellow sticky blood dripping down my hand as I run across the ruins to Nerelyth. Somehow, she has gotten herself under a large piece of stone barely propped against a wall where she's hiding, and the monster is on top of it, clawing at the gap and nearly squishing her. I see her wave her arm at me from the small gap, and I sigh. There is only one way to capture a monster. Get up close and personal, and hope it doesn't eat me.

Thankfully, with Nerelyth's distraction, the monster's back is to me as I pull out my enchanted rope and let it wrap around my leg as I run across the ruins and close the gap between us, keeping my footsteps silent. Nerelyth's eyes widen when she spots me, but I don't pause as I leap off a fallen ledge and land on the creature's back, grunting at the impact on my swollen ribs, but my dagger easily slides into its back. Its skin is like goo, and I struggle to hold on as it straightens with a roar, but I lasso my rope around its neck with my other hand. The monster almost screams like a mortal as I let go, sliding down the monster's back and landing in a heap on the ground. I crawl backwards as the rope magically wraps itself over and over around the monster until it ties its legs together and it falls to the side.

The rope won't kill it, but it will stay locked up like this for hours, depending on how good the enchantment is.

With a grunt, I stand up and wipe the goo off my hands and walk over to where Nerelyth is still hiding. I tilt my head and look down at my partner, who has her eyes closed. "It's sorted now."

Nerelyth is lying face up under the stone, her red hair splayed around her. Her chest is moving fast as she finally opens her eyes and looks over at me, arching an eyebrow. "Thank you. Again," I tell her. "We might have fucked up." I offer her my hand as she brushes the dust off her leather clothes. "Any chance you love me for saving you and you will explain it to the boss?"

"Not a chance," she chuckles as I help her climb out, light shining in from the bright sun hanging over us. We both stop to look over at the monster, who is trying to escape the rope. "Third one this month. Where do you think they are coming from?"

"Not a clue," I mutter, eyeing the monster suspiciously. "I'm not sure M.A.D. even knows where the hybrids are coming from. They still happily send us out with no warning that this wasn't a normal job. Assholes."

She shrugs a slender shoulder, picking out flecks of dust from her flawless waist-length dark red hair that matches the red curls of water marks around her cheek that go all the way down her neck to her back. I'm certain I look much worse than she does, and I'm not even attempting to take my hair out of my braid to fix it. "The money is worth it."

Lie. I've been in the Monster Acquisitions Division, aka M.A.D., for three years, and the pay has never been good compared to the other divisions, and we both know it. Like everyone says, you have to be literally mad to make it in M.A.D. for more than a month.

Most enforcers, like us, are sent here as a punishment for fucking up. I had no choice but to take this job, as it was all I could get with my background, lack of money, and young age when I started at only eighteen. I glance at my partner of just one year and wonder again why a siren is working in one of the shittiest divisions in Ethereal City. Sirens are one of the wealthiest races, and the few I know work at the top of the enforcers. Not at the bottom, like us, which makes me question my friend's motives for being here with me once again. "Drinks tonight?"

"You know it," she says with a friendly smile and tired viridescent green eyes. "I'll send a Flame to get some enforcers down here to take him in. You get back to the office and good luck."

I groan and send a silent prayer to the dragon goddess herself to save me.

I head across the busy market street and look up at the Enforcer Headquarters as I stand on the sidewalk. The streets around me are filled with mortals and supernaturals heading to or from the bustle of the market to buy wares, food or nearly anything they want. The market hill is right at the top of the city, and it's the biggest market in Ethereal City. Fae horses wait by their owners' carts at the side of the main path, and I eye a soft white horse nearby for a moment and admire its shiny coat.

From this point, I can see nearly all of Ethereal City, from the elaborate seven hundred and four skyscrapers right down to the emerald green sea and the circular bay at the bottom of the city. Ethereal City was created over two thousand years ago, and the bay is even older than that. Dozens, if not hundreds, of ships line the ports, and they look like sparkling silver lines on the crystal green sea. Beyond that, the swirling seas of the largest lake in the world stretch all the way to the horizon and far beyond.

Most of Wyvcelm is this land, wrapped around the jeweled seas between Ethereal City and Goldway City on the other side. There are a few islands off the mainland, and one of them I want to go to one day—when I'm rich enough. Junepit City, the pleasure lands. I shake my head, pushing away that dream to focus on the Jeweled Seas, and I think of Nerelyth every time I see it.

The Jeweled Seas are ruled by the Siren King, and no one ever travels through them unless you are a siren, escorted by sirens, or want to die. Nerelyth told me once about how going through the fast, creature-filled rapids and the narrow cliff channels makes it nearly impossible to survive for long unless you know the way and can control the water. Above the sea level is worse as enchanted tornadoes reach high into the sky, swirling constantly over the waters controlled by the sirens themselves. That's why they're one of the richest races in Wyvcelm, because if the sirens didn't control the tornadoes, they would rip into both Ethereal City and Goldway City, ending thousands of lives. But they are not richer than the fae who rule over our lands and pay them to keep us safe.

I turn to my right, looking up at the castle that looms above the entire city. Its black spiraling towers, shining slate roofs and shimmering silver windows make it stand out anywhere that I am in the city. It was made that way, to make sure we always know who is ruling us. The immortal Fae Queen. Our queen lives in that palace and has done her entire immortal life. Thousands of years, if the history books are right and our longest reigning queen to date. She keeps us safe from the dangers outside the walls of the city, from the Wyern King and his clan of Wyerns who live over in the Forgotten Lands. They are the true monsters of our world.

A cold, salty breeze blows around me, and I shiver as I pull myself from my thoughts and look back up at the building where I go every single day. The Enforcer Headquarters, one of twelve in the city, and they all look the exact same. Symmetrical pillars line the outline of the two-story building that stretches far back. Perfectly trimmed bushes make a square around the bottom floor, and three staircases lead up to the platform outside the enormous main door. All of it is black, from the stone to the bushes, except for the white door, which is always open and always guarded by new junior enforcers. I walk up the hundred and fifty-two steps to the doors, and both the enforcers nod at me, letting me in without needing to check my I.D. I'm sure they have heard of me—and not in a good way. My list of fuckups is a mile long.

I glance at the young enforcer, a woman with cherry red lipstick and black hair, and wonder why she chose to sign up to be an enforcer. I doubt she was like me, fresh out of the foster system and left with no other decent options but this. Many don't want this job, and with the right schooling, they don't have to take it. It's hard work and long hours... and we die a lot. I've been lucky to skirt death myself a few times, and each time, I thank the dragon goddess for saving me. I smile at the junior enforcer and walk into the building, across the shiny black marble floors and up to the receptionist, Wendy, who sits behind a wall of glass and a small, tidy oak desk. I like Wendy, who is part witch, but I don't hold that against her. Her black hair is curled up and pinned into a bun, and she is wearing a long blue skirt and a white chemise top. "Hello, Calliophe. I missed you yesterday during the quarter term meeting."

"Sorry about that. Monster hunting and all," I say with a genuine smile even if I'm not sorry at all for missing another boring meeting. "Is he in there?"

She nods at the steps by the side of her office that lead up to the only full floor office on the top level. All the rest of us have our offices below his. The boss made sure that he had the only room above when he was transferred here a year ago. Her dark, nearly black eyes flicker nervously. "Upstairs. He's not in a great mood tonight."

"Brilliant," I tightly say and take a deep breath. "Thanks, Wendy. See you around if I survive the boss's bad mood."

"Good luck," she whispers to me before I walk to the stairs and head up to the top level. I'm glad I took the time to quickly get changed into a black tank top and high-waisted black jeans. My pink hair flows around my shoulders to the middle of my back, reminding me that I need a haircut soon.

When I get to the top of the stairs, I pause to look over the gigantic space that I'm rarely invited into, noticing how it smells like him. Masculine, minty and cool, which suits the space he has claimed. Massive floor-to-ceiling windows stretch across the back area, giving magnificent views of the fae castle upon the hill and the rest of the city below it. The towers, the small buildings, the people are easy to see from this vantage point. The sun slowly sets off in the distance, casting cascades of mandarin, lemony yellow and scarlet red light across the tips of buildings and across the shiny black floor. The light spreads across my boots as I walk into the room and finally look over at him. He is sitting at his desk, the single piece of furniture in this whole massive space, and on the desk is a Flame.

Flames are small red gnomes that use flames to travel from one place to another, and in general, are useful pests. The city is full of them, and for a coin, they will send a message for you. I've heard that you can ask the Flames to send anything you want, even death, to another, but it comes with a price only the dragon goddess herself could bear. They are ancient creatures and not to be messed with. I wouldn't dare ask for more than a message, and not many would. The Flame looks back at me with its soulless black eyes, and then he disappears in a flicker of flames, leaving embers bouncing across the desk.

Merrick looks up at me with his gorgeous dark grey eyes, and the room becomes tense. Some would say his eyes are colorless, but I don't think that's true. His eyes are a perfect reflection of any color in the room, and there are others that claim his grey eyes suggest he has angelic blood. Which is laughable. The Angelic Children, a race so rare we hardly ever see them, are said to be endlessly kind.

There's nothing nice or kind about Merrick Night. My boss. His dark brown hair is perfectly gelled into place, not a stray daring to be wrong, and it's much like the expensive black suit, the perfect black tie, flawless white shirt tucked into black trousers he wears, all of it expensive. He doesn't wear the enforcer leathers, magically made material, and he has never explained why.

I stop before his desk and cross my arms.

"Do you want to explain yourself, or should I start, Miss Sprite?"

His deep, cocky, arrogant voice irritates me as we both know he knows what happened—and why. But fine, if we are going to play this game.

I resist the urge to glower at my boss, not wanting to get fired, as I lift my chin. "I'll start, boss. We were told it was a simple monster on the loose on the left side of the city—Yenrtic District. It was suggested that an exiled werewolf had murdered mortals, and they called us to take him in. That was all that we were told, and we went to hunt him as per our job. He might have been part werewolf once, but he wasn't anymore when we found him. He was a hybrid, twisted and changed into something indescribable, but I'm sure we can go take a visit if you wish to see it."

"That won't be necessary, Miss Sprite," he coldly replies, running his eyes over me once.

I grit my teeth. "It was a difficult mission. We were underprepared for it, and none of the usual tactics for taking down a shifter worked. It went a little wrong from the start, and I do apologize for that."

"A little wrong," he slowly repeats my answer.

Here we go.

He stands up from his desk and walks over to his window. "Come with me."

I reluctantly follow him over, standing at his side as he towers over me. I hate being short at times. "A little wrong is when you make a small mistake that no one notices what you did and it doesn't attract attention. M.A.D. is known for discreetly dealing with supernaturals who have turned into monsters, for the queen. Destroying two buildings would suggest it went very wrong and quite the opposite of what your job stands for."

"Boss—"

"And furthermore, my boss is breathing down my neck to fire you. He is questioning why two of my junior associates have somehow managed to destroy two fucking expensive buildings. Explain it to me. Now, Miss Sprite."

"Technically, the monster destroyed the buildings when it had a tantrum and reacted badly to the enchanted wolfbane," I quietly answer.

"If you were struggling, you should have sent for help," he commands. "Not taken it on yourself with a new enforcer."

"We didn't have time, or it would have escaped and killed more mortals," I sharply reply. "Isn't that the real job? To save lives?"

An awkward silence drifts between us, and I steel my back for his reply. "You're meant to be instructing your partner on how to responsibly take on monsters. What you did today was teach her that you can take on a hybrid, alone, and somehow survive by the skin of your teeth. When she goes out and repeats your lesson alone, she will be hurt. Even die."

Guilt presses down on my chest. "But, boss——"

"Yes, Miss Sprite?" he interrupts, challenging me to say anything but *I'm sorry* with those cold grey eyes of his. When I first met Merrick Night, I thought he was the most beguiling mortal I'd ever met. Then he opened his perfectly shaped lips and made me want to punch him.

I look away first and over the city, the last bits of light dying away over the horizon. "There's been so many of these hybrid creatures recently, all over Wyvcelm. I have contacts in Junepit and Goldway City who told me as much. Where are they coming from? What caused them to be like that?"

"That is classified, Miss Sprite," he coolly replies. Basically, it's well above my pay grade to ask.

"It's probably not safe for everyone to go out in twos on missions like this anymore," I counter.

"Your only defense is that you secured the monster without Miss Mist using her voice," he says with a hint of cool amusement. "That would have been a real fuckup for us all to deal with."

Fuckup would be an understatement. The sirens' most deadly power, among many, is their enchanted voice when they sing the old language of the fae. Instantly, she would lure every male in the entire vicinity towards her, monster or not, and they would bow to her alone. Mortal females like me would be left screaming for the dragon goddess to save us, holding our hands over our ears, begging for death. Her voice stretches for at least two to three miles, and only a full-blooded fae can resist it. I've only heard it once, and personally, I never want to hear it again. I can still hear it now, like an old echo that draws me to her, a flash of the old power of the sirens who used to rule this world before the fae rose to power.

"Am I fired or can I leave, boss?"

He links his fingers, leaning back in the chair, which creaks. "I'm itching to dock your pay for this. But I won't. Not this time. You can go."

"Thank you," I say sarcastically and turn on my heel.

"Miss Sprite?" I stop mid-step and look back at him. "Don't make me regret being lenient on you today. You should know better."

I nod before turning away. "Fucking asshole," I whisper under my breath. He's not supernatural, and I know he can't hear me, and it's not like I can actually call him that to his face. Then I'd be fired for sure. Still, I'm sure I hear him chuckle under his breath.

I rush down the steps and say goodbye to Wendy before leaving the enforcement building and going to the Royal Bank on the other side of the market. I withdraw my day's pay, wincing that it's not nearly as much as I need, but a few hundred coins will sort everything out, and I'll work a double shift at the end of this week so I can eat for the rest of the week.

After making my way through the market and grabbing some dried meats, I head into the complex where my apartment is, listening to the old tower creak and groan in the wind. My apartment is four hundred and seven out of eight hundred flats in the entire building, and it is owned by the Fae Queen, like everything else. I'm lucky I got a place here, in a decent side of town, and it is everything I've worked towards for a very long time. I take the steps two at a time until I get to the hundred level. The corridor is littered with bikes, toys and plants, like every family level.

I knock twice on door one hundred and seven before opening it up with my key and heading inside.

"It's just me," I shout out as I feel how cold it is in here and flick on the magical heating. The weather is always changing so quickly. Some say it's the old gods anger that changes the weather from hot to cold all within a day. I'll pay that bill later, either way. "Louie?"

"Here," Louie shouts back, and I follow his shout to find him in the open-plan kitchen-living area, also where he has a small bed pushed up at the one side. The walls are cracked, the cream paper peeling off, but it's the same in most of the apartments. Louie is sitting on the bed, throwing an orange ball in the air and catching it over and over. Louie catches the ball one more time before sitting up, brushing locks of his black hair out of his eyes.

"How was school?" I question, leaning against the wall.

"Boring and predictable. Mr. French told me I was too smart for the class and suggested I join the fae army. Again," he tells me, and my heart lurches for a second until I see him chuckle. "I'm not crazy. Obviously."

After the age of ten, any male or female can join the fae army and be trained to fight for the queen, but they have to take the serum. The serum is an enchanted concoction that turns any mortal into a full-blooded fae and forces a bond between whoever takes it and the queen. Meaning that no one who takes the serum can ever betray her. I once thought about joining the fae army myself when things were rough and I was starving, but I will never forget the other foster kids in the homes who died from the serum. Roughly ten percent survive. I will never let Louie take a risk like that. Not even for the riches and security and the promise of power that the Fae Queen offers up.

I'm lost in my thoughts. I don't even notice Louie climb off his bed and come over to me. His eyes are like molten silver, just like his father's were. "You look tired."

"Hello, good to see you, too. How's your mom today?"

"The same," he quietly says, walking past me and opening the door to her bedroom. His mom was once a foster mom of mine, and the only one alive. I look down at her in her bed, her thin body covered in an unnatural blue glow as she lightly hovers off the bedsheets. Five years ago, we were attacked by the monster who has hunted me my entire life. Five years ago, her mate jumped in front of her to save her life, they smashed through a wall, and she hit her head on the edge of a door. My foster dad was the only reason I became an enforcer—because he was one. The Enforcer Guild paid for this apartment and a magically protected sleep until she can be woken, not that we can afford to do that, and the Guild's sympathy only stretched so far.

This was my eleventh foster home, the very last one I went to before I turned sixteen and aged out. I remember coming here, fearful, and meeting Louie, who hugged me. I hadn't been hugged in years, and it shocked me. It was still one of the happiest days of my life.

I go over to her side, stroking her greying red hair and sighing. I'd do anything to be able to afford to wake her up. For Louie. For me.

I leave three quarters of my wages on the side, and Louie looks down at the money, right as his stomach grumbles. I smile and nod. "Should I go and get something for us?" he asks.

"And for the week. For you," I tell him, ruffling his hair.

"Thank you," he says quietly. "One day, I'm going to be an enforcer like you and pay you back for all these years. I'm going to protect you."

"You're my brother in every way that matters, and family don't owe each other debts like this," I gently tell him. "And with how smart you are, I hope to the goddess you become someone so much better than me."

"Impossible," he says with a grin.

"Be careful on the streets," I warn him as he picks up a few of the coins and shoves them into his faded brown trousers. I need to buy him some new clothes soon, judging from the tears and holes in his blue shirt. One thing I love about Louie is that he never complains, never asks for clothes or for anything that costs money except for food. I wish I could give him more, but I can't.

"The monsters can't catch me, I'm too fast," he exclaims before bolting out of the door.

I chuckle as I sit down in the chair by the side of her bed, picking up her pale hand. "He doesn't have a clue, does he, mom? But he looks so much like dad."

Silence and the gentle hum of the magic surrounding her is my only reply, and I can't even remember what her voice is like anymore. She was my foster mom for a few years, far longer than any of the other ten before her, and she always asked me to call her *mom*. "One day, I'm going to wake you up so you can see Louie growing into a strong man. I'm going to make sure he gets a good job and stays far away from the true dangers of this city."

I hope she can hear me. I hope it gives her some comfort to know I'm here, but a part of me wonders if she would resent me. I'm the reason she is like this. I'm the reason her mate is dead. I close my eyes and blow out a shaky breath. The monster hasn't come back, not for years, and I have no reason to suspect he will now. But if he does, this time, I won't be a helpless child, unable to stop him from murdering my foster parents. I don't know if he killed my biological parents, no one does, but he killed every enforcer family that took me in. I try not to think of it, of all the death that haunted me like he did. My monster, my lurking shadow. I stay with my foster mom for a little longer before cleaning up the house, doing the washing and tidying in her room before Louie gets back, and then we cook dinner together before eating.

"Can I come to yours to play a game of kings?" he asks, referring to the card game we play on quiet nights, especially weekends like today, as I wash up and he dries the plates.

"I'd usually have you over, but I'm meeting Nerelyth for drinks tonight. It's her birthday," I tell him softly. Most kids his age would prefer to play with their friends and have them over, but Louie has never been good at making friends. He keeps to himself.

"Okay," he replies, his voice tinged with sadness. Loneliness. He only has me and his mom, but she can't read him stories, play games and help with the complicated enchantment work he is learning at school. After grabbing my bag, I kiss the top of his head before I leave, closing the door behind me and resting my head back against it, my eyes drooping. I'm so tired and I could use a long nap, not a night of partying for Nerelyth's birthday.

I sigh and push myself off the wall before heading up to my apartment. It is partially paid for by the Enforcer Guild, one of the half decent things they do for their employees. The night sky glitters like a thousand moons as I get to my floor and look up at the sunroof far above. Three actual moons hang in the sky somewhere, but I can't see them from here, and I wish I could. They say looking at the three moons and making a wish is the only way for the dragon goddess to hear you. I'm sure it's not true, but I still look up sometimes and wish. I shove my key into the lock, wondering if I have any enchanted wine left over from last time Nerelyth came over, and push into my cold apartment. If I get dressed quickly, I might even have time to finish the extremely spicy romance book I was reading last night, on the way to the bar.

"Posy, where are you?" I shout out as I head in. "I bought some of those meat strips you like from the market, as I'm going out tonight with Nerelyth. It's her birthday, remember?"

I've been mostly absent for the last two days and not had much time to spend with Posy—my roommate who happens to be a bat and stuck that way thanks to a witch's curse. I drop my bag on the side and look around in the darkness before sighing. Clicking my fingers, balls of warm white light within small glass spheres flood my apartment with light from where they are attached to the wall. I search around the main area, a small kitchen with two counters, a magical food storage box, and a large worn sofa pressed against the wall. It looks nearly the same as when I moved in, I notice, except for my two bookcases in the corridor leading to the bathroom and bedroom, full of romance books I've collected over the years. My prized possessions.

Escapism at its finest.

"Posy, come on. You can't still be mad at me?" I holler in frustration as I walk into the tiny bathroom, which is empty. "Bats are nocturnal, so I know you're awake and ignoring me, but I don't have time to chase you around this apartment all night."

I hear a small rustling noise from my bedroom, and I smile as I walk over and push the door open.

Clicking my fingers, two lights burn to life above my bed, and I go still. My heart nearly stops because it's not Posy in my bedroom.

There's a monster sitting on my bed.

CHAPTER 2

*L*arge wings.

Grey skin.

Muscular, massive shoulders and thick arms.

"Get the hell out!" I shout, a scream dying in my throat as I take a step away. I pull my dagger out from the clip on my thigh and hold it out between us as I quickly look for Posy, not seeing her anywhere. There's a friggin' monster in my room.

A wave of magic whips into my hand, the sting of it cold and piercing. My dagger flips across the room as I flinch, and it embeds itself in the wall with a thud. The monster doesn't even lift its head. He's... reading—my spicy romance book, of all things—as he sits on my bed. My double bed looks tiny with him sitting there, his dark hair soft and curling down his shoulders.

What the fuck?

My eyes widen as I look at this monster. He's a male. That much I'm sure of, and he's huge. He's sitting in the middle of my bed, reading my book from last night, looking like he's meant to be there. His skin is dark grey and almost velvety. Massive black wings stretch out of his back, but they're pulled in at his sides. Black horns curl out of the top of his thick black hair on his head, and if he wasn't a monster, I might even say he's handsome. He's shirtless, and he has pants on, but a tiny weird part of me focuses on the lack of a shirt for a second. No one looks that good shirtless —except this monster, it seems.

He is so big, and I'm sure he could snap me like a twig. Who the hell is he? What is he? More importantly—why is he in my bedroom?

"This is an interesting book for an innocent doe like you to be reading, Calliophe Maryann Sprite."

I freeze, my heart pounding as his deep, sensual voice fills my room. How does he know my full name?

He looks up at me with hauntingly beautiful amethyst eyes and smirks. "Speechless, Doe?"

"Get the fuck out of my room!" I shout, grabbing the nearest thing on my side table and throwing it at him. He catches the stuffed purple teddy bear in his hand, then raises an eyebrow as his lips twitch with humor.

"Don't run," he purrs.

I glare as I grab the next thing, which is a cheap statue of the goddess, and I throw that straight at him instead. The statue crashes into his hand, smashes into pieces on impact, and he simply sighs in annoyance as he begins to stand. My old bed creaks as I grab my precious books from the corridor as I back away and throw them at him as I retreat. He catches them all like it's a game. I can't hear anything but my heartbeat, and I can't see anything but those wings that have haunted me for so many years. My monster had wings. It's all I can remember of him before he killed every parent I ever had.

Wings. The beat of wings fills my ears as I burn with anger. My monster is back to kill me. I turn and run to the sofa, jumping on it as I pull out the two daggers I have hidden down on one side and crouch down in the corner. He casually strolls down the corridor, and he blocks the way to the only exit from my apartment as he faces me and crosses his arms. "Do you really believe that you, a tiny little mortal, will be able to stop me?"

"Come closer. Find out," I taunt. If he is going to kill me, I'm going down with a fight. I haven't survived monsters all these years, my entire life, to die easily at the hands of one.

He laughs, the sound deep and frightening. Arrogant son of a bitc—

I see a flash of black right before Posy flies straight into his face, clawing at him with her tiny, almost purple, bat wings. Posy is only a tiny bat and no more than the size of his hand as he grabs her by the scruff of her neck and holds her up in front of him. She still fights. The more I look at him, I realize he can't be the monster who hunted me. Those purple eyes aren't black, dark and cold like my monster's were. Still, those wings... my monster must be what he is. "What is this thing?" he asks.

I would laugh if he wasn't trying to kill me. Posy yells, "Die, die, die. You supernatural monster! This is my home, and I don't care how horny my roommate is. She is not fucking a monster when I'm living here!"

By the old gods. My cheeks burn.

The monster smirks and looks over at me. "You have a talking bat."

"Let her go!" I demand as I look between them and the door. I don't know how I will make it to the door to run if I go for Posy.

He sighs, and Posy is still ranting away, unaware that no one is listening to her anymore. Or the fact this monster isn't my date and that he is here to kill me. "No. We are leaving."

"We are not," I say at the same time Posy declares, "Finally. Go to the monster's place and do the dirty. Between keeping me here as your pet and your new fuck buddy, I think you have a weird thing for bats."

"We bats can be very fun," the monster agrees with a hint of dry amusement that makes him seem almost mortal. Almost. He is very much not.

He lets Posy go, and she flies into my bedroom, slamming the door shut. I need a better room-mate/pet. Posy sucks.

"Then go and have fun somewhere else, or I'm going to pin those nice wings of yours to my wall," I say, holding the daggers up higher. Why he hasn't used his magic to rid me of them yet floats into the back of my mind. Maybe he is playing with me. "What are you, anyway?"

"Wyern," he coolly answers. "Haven't you seen any in your career?"

No, I haven't, or I'd be very dead. My blood runs cold as I take him in, a Wyern male, in my living room. The Wyerns are immortal, deadly, and everyone knows they are forbidden from entering Ethereal City. Some say they are fae—an old race of them. Some say they were created by the fae and are born monsters.

I should have known he's not a monster. Not exactly, but not far from one. From what I know, the Wyerns live in the Forgotten Lands, a punishment from my queen for the war they started thousands of years ago. Some say the sirens siding with the Fae Queen was the only way we won.

One trained Wyern male can slaughter ten trained fae in minutes.

My heart races as I take all of this in. If I call for help and they find me here with him, even if he is trying to kill me or take me somewhere, the queen will execute me for treason. "If the queen finds you here, which she will, we are both dead. Leave."

He steps towards me, an amused smirk on his lips. "Your precious queen would be very honored if I turned up in her city, but perhaps a little angry I came for you and not to see her."

"What?"

He glowers at me. "Are you mortals truly this dense? We. Are. Leaving."

"We certainly are not going anywhere!"

He takes another step forward, and I start to back away until the back of my knees touch the sofa.

I lash out at him with my daggers, cutting through his arm, and it bubbles with blood. He doesn't even notice as he grabs my hands, squeezing tight enough I'm forced to drop the daggers with a yelp. I kick at his shin, which is like a rock and only hurts me, and he grabs me by the waist and throws me over his shoulder like I weigh nothing. I scream and kick him in the stomach and slam my hands on his solid back, but nothing makes his arm shift from his iron tight grip on me.

Magic wraps around me firmly, its icy sting burning into my skin, and I hiss in pain as my head spins. I hate magic.

"Let me go!" I scream over and over. He only laughs like it's deeply amusing to him as he walks out of my apartment by kicking my front door open. I look up in horror as he spreads his massive wings out, and magic lashes around us as he shoots up the flights of stairs. The stairs whip up around us as I scream, ducking my head as my stomach feels like a million butterflies have burst to life. He crashes through the glass, bits of it cutting into my arms, and launches us into the night sky above the city. His wings beat near my face, and I stop trying to fight him. If he drops me, I'm dead.

It doesn't stop the lash of magic that slams into my head and knocks me out cold seconds later, leaving me dreaming of wings and star-filled night skies.

CHAPTER 3

"*Take her, Vivienne. Just take her and run!*"

I snuggle down into my bed, clutching the sheets tighter as I hear crashing noises, shouting and doors slamming. It's happening again. He has come for me again. No, no, no...

"*We both can run and fight him,*" my foster mom pleads. I've only been here a year. It's too soon for the monster to come for me.

"*No. She needs someone to live for her,*" my foster dad exclaims, and the door to my room slams. "*She is just six years old, and all she has known is death. Someone has to tell her why, someone has to explain the truth.*"

"He'll never stop," Vivienne cries. "We shouldn't have taken her in after—"

"I have no regrets. We do this for the Guild. For our queen and what she gave," he interrupts her. Hands pull my quilt back, and I look up at my foster dad with panicked eyes. His voice is gentle and as soft as his brown eyes as he stares down at me. "You need to go with Vivienne and run. It's here, and I'm going to stop it."

"But—"

He hushes me, kissing my forehead. "It's been an honor to care for you, Calliophe Maryann Sprite. Live."

I gulp, tears falling down my cheeks as Vivienne picks me up, holding me to her. She always picks me up, telling me how small I am for my age, and I cling to her neck, wishing this is all a dream. It's not real. The monster isn't real.

I hide my head in her bright red hair, peeping out to look at my foster dad standing by the door. He looks over his shoulder, holding a silver sword in front of him, an enchanted rope dangling from his fingers. "Live for all of us, Calliophe."

Vivienne and he share a look for a moment before she carries me to the window, and my foster dad opens the door, *shutting it behind us. Vivienne opens the window before sitting on the edge, the icy wind blowing around us, snowflakes littering the air. My breath comes out like smoke as I shiver. "Hold on to me and don't let go."*

I nod against her shoulder as she jumps off the window ledge into the snowy night, and I cling to her as she lands in a thump on the ground. Vivienne wraps her arms around me before she sprints across the grass, leaping over the small brown fence and past the swing tied to the old oak tree. I keep looking over her shoulder for the monster inside my home, but no lights are on, and there is nothing but the glittering night sky until I hear a male scream.

Vivienne stops and slowly turns back, holding me tightly to her. She puts me down on the ground and points at the woods a few feet away. "I have to go back for him. I love him. You have to run. Don't stop running. Find someone, anyone, and tell them to call the Guild. Tell them we're in trouble, but you need to run."

"I don't want to be on my own," I wail as she lowers me to the ground, pulling my arms from her and stepping back.

She kisses my forehead. "I'm so sorry, but he is all I have."

"You have me."

I try to catch her hand, but she pushes me away before she runs back to the house. Tears fall down my cheeks, and I shake from head to toe as I turn and run into the tall, dark trees. I cling to the nearest tree, the bark scratching my hands and the branches snatching in my hair. Everything is silent for a moment before I hear Vivienne scream and cry out, and then there is silence once more. I hear a door being smashed open, and I turn to see a male stepping out into the shadows. He has gigantic wings that spread out like shadows in the night, but I can't see anything else as he turns my way.

Terrified, I run deep into the forest, letting it swallow me in its darkness.

I wake up with my heart racing fast in my chest as I blink and look around, tasting the icy sting of magic on my tongue. It was just a dream. I click my fingers, and lights burn up in the room, and I go still.

It wasn't a dream.

I've been kidnapped by that arrogant, and a little beautiful, monster. The bat guy. Shit. I take in the scents around me on the soft sheets, and I frown. Masculine. This is that monster's bedroom. By the goddess. I push the dark midnight blue sheets off me, noticing my boots are missing as I look at the bedroom. Expensive and exotic wood makes the massive bed I'm on, and there are matching wardrobes and a dresser. They go well with the dark red walls and polished oak beams that run across the ceiling and the carmine curtains. I look back at the headboard, which is one magnificent piece of wood carved and polished.

My legs are shaky from the magic and a little fear as I walk across the hardwood floors and to the window. The window is massive, ceiling to floor, with black squares all over it. My heart stops as I look outside at the unfamiliar mountains.

We aren't in Ethereal City.

If I had to guess where I am… The Wyern are said to live in the Forgotten City, in the thick mountains to the north of Ethereal City. I've only ever seen these mountains from a far distance, and then they were nothing more than a dot on the horizon. Now, I'm in the middle of them. The mountains are steep, covered in jagged spikes and snow. It's kind of pretty, with the night sky hanging behind, the sun slowly rising.

I think it's safe to bet I'm not going to work today.

My heart is still racing, and I will myself to calm down. If the Wyern wanted me dead, I would be dead. No, he must want me for something else, and that gives me time to make a plan and escape.

Somehow.

I glance around to see if I can find anything useful to defend myself, but there isn't much, just a dresser, two wardrobes, and a rug. I search the wardrobe and drawers, finding male clothes and nothing else. Unless I plan to throw socks at him, my search isn't going well. I find my boots by the end of the bed and slide them on, finding the two small knives I hid in the heel have been taken. My mouth feels dry as I go to the dark wooden double doors and test the silver handles to see if I'm locked in. The doors click open to my surprise, and I peek out into the corridor. The same dark wood floor stretches down a long and wide passageway, and there's a dark red, patterned runner running down the entire length of it. There are endless doors on either side and more light orbs lighting up the space on the ceiling. I hear vague scuffling, voices and music from the left side, and the right is completely empty and silent but a dead end by the looks of it.

I quietly shut the door behind me as I step out and head down the passageway, wishing I had some of my weapons on me. I try a few handles on my way, but all of them are locked, to my annoyance.

I blow out a shaky breath when I see a door open a few feet away, the noise coming from in there and orange light shining out the gap. My hair falls around my shoulders, and I tuck a strand behind my ear as I follow the sounds of the music. It's old music, but it's sensual and soft and not what I expect to hear. I walk the final steps to the door and peek into the massive room. Pillars and tapestries line the walls, all of it old and stunning, and the soft music is being played by magic throughout the air, the taste of it coating my tongue. Several cushioned areas lie around three giant waterfalls with statues of the goddess in the center of them, water pouring out of her hands. The room is warm and cozy, but maybe not the people inside it. Wyerns. Each one of them looks slightly different, all dark or grey skinned, and there are at least twenty female mortals in here with them. By the moans, they're clearly having fun, and I try not to look too long at any one of them. They are all having sex.

Except a few. Like the male on the seating area nearest me. He is different from the others; his light grey skin is littered with small and large scars, and his horns have been cut off. He doesn't have wings, and his eyes are a soft forest green as he looks my way. He has a grey shirt on that a female with long brown hair is pawing at. In fact, he has three females lying on his lap, and one of them is stroking him underneath his trousers. He still watches me, tilting his head to the side with a little smirk on his lips as one of the other females runs her hand through his short brown hair. Dear god, I just walked into a monster orgy. Absolutely brilliant. I really hope that is not what they brought me here for. I haven't had sex with anyone for over two years thanks to my work. And even then, I prefer a heated few hours at their place and then I disappear. I don't do long-term anything.

I'm certainly not staying here if this is the plan.

"The doe is awake," the male shouts, and many male laughs follow. Fuck it.

I push the door open and head inside, letting the door slam against the wall. "Kidnapping is illegal.

I'm leaving if one of you will be kind enough to show me the door."

"I don't think so, little doe," the male says, gently pushing the females off him and standing. He walks up to me, towering over me. "We've been waiting for you to wake up. Do you want a drink?"

I glower at him. "No."

"Come on, relax. Have you never seen a royal court having fun before?"

"This is a royal court?" I say dryly. "Looks more like—"

"Ah, be nice. You don't insult someone's home when you're a guest," he interrupts.

"I'm not a guest. I didn't come here willingly!" I protest.

"Still, be nice, little mortal."

He pats me on the head and looks back at the beautiful females on the sofa, who giggle. By the goddess. It stinks of sex in here, and the moans are getting louder than the music. "No."

"How about that drink?"

"No," I repeat, and he smiles at me. "I want to know why I'm here? Where's the male that kidnapped me and took me?"

He sighs, stepping closer, and offers me his hand. He smells of wine and bad decisions. Nerelyth would love him. "My name is Lorenzo Eveningstar."

I don't take it, considering what he has just been doing, and raise an eyebrow. He chuckles deep and low. "Usually when someone tells you their name, you shake their hand and tell them your name. Do mortals like yourself no longer know manners?"

"So you don't know my name? After kidnapping me—"

"I didn't kidnap you," he quickly corrects me.

I rub my forehead. "My name is Calliophe."

"Ah, I did wonder if it was Doe," he smiles and looks me over. "I don't know what my king is thinking."

King?

The Wyern King kidnapped me?

By the goddess, I'm dead. I'm so dead.

I cross my arms with bravado I don't have. "Why am I here, Lorenzo?"

"I believe that is for King Emerson Eveningstar to answer," another voice answers.

I turn to look over at the female walking towards me. She's fae. This female is a full-blooded fae. She's wearing pretty much nothing but a slip of silver sheer fabric that makes up a dress that is wrapped around her large breasts and thin waist before falling to her feet. She is flawless. Fae always are. Everything about them is designed to trick mortals like myself into trusting them. Her beautiful silvery blonde hair that is loosely held up, curls and falls around her shoulders and slender face. She stops in front of me, and her eyes light up in different shades of purple and blue.

Lorenzo smiles at the fae female. "Calliophe, meet another member of our court, Zurine Quarzlin. Rine, she is looking for Emerson."

Zurine looks me over from the top of my head to my feet, focusing on my eyes for a second. I search her eyes and see nothing but sadness hidden within them. "Why don't I show you the way?"

My smile is tight. "Alright."

She waves her hand at the door, and I follow her through, glancing back to see Lorenzo swaggering back to the females. "I imagine you're confused and worried, but ignore the males here. As usual, they think with their cocks and not their minds half the time, much like the rest of our court. That's not why he brought you here. The mortal females come to our court willingly for the pleasure."

I dryly chuckle. "Confused? I was kidnapped by a monster."

"My king isn't a monster," she says softly, her voice full of affection. "Even if he appears as one."

"I hadn't seen a Wyern before, so to me, he looked like one. Then he kidnapped me...," I drawl.

She laughs lightly as we head down the corridor, and our conversation drifts off until I need to fill the silence instead of feeling so nervous. "I haven't seen many fae before. Only one or two. Most don't come down to the lower parts of Ethereal City, and my work doesn't lead me anywhere near the castle or the fae district."

She doesn't look down at me. "Then you are lucky, mortal."

"Perhaps," I mutter. "So you're part of this court even when you're not one of them?"

She looks at me this time as we go through a door and into a corridor with long windows on each side. "Yes, and for what it is worth, you can trust me. You won't be able to trust many here."

One of these Wyerns is my monster, hunted me from birth, and I won't trust anyone here until I find who it is. And kill them.

"For what it's worth, I don't believe trusting anyone here is going to end with anything but my death."

She smiles at that. "You're a smart mortal."

Weird compliment.

"Although you're not all mortal, are you? You definitely have a bit of fae in your bloodline with those eyes. Who was it?"

I look at the shiny floor. "I don't know any of my family."

"Oh, I'm sorry. Is your hair natural or enchanted?"

"Enchanted by a dodgy spell, and I haven't been able to change it back since I was fifteen," I explain with a chuckle. "It was a lesson in why you don't buy enchantments from strangers on the market."

She laughs. "I think pink is your color."

I smile for a moment at the fae female. "Thank you."

She leads me down several corridors, through a few more empty rooms, each more confusing than the last until I'm thoroughly lost. We both stay silent until we come to a massive pair of imposing doors at the end of a corridor. These are curved to almost look like bat wings, and they are old, much like the walls around it. Zurine pulls the doors open and moves to the side. "I'll leave you to him. Remember, with these males, they will bite if you push too much."

She lowers her voice. "But most of them have a soft heart underneath it all. Especially the king."

I walk into the gigantic room, eyeing the red carpet that runs up to a platform at the back of the room, where a king sits on a massive throne. The throne is made of black oak, with five long spikes making the headboard that looks like the spiked mountains outside. The throne room, which I'm guessing this is, is magnificent. Pillars line the walls with windows between them, lined with black squares. Fae light, a rare and expensive form of magic, hovers in tiny little stars across the entire ceiling, and it makes it look like the endless night sky.

Beautiful and daunting.

I turn my gaze to the throne, pulled towards it with an invisible tug deep in my chest.

The king sits on his throne, his legs spread wide, his wings hanging off the sides of the seat. Tight black leathers spread across his chest and down his arms, and into his leather trousers. The shine of the leather reminds me that they must be enchanted, maybe by himself. I'm not sure what powers the Wyerns have, but if they can effortlessly fight the fae, making enchantments should be nothing. His hand is dug into the brown hair of a female between his knees, her head resting on his knee. The room smells of sex, and looking at the pair of them, it's clear what they have been doing. The female doesn't even look at me as she stares up at Emerson, and he tilts his head to the side as his eyes lock on mine. The move is pure predator-like with a stillness only an immortal can have. "What do you want?"

I shiver from his deep, cold voice, but I don't cower. "That's the very question I came to ask you. Considering you kidnapped me."

He stands up off his throne with fury in his eyes, leaving the female on her knees, and walks towards me with a casualness that makes me fear him. He is so tall I have to arch my neck to look at him as he stops close. "Mortals bow to kings. Get on your knees."

"No," I bite out.

A lash of magic slams into my knees, and I fall to my knees before the king, unwillingly, and I glare at him as his magic surrounds me, holding me in place.

He looks down at me like I'm a bug to a bird flying high above. To him, I might as well be. "Next time I tell you to bow, you bow. Next time I tell you anything, you do it. Welcome to my court, Doe. Stay here."

He walks past me, leaving me locked in his magic as the mortal female rushes past me to follow him out. Only when the throne room doors slam shut behind me does the magic fade away, and I bite back the urge to scream.

I really, really hate the king.

CHAPTER 4

*T*slam my fists repeatedly against the throne room doors in frustration. "Let me out! Let me out!"

The doors don't budge, neither do the handles, which feel like ice to touch. Magic.

I scream in frustration, but no one comes for me, and I swear I hear a male laugh on the other side of the door. Eventually, I give up when my hands start to hurt, and back away from the door.

Wrapping my arms around myself, I look around the room before walking over to the windows. Wherever this is inside the castle, it's definitely at the highest point or near it. The mountain spikes look lower, and I know if I jumped out this window somehow, I'd impale myself on one of them. Birds duck and dive through the air on the breeze, dancing to an invisible element, and I watch them for a long time until they disappear into the black mountains.

The sun is shining high in the sky, climbing with every hour that passes as I stay locked in here. My stomach is rumbling and my mouth is dry when the doors finally open, and I climb up off the floor. I cautiously watch as Lorenzo walks in, followed by four Wolven males. I recognize some of them from the first room I saw, but now they have clothes on at least. Lorenzo flashes me a toothy smile, and I glare at him as Zurine wanders in after them. She walks my way, smiling softly at me.

I cross my arms. "He locked me in here."

"He's not in the best of moods today," she tells me gently with amusement in her eyes. "Seems you've riled him up."

"It wasn't me. It looked like he was in a foul mood well before he kidnapped me and locked me in here."

"You will understand why you're here in a moment. We're about to have a court meeting, and you're invited as a guest," she kindly tells me, waving in the direction the others went. "Please, come and sit with me."

I do not have a choice, and we both know it. I reluctantly follow her behind the throne room where there is a large circular slate table and brown leather, backless stools spread around it. Lorenzo and the others are talking quietly by the side of the table, and they go silent when we get close.

Zurine takes a seat, and I sit down next to her, crossing my legs and resting my hands on them to stop them from shaking. Lorenzo comes and sits next to me, close enough his arm brushes my arm, and I move away.

The four other Wyerns take some of the remaining seats while we wait for the king, and I feel them all staring at me as I keep my eyes straight ahead.

"Let me do some introductions. Everyone, this is Calliophe Maryann Sprite. She's a mortal who works at Monster Activities Division of the

Enforcer Guild and is considered one of the best they have," Lorenzo states.

I turn to look at him. "Someone's been doing their homework."

"Only when young, beautiful mortals are the research topic," he replies with a flirty tone.

"Charming, but don't waste your flirting skills on me. I'm sure there are other poor mortals for you to bless," I coolly reply, because he is charming, and good looking, but he is one of them. I've never been good at flirting, and as Nerelyth tells me, I don't need to flirt when I'm pretty and want nothing long-term with anyone. Long-term means there is a risk of my monster coming and killing them. I can't have the happy ending, the family and one true love. I've been on four dates, had three lovers, and that has been enough. Still, I can see why willing mortals wish to come here and be with them. The Wyerns remind me of the male fae: beautiful, alluring, and likely much better in bed than mortal males.

One of the other Wyerns chuckles low. "She has you sussed, Lorz."

This one is shorter than the others as I turn to face him. His wings are near pitch black and tall, and his skin is a similar tone. His eyes are like melted honey as he looks over at me and warmly smiles. His head is completely shaven, and three silver earrings are clipped to the tip of his left ear. "I'm Felix Masterlight. This is my brother, Nathiel. It's a pleasure."

His voice is like honey, too. His brother looks nearly identical. So much so, I would say they might be twins. Nathiel doesn't smile at me, but he simply inclines his head.

I nod mine back. "I would say it's nice to meet you, but..."

One of the Wyerns on the other side of the table coolly chuckles. "You've been kidnapped and dragged here, and you believe we are monsters."

I look over at the male who spoke, his voice gruff and playful, and the fourth court member. These Wyerns look like the opposite of each other. The one who spoke has dirty blond hair that hasn't been brushed and falls down to his ears, and he has more of a slim build. The male next to him has jet black hair, is more muscular than even the king, and his face is littered with small scars. He scowls at me, and it doesn't faze me like it would do most people. I face monsters every day.

"You're right, Ferris. I don't believe she likes us," the scowling one says.

The blond runs his eyes over me. "I'm sure I could find a way to encourage her to like us."

"Mortals are a waste of everyone's time unless they are on their knees. Begging," the other male coolly states to his brother, not even bothering to look at me.

Ferris laughs low. "True, Julian. True."

Bastards.

We sit in silence for a while, the silence getting more and more daunting, until I hear the doors slam open and his footsteps echo across the floor. He storms into the throne room, and I twist my neck to watch as he walks in, past me and around the table, before taking a seat.

Everyone bows their head once, and he looks directly across at me when I don't bow mine.

He may have forced me to my knees, but I won't willingly ever bow to him.

I look away first, needing to or it's hard to breathe, and find Zurine carefully watching me.

"We're going to make it simple for you to under-stand," King Emerson begins, his tone bored. "I brought you here—"

"Kidnapped," I correct.

"Don't interrupt the king," Julian growls at me, making the hair on my arms spike up.

"We brought you here," King Emerson continues, no amount of sarcasm missing from his words, "because you've been hunting hybrids and capturing them."

I furrow my brow. "The hybrids? That's why I'm here?"

"Yes," Lorenzo takes over. "Our information states you've caught three of them without dying."

I nod. "Do you know where they're from?"

"No. We want to hire you to find out where the hybrids are from, to hunt them privately for us.

You can work alongside your division if you wish, but this would be a private matter for you and not to be discussed with anyone," Lorenzo explains.

I look at the king, who is sitting with his arms crossed, watching me with the same bored expression he had when he got in here. He kidnapped me to ask for my help. I almost laugh. "Why would I do that? I don't want to help you and end up killed by the Fae Queen. She would kill me for even considering helping you."

The king tilts his head to the side. "You have a ward, do you not?"

"Yes," I bite out.

Zurine places her hand on my arm, and I nearly jump. "What my king suggests is that the young boy who you look after and his mother in the medical sleep might do well if you took our job. It is a job, not a favor, and you will be heavily paid."

King Emerson slides his eyes to me. "Find out who did this and find the hybrids' leader, and we will pay you an exorbitant amount. So much coin that you can move out of that hovel you live in and buy somewhere nice to live out your mortal life. Do we have a deal?"

I feel like King Emerson might not have heard this word often in his life, but here goes... "No."

His eyes narrow into sharp blades. "You would let your ward and his mother suffer? You would let the hybrids continue to rip apart your fellow mortals, out of what? Pride?"

I glare right back as I stand up and place my hands on the table. "I would do anything for Louie and my foster mom, but helping you will end up getting me killed. I'm not stupid. It's why you're asking me in the first place. Because you can't search in Ethereal City. The Fae Queen—"

He frowns and cuts me off midsentence. "You're a coward, Calliophe Sprite. How disappointing."

"Calliophe, we will protect you from the queen and her spies in the city," Zurine softy warns as I sit down . "Yes, there is a risk, and it is your choice. We are not here to force you into helping us."

Lorenzo looks at the king, and some kind of silent message seems to spread between them before he speaks. "You will receive ten percent of the million coins we will pay you. You will get the other ninety percent when you find out who they are. If you're not dead, that is."

A million coins. By the goddess. With that sort of money, I could wake my foster mom and take them both to live happily in Junepit City for the rest of our lives. I wouldn't have to wake up at the crack of dawn every day, fight and risk my life for scraps of coins to get us by. I could live and choose a real future for myself that isn't just a life I have to live to survive. All of it lies right in front of me, as risky as it is. Also, this is the closest I have ever gotten to finding out who the monster is that hunted me as a child and killed everyone I ever loved back then.

"But if I die," I say, leaning forward, "it's all for nothing, and my ward is left alone. I have too much to lose. Find someone else."

"I knew the mortal would be too selfish to do this," Julian sneers. "If we—"

King Emerson cuts him off. "We are not discussing that option again, Julian. Your anger with mortals clouds your judgment."

I rub my forehead. "Why do you want to know who is making the hybrids? How does it affect you?"

King Emerson barely even glances at me as Lorenzo answers. "We want to know because they took one of our people. Our sister, the princess of our race. She was taken three days ago, and we can't find her."

I look between King Emerson and Lorenzo... who never mentioned he is a prince. "Our sister?"

Emerson's eyes are like icy frost blowing over my skin with pepper sweet kisses. "Is there a problem?"

I'm in too deep because I'm actually considering this. Nerelyth is going to drown me in the seas when she hears about all of this. "How old is your sister? Why would they take her? How was she taken exactly?"

King Emerson looks like he has won, and I hate it. "She's young, nearly your age, and inexperienced in combat. They came, and they took her when we were away. Those left killed at least twenty of the hybrids, but there were endless amounts of them. They knew how to get in, where to find her, and how to get her out without alerting many."

I point out the obvious. "Someone fed them information, then?"

"My people are bound to me and cannot betray the royal blood. Whoever it is must have walked these halls at some time. Perhaps when my father or grandfather ruled the Forgotten City," he informs me.

Lorenzo's chair groans as he moves. "We want her back alive and will pay you. What have you to lose?"

I hate that he has a point in a way, but this is a risk. I'll be working with monsters to hunt down a bigger monster.

I sigh. "Why bother kidnapping me and not just asking me nicely back at my home?"

Emerson doesn't look remotely sorry. "Because you'll be staying here. It's safer for you while you are under our protection and working for us."

"I really don't think so. If you want me to work on this case, I'll need to be in Ethereal City, not here in the mountains. Plus, people are going to realize

I'm missing, and that's going to draw attention," I counter. "I will take this job, but the condition is that I stay in my apartment."

He throws his own condition right back at me. "For the week. The weekends you spend here."

"Fine." I grit my teeth. The weekends, I can spend investigating the Wyerns and who might want to hunt down me.

He crosses his thick arms. "There was never an option. You work for me or you die."

"You're not my king," I remind him. "But I'm no coward, and I will find your sister. I want to stop whoever is creating the hybrids just as much as you. They are killing innocent mortals and super-naturals. This is my work, and you're right, I'm damn good at it."

His lips tilt up. "Still a coward under all that pretty pink hair. Pretending to be brave won't stop that fear in your chest from crawling itself out."

"Says the heartless monster king on a cold throne, hidden in a corner of the world, asking a mortal to help him because no one else would dare."

The room goes deadly silent.

Shit. Maybe I shouldn't have said that. I don't have it in me to apologize, but there is a little fear that crawls up my throat with how Emerson's eyes narrow on me. He looks at Lorenzo. "Have her trailed in the day, and one of us sleeps at hers at night. She is not to be left alone."

I want to argue I can look after myself, but the truth is, if the hybrids are working in groups, I'll take whatever protection I can get.

They can take the bumpy sofa and deal with my psychotic bat roommate.

She loves guests. Not.

Lorenzo nods sharply. "I'll arrange it all, brother."

"Everyone leave. Except you, Doe."

My eyes widen as they all stand and leave, and I don't even try to stand up. Lorenzo pats my back once before leaving. I assume it's some sort of good luck pat. I keep my eyes on the king, my hands gripping the seat of the chair tightly as he stands up and walks around the table. When the throne room doors are shut, he pushes the chair to my right aside and sits on the edge of the table next to me, his wing brushing so close it could touch my hand.

I lift my head. "What else do you want?"

He leans down, leaving our faces inches apart. This close, I can only smell how good his scent is and see how the leathers are tight across his body, his face smooth and sculpted into perfection. He is a beautiful monster indeed. "If you're caught by any fae, you do not mention my name. You do not tell a single fae a word of this, or I'll kill you myself. Do you understand?"

"Threats are idle. If a fae knew of this, I'd be dead way before you'd get to me."

And I'd be thankful for it, I bet.

His eyes seem to swirl like rippling water. Still shallow water that you'd walk into, unaware of the current underneath waiting to snatch you up. "Watch your back, mortal. Make one wrong step, and death will seem like a mercy."

My heart is racing fast as he leans back and then pushes off the table before walking away. Only when he is gone do I remember to breathe.

ABOUT G. BAILEY

G. Bailey is a USA Today and international bestselling author of books that are filled with everything from dragons to pirates. Plus, fantasy worlds and breath-taking adventures.

G. Bailey is from the very rainy U.K. where she lives with her husband, two children, three cheeky dogs and one cat who rules them all.

(You can find exclusive teasers, random giveaways and sneak peeks of new books on the way in Bailey's Pack on Facebook or on TIKTOK—gbaileybooks)

FIND MORE BOOKS BY G. BAILEY ON AMAZON…

LINK HERE.

MORE BOOKS BY G. BAILEY

HER GUARDIANS SERIES

HER FATE SERIES

PROTECTED BY DRAGONS SERIES

LOST TIME ACADEMY SERIES

THE DEMON ACADEMY SERIES

DARK ANGEL ACADEMY SERIES

SHADOWBORN ACADEMY SERIES

DARK FAE PARANORMAL PRISON SERIES

SAVED BY PIRATES SERIES

THE MARKED SERIES

HOLLY OAK ACADEMY SERIES

THE ALPHA BROTHERS SERIES

A DEMON'S FALL SERIES

THE FAMILIAR EMPIRE SERIES

FROM THE STARS SERIES

THE FOREST PACK SERIES

THE SECRET GODS PRISON SERIES

THE REJECTED MATE SERIES

FALL MOUNTAIN SHIFTERS SERIES

ROYAL REAPERS ACADEMY SERIES

THE EVERLASTING CURSE SERIES

THE MOON ALPHA SERIES

Made in the USA
Las Vegas, NV
15 September 2024

95339666R00225